SUBMARINE I

'Reload tubes one to three!' he barks.

It is laborious, dangerous work. The torpedo squad complete it in twelve minutes, a new record for U-47. Meanwhile, the boat has gone about again and is moving towards the *Royal Oak*. Prien creeps closer and closer to his 29,000-ton victim and its thousand-strong crew.

And still the harbour is deceptively peaceful.

Range: 1,000 metres.

'Closer!' Prien orders, like a man possessed. Neither he nor his First Mate, who is in charge of the torpedoes, are taking any chances this time.

At last he rasps the command, 'Fire torpedoes!'

No duds. All three hit their targets. A huge wall of flame shoots skywards. Seconds later comes another, and a third.

Prien has no time to observe the death-throes of the *Royal Oak*. Full speed ahead. The screaming jumbos struggle against the current. The chase is on.

Also by Will Berthold in Sphere Books:

PRINCE-ALBRECHT-STRASSE
DEATH'S HEAD BRIGADE
EAGLES OF THE REICH
LEBENSBORN
BROTHERHOOD OF BLOOD

Inferno I: Blitzkrieg!

WILL BERTHOLD

Translated by Fred Taylor

SPHERE BOOKS LIMITED
30–32 Gray's Inn Road, London WC1X 8JL

First published in Great Britain by
Sphere Books Ltd 1984
First published under the title
Inferno: Die Ersten Blitzsiege

Set in Plantin

Printed and bound in Great Britain by
Collins, Glasgow

Inferno I: Blitzkrieg!

Attack Poland!

The sun is burning down out of the heavens, though it is almost autumn. A late August day, and the country east of the Oder river is crammed with German soldiers. The punishing heat has transformed its water meadows, grasslands and patches of woodland into one big hot-house, one seething with rumours – that wilt and fade even more quickly then the oak leaves that the young Panzer troops use to camouflage their vehicles.

The vehicles block each other's ways. The sallow-faced soldiers live in crowded conditions, jammed together in fields of stubble, in barns and in pine copses. Units such as the 46th Infantry Division are jumbled in with the likes of the 35th Panzer Regiment; the different branches of the Wehrmacht mingle like the plums, pears and apples in what passes in the army for a fruit pudding.

But lately that pudding has improved; the non-commissioned instructors, who not so long ago were telling their groups that they would 'boil their arses' have become friendlier; and even the officers seem more approachable.

'From that we can conclude,' says Kudritzki, a sharp lad from Essen, 'that there'll soon be war.'

'If it comes, it comes,' answers the freckle-faced Haselmann. 'The main thing is: no more bull.'

'And it's high time we shut the Poles' big mouths for them,' chips in Kienbaum, officer candidate and former Hitler Youth leader. 'So far as I'm concerned, the balloon can go up tomorrow.'

But he is wrong. The next day is like any other, and so is the next and the next. Nothing seems to change.

For the moment, the troops' main battle is against unsanitary conditions and swarms of flies. Most of the members of this company of sappers have six months in the Labour Service behind them and another two years with the Wehrmacht besides. They would have been due for demobilisation – but there's no prospect of that, because the Führer intends to make history.

The entire region between the Carpathians and the Masurian marshes is one huge, grey army camp: in East Prussia the 3rd Army is preparing to smash through into the Polish Corridor along with the 4th Army, which will attack from Pomerania. From there they will advance together. In the south, the 8th, 10th and 14th Armies – massing in Central and Upper Silesia and in Slovakia – are also getting ready to attack. Their two Panzer Divisions are to thrust beyond the Vistula and head for Warsaw once war breaks out.

The fuelled and armed combat vehicles stand around like beached ships, guarded by their crews as if they were likely to be stolen. Nearby there are weapons inspections in progress and trenches being dug, but the men seem phlegmatic. There is no great sense of pressure, no evidence of bull. A few hot-heads are blabbering about the glories of a war they have not yet experienced. Most of them have found the past six days stupefying. In the evenings they manage a few hands of *skat*. And towards midnight, when the air starts to cool off a bit, they talk about their girls.

They are in the assembly area of the 10th Army, only a few kilometres from the Polish border. As soon as the attack order comes, they will move forward as quickly as possible, giving the Poles no warning. The civilian population has been evacuated from its villages. Special units from the Wehrmacht are caring for their farm animals. These soldiers are living as if they are at the ends of the world, without sight of civilians and certainly not a glimpse of womankind, in a sort of organised chaos. No leave, no chance of an evening out. All they have to provide some excitement in their lives is the food – which is boring, unimaginative, and plentiful.

'Stew again,' Private Haselmann growls, gazing disgustedly at the huge cauldrons being carried across to them by the cooks.

'Pea soup with a few bits of pork belly,' says Kienbaum, the Nazi enthusiast, knowingly.

'Come on, I can see you're all dying to get your snouts in the trough!'

The voice belongs to Feldwebel Sagorski, a man in a hurry but at the moment studiedly casual, waving a dismissive hand before anyone can call his platoon to attention. His square, good-natured face can change expression very quickly; the platoon commander, who saw action in Spain, is subject to outbursts of rage that come without warning. But there are worse commanders; Sagorski is not unpopular. The young conscripts cluster round him like chicks round a hen, because they know that his worldly-wisdom wasn't learned on the barrack square.

'Green beans,' Haselmann observes contemptuously. 'For the hundredth time ...'

'Aha. Can I take it, then, that you would prefer a plate of pork and sauerkraut, friend Haselmann?' Sagorski asks, putting one meaty hand on his shoulder.

'Yes, Herr Feldwebel.'

'Then round up some transport and a couple of other men and come with me.'

A few of his mates grin sadistically, but others envy him and Kudritzki and Kienbaum, because at least they will get a change of scene. The Kubelwagen jeep that they are about to drive off in will take them to the base area, where there are bars, cinemas and waitresses. Rumour has it that Sagorski – who has proved more than once that he learned more in Spain that just killing and being killed – is out to organise himself some canteen stores at knock-down prices. Then again, maybe it's just latrine duties, but in any case Kudritzki, Kienbaum and Haselmann will get a few hours away from that great mass of humanity, away from the endless *skat* games, the stink and the Big Obsession.

The Big Obsession is women. A subject that never tires these men, that never loses its attraction. Sex is a comfort of sorts, and sexual freedom is the only freedom these young soldiers have – so long as they keep to the medical regulations.

'It was a trick,' says Sagorski as soon as the three of them are out of earshot of their mates. 'No pork, no buckshee stores.' An evil smile flits over his face. 'I just didn't want the others to get any ideas.' His voice is that of a conjuror pulling a rabbit out of a hat. 'I'm looking for volunteers for a secret mission.'

'There's going to be a war, then,' Kudritzki says.

'How the hell am I supposed to know?' growls the Feldwebel. 'Am I Jesus Christ Almighty?' He offers round cigarettes. 'I'm looking for real men,' he says challengingly. 'Not milksops.'

'Understood,' Kienbaum answers. 'And I thank you for thinking of us, Herr Feldwebel.'

'Sure.' Sagorski grins and jabs a finger at the Hitler Youth Achievement Badge in silver on the officer-cadet's battle dress. 'You don't want to run around for the rest of your days with that thingummy there all alone on your chest, eh?'

'No, Herr Feldwebel,' says the hundred-percent Nazi, blushing beetroot-red.

They drive off.

'Where to, then?' asks Haselmann.

'I ask the questions,' Sagorski spits back, and then adds none too logically, 'First to Kreuzburg. There we'll report to Leutnant Leimer. Heard anything about him?'

'No, Herr Feldwebel,' chorus the trio.

'Glory-hungry,' Sagorski explains. 'Cold-blooded type. I was with him in the Condor Legion.'

'Don't we have to report absent from the Company, Herr Feldwebel?' Kienbaum asks.

'Not necessary,' says Sagorski. 'To save time, I signed your volunteer documents straightaway.'

At first it looks as though they will never reach their objective; even the tracks through the fields are congested. The 10th Army, along with the 1st and 4th Panzer Divisions, will form the spearhead of the 16th Corps in the event of war, which means that they are among the best-equipped forces in the entire Wehrmacht. The foot soldiers still stand and stare at the Panzer Is – which even their own two-man crews call 'sardine tins' – as if they were still made of cardboard and canvas, as they used to be during the old Reichswehr manoeuvres, where they were treated like dodgem cars.

The six-ton, thinly armoured vehicles are really little more than mobile machine-gun nests. They won't win any wars, but they make up almost half of the 3,195 combat vehicles under the sign of the Swastika. Their reputation is not of the best. During the invasion of Austria, one Panzer I in every three went out of action without any enemy lifting a finger – but then they'll do to deal with the Poles and their tired old horses, or so the crews tell themselves ...

Artillery positions have been dug in between the chains of low, dune-like hills. The probing antennae of armoured scout cars are visible among the stunted fir-copses. It is already getting dark when the three men arrive in Kreuzburg and ask their way to the barracks.

'Listen, you rookies,' says Feldwebel Sagorski. 'Nothing is so urgent that it can't wait a little. And you won't get far on an empty stomach.'

They end up in the canteen. There's no pork, but there's beef stew and even boiled potatoes, a treat usually reserved for Sundays in the Greater German Wehrmacht.

Kudritzki comes back with his mess-tin full to the brim with schnapps.

'Boozing on active service?' says Sagorski harshly. 'Don't let yourself get caught!' He takes the tin container from the man's hands and allows himself a few good swallows. From the corner of his eye he is watching a well-upholstered redhead, who is selling cigarettes and filled rolls.

'Red-haired and randy,' Kienbaum declares. 'Otherwise, though, nothing special.'

'Idiot,' Sagorski retorts evenly. 'That vixen could drink you dry.' He reaches for the mess-tin, as if about to show how it's done.

'How was it in Spain?' Haselmann asks boldly.

'Hot,' the Feldwebel says. 'And dusty.'

'And the girls?'

'Great from the waist up. But from there on down, sewn up tight.'

'Sewn tight?' says Kudritzki, to encourage him to talk more.

'Well, down in Spain it was easier to catch a bullet in the head than a dose of the clap, I'll tell you,' says Sagorski, tossing out a little morsel from his rich store of experience.

The redhead on the cash-desk shuts up shop for the night. She sits down at a nearby table and lights a cigarette.

'A German woman does not smoke,' Sagorski mocks, his version of an opening gambit.

'True,' she says, and blows a small cloud of smoke. 'She also doesn't put out,' she adds, 'and especially not for the likes of you, Herr Feldwebel.'

Sagorski shows himself as fearless as a man throwing back a hand grenade. 'I haven't got the time,' he snarls. 'And my taste doesn't run to second-hand goods.' He gestures to his companions to stay seated but stands up himself; it's time to report to the mission commander. 'And they say that blondes do what redheads only promise,' he says, and makes a triumphant exit.

He arrives back twenty minutes later. 'We're in completely the wrong place. I hope we can find the dump,' he says, peering at his map.

Leimer's mission headquarters is in the schoolhouse of a village near the border. When they report to the Leutnant, it turns out that the Feldwebel has brought one man too many. One officer and twenty-nine men are needed. No more, no less.

One will have to go back.

They toss for it.

Kudritzki loses. He is to drive the Kubelwagen straight back to his unit. Well, not exactly straight: even a raw recruit knows that it pays to stretch your luck as far as possible.

The future heroes' first reward is a handshake from the mission commander. Leutnant Leimer is tall, thin, his hollow features seem emaciated, and certainly his feelings are equally sparse.

'Now, listen to me,' he begins. 'Top secret business. Once I've told you what it's about, there's no turning back. But I don't intend to be unfair,' he continues. 'You've got five minutes to think it over. A smoke-break.'

More than one of them gets through a couple of cigarettes during the five minutes, but no one pulls out. Some maybe just because they don't have the guts to look like weaklings.

After the break, the Leutnant unrolls an enlarged staff map onto the table.

'It's to do with the strongpoints at Lublinitz,' he explains. 'They're right behind the border.' His swagger-stick ranges across the map. 'Roughly here. Not the greatest of fortifications, but they're in the way of our Panzers. Our job will be to smoke the bastards out with flame-throwers, smoke-grenades, explosive charges, grenades, and so on.' The list is like a savage litany. 'You're all trained sappers, and you know the drill.' He pauses briefly, waits for questions, gets none, and so continues. 'When we clobber these strongpoints - and we will - our Panzer spearheads will be able to roll through without opposition, encircle Tschenstochau and,' the stick wanders on further, 'cross the Warthe river at Radsamsko, ready to bust their way through to Warsaw. All right?'

'Yes, Herr Leutnant,' they all chorus enthusiastically, as if they had already blown the strongpoints to kingdom come.

'Any last questions?' says the mission commander, and looks hard at his men. He is sure that he can rely on them, because they were nominated by their units and not just taken at random. And all of them have been given extra training in taking out concrete bunkers.

'When is the mission due to take place, Herr Leutnant?' asks Kienbaum.

'God alone knows,' the officer responds. 'About a minute before the entire balloon goes up is all I can tell you. We'll sneak up on the bunkers a few hours beforehand, hauling along all we can in the way of weapons and ammo, and then our Polish campaign will have started.'

'You mean, the mission is taking place before anyone's declared war?' Haselmann asks naïvely.

Leimer grins. 'That's the fun part of it. You've got the point.'

'And if we're taken prisoner?' the freckle-faced boy asks.

'Firstly, we'll be wearing windcheaters over our uniforms. Secondly, we'll be blacking our faces. And thirdly, the entire operation will be run according to the eleventh commandment: Thou shalt not get caught.'

They laugh nervously, because they know there's nothing to laugh about.

'Any more problems?' asks Leimer.

'Not a problem, just a question,' says Kienbaum. 'How do we get out again afterwards?'

'Use your head,' the officer answers. 'Christ, you'll have seventy-five German divisions at your back. D'you think they'll sleep through the order to attack?'

'And if they're held up?' Private Haselmann asks.

'Blimey, Haselmann,' Sagorski chips in. 'You're pretty good at making yourself scarce. You just take cover and wait for your commander to congratulate you on your heroism.'

'Very good, Herr Feldwebel,' the freckle-faced boy bellows, and suddenly they're all as happily expectant as if they were about to leave on a Strength through Joy holiday tour.

'One more thing, gentlemen,' the Leutnant says. 'We maintain radio silence. And no talking throughout the entire mission. I don't want to hear a single word. No sneezing, no belching, no cursing, not even a fart. Is that clear?'

'Very well, Herr Leutnant.'

Feldwebel Sagorski asks the final question when he is alone with the commander, 'The Poles have surely put forward sentries in front of the strongpoints?'

'We must reckon with it,' Leimer answers with a grimace. 'Naturally, they will have to be dealt with. Silently, Sagorski. A knife job. Keep your arse tight and think of what these Polacks are doing to our poor ethnic Germans.'

The volunteers are divided into two squads: Leimer will lead the first, while Sagorski will take charge of the second. They learn the route thoroughly from the staff map, commit it to memory, follow it a hundred times and come back in one piece again and again. They have the time. Plenty of time, for these hot August days are heavy with inactivity, the kind of waiting idleness that tears at the nerve-endings. They stock up with ammunition, weapons and explosives, keep their civilian outfits ready. They play *skat*, tell jokes, curse the food and fill themselves with beer.

And then one day Leutnant Leimer turns up, nice and easy, as if he were about to suggest a night at a beer hall. 'Get your stuff together, boys,' he murmurs. 'Tonight's the night.'

That afternoon, in the Reich Chancellery in Berlin, Hitler had given the word for 'Case White'.

The simple radio message, 'X-Time: 26, August 39, 4.30' concealed the long-awaited confirmation that the Führer intended to solve the Polish problem by force.

Radio operators pound their keying devices. Messengers flit here and there. Panzers are warmed up. Dust is stirred up, combining to form a great cloud hundreds of kilometres long. The Panzers move into their positions close to the front. The forest north-east of Oppeln is seething with infantry.

In the 16th Army's assembly area surrounding Rosenberg, the district capital, unit after unit moves into its attack position. It takes hours, and no one seems to be getting any confirmation reports. The telephone network collapses. Radio traffic is restricted, so as not to warn the enemy. Often orders simply do not reach their recipient. Commanders go off to hunt for information, and end up losing their units.

The 46th Infantry Division slots into the southern sector, close to the border. Their forward units have a clear sight of the Polish patrols. Squadrons of the German Luftwaffe leave their bases in the rear and establish themselves at temporary airstrips close to the front. The crews are cursing. No proper preparations, God knows where the fuel trucks have got to. No one thought of laying down slit-trenches, and there is nothing to transport the bombs with.

The situation is chaotic. Improvisation becomes the order of the day. And the ridiculous insistence that the army make itself invisible wastes even more time. But somehow it works, though often only at the last moment. Germany's generals, with power over a cast of hundreds of thousands, are about to put on a spectacular new show called: *Blitzkrieg.*

Leimer's men are piled into a truck, covered with a tarpaulin to keep them away from prying eyes, guided through the 46th Infantry Division's attack positions. They are established at their jumping-off point close to the border hours before the main attack is due. Well-camouflaged, the men wait for darkness, huddled directly by the barbed wire. They have pulled on their windcheaters and blacked their faces with charcoal. The first of them are already cutting their way through the wire at two pre-arranged points.

Leimer is the first to reach the other side. He sniffs the air, waves to the next man, who immediately squirms through the gap to join him. The next, the next, the fifth, the sixth . . .

One after the other – wolves on the prowl.

The Leutnant looks at his watch. Another five minutes and a diversionary action will begin some 800 metres away: a shooting-match. In four, three, two, one . . .

Just about on the button, a machine-gun splutters into life.

Grenades are thrown. Searchlights probe the night. The shoot-out makes it easier for them to make progress.

The first squad hurries forward. Feldwebel Sagorski and his men give them cover, then slowly move to follow. Heroism is a heavy burden. Against orders, they pant loudly; lungs know no regulations.

The stamp of horses' hooves.

They hurl themselves into concealment. Their silhouettes merge with the shadows of the night. A Polish cavalry patrol gallops by them, so close that the horses spray sand in the Germans' eyes. A big grey horse rears and whinnies. Then the danger is over. The men get to their feet and push on.

Leutnant Leimer looks at his watch again. They have time. They'll get there before the war starts all right. He allows his men a short rest, then urges them forward again. They have already penetrated three kilometres into Poland. They hardly dare put one foot in front of the other. Haselmann stumbles, falls flat on his face and mutters a curse. Sagorski boots him in the backside and drags him to his feet.

Onward.

Another three kilometres. A wide ditch. A dog barks at a lonely farmstead. Somewhere a few drunks are singing. Then it is back to being so quiet that a man can hear his own breathing. The Leutnant sniffs the air again. It is now long after midnight; he will reach his goal on time. Exactly according to plan – and five days too early.

The young warlord has no idea what is happening behind him, on the German side of the border.

The spearhead units are by no means all in position when, without warning, shortly after 20.00 hours, the first report comes in. Luftwaffe General of Fighters, Wolfram von Richthofen, quartered with General Walter von Richenau of the 10th Army at Schönwald Castle near Rosenberg, only ten kilometres from the border, receives a message to the effect that the 'Eastern Excursion' has been postponed. This can only mean that war will not break out the following morning.

The general acts immediately. He informs his advance squadrons of the unexpected turn of events by coded radio messages, improvised field telephone links, and then through messengers. Even at this stage, the Luftwaffe possesses an excellent, efficient Intelligence branch. After a few hours, Richthofen can rest assured that his winged gladiators will not take off in the dawn light.

'Then, my dear fellow, we shall have to fight our battle tomorrow without the Luftwaffe,' declares the commander-in-chief of the 10th Army to the fighter commander. The order has not yet reached von Reichenau. He is still letting his units advance, because the army is the army, the Luftwaffe is the Luftwaffe, and orders are orders.

At 21.30 hours the Panzers are still rolling towards the border. Not until an hour before midnight is the 10th Army informed by the Wehrmacht High Command that the attack on Poland has been postponed for them, too. Reichenau is forced to stop the war machine – easier said than done. Dozens of dispatch riders and messengers are sent out to inform the local commanders. Unit after unit can be struck off the list, but in the Tatra Mountains a single motorised regiment continues to roll towards the Poles. Radio contact has broken down. The messengers arrive too late. Save for a last-minute miracle, one regiment will end up taking on the Polish Army all alone.

A staff officer hurries to a Fieseler Storch, probes the mountains in the fast, light plane, is almost out of fuel when it lands just in time on a narrow, dusty road between the border and the advancing column. At first it seemed as if the leading vehicle must ram the unexpected aircraft . . .

There are enough difficulties warning ordinary units; it is well-nigh impossible to halt the special commando units that have gone out in the course of the night. A few are fetched back by messengers. But one is on its way from Slovakia to take possession of a key railway tunnel inside Poland.

These men are not so pedantic about timekeeping as Leutnant Leimer farther north. They quickly take the tunnel, which is to be an important route for the motorised and armoured reinforcements.

Suddenly the order arrives to give it up unconditionally. They make their way back to the German lines before the Poles can mount a counter-attack – but now the enemy has been warned, and they blow the tunnel to smithereens.

Leutnant Leimer has reached his goal.

The strongpoints are in sight. Sagorski will take the left-hand bunker, he will take the right-hand one. First, however, the sentries must be dealt with. He takes on the dirty work himself, prepares to launch himself down on the first candidate.

But just at the moment that he is about to drop down, the man crouched over his machine-gun happens to stand up. A chance decision that sends Leimer plunging into nothingness. Alarmed by the sound, the Pole grabs his weapon back, and before the Leutnant can get to his feet he has fired a warning burst.

Leutnant Leimer lunges at him, knocks him to the ground, has the knife at his throat, and all hell breaks loose.

Searchlights cut the night. The beams meet, bathe the spot, and from now on even blackened faces will do these men no good. A Leutnant and twenty-nine men served up on a plate: agents, saboteurs, spies. The laws of war will not protect them for, technically, it is still peacetime, by the Führer's grace . . .

Sagorski, the perfect soldier, sees that he is caught in a trap. No way out, and his only desire is to sell his life as dear as he can.

'Target. Three hundred metres to the right!' he bellows. 'A machine-gun nest!' he screams at Kienbaum. 'Off you go! We'll put the bastards through the mangle!'

They follow the Feldwebel mechanically, as if they were on the barrack square, because training is training: one rolls, the other shoots.

Tracers zip over above their heads, but they keep moving forward. Seventy metres to go, then forty. Sagorski pulls out a hand grenade, throws himself into the air. A machine-gun catches him there, slices him in half as he soars headlong between heaven and earth.

Haselmann sees it and throws himself to the ground. Bursts of enemy fire scythe the air above him. Grenades tear up the Polish earth. He is half-blinded, but somehow he makes it to the cover of a thicket. Sweat is pouring from his forehead. He makes to wipe it away with one hand, and it is then that he sees not sweat, but blood. And his windcheater is suddenly crimson. And he knows that they got him too . . .

Haselmann must lie there, waiting for them to find him and give him the *coup de grâce*, but meanwhile he has to watch the annihilation of his comrades. The place is thick with Poles: Poles coming from positions in the forest, from bunkers and trenches. They have realised that the attackers are wearing German uniforms under their windcheaters, and there is hate burning in them like a forest fire. Three of them grab Kienbaum, the officer cadet.

They shove him up against a tree, set into him.

'You can't do that,' he howls. 'Swine! It's against the –'. Kienbaum gets no farther. The Poles riddle him with bullets.

Three or four men manage to make some kind of escape from the scene, but they are pursued and hunted down mercilessly. Leutnant Leimer realises that he has no chance. He kills himself, like a scorpion at bay, putting his gun against his own temples and pulling the trigger. No Polacks will take him alive.

Not that it makes much difference. The Poles kill everyone who crosses their path, whether they try to surrender or not, whether they are wounded or in flight. There are no survivors except young Haselmann, who continues to lie undiscovered in his thicket – but will bleed to death if he does not get urgent medical attention.

Leutnant Leimer and his men are the first dead of a war that has not even broken out yet.

During these tense hours, the ministers of the Reich government have been cowering in their luxurious offices every bit as fearfully as the infantrymen in their forward trenches by the Polish border. The first break comes when the hotline buzzes in Göring's palace, which has a direct connection to the Reich Chancellery and the Führer himself.

'I have postponed "Case White",' says Hitler to his chief henchman.

'Permanently?' the Luftwaffe commander asks quickly.

'No. I simply wish to try to prevent British involvement.'

Göring is relieved. The delay gives him time to negotiate with the British through his contacts in Sweden.

The last-minute postponement had been caused by a message from their ally, Mussolini, to the effect that the Italian army was nowhere near ready for war. Hitler was forced, however reluctantly, to take this fact into account.

All through that endless, baking summer the talk had been of peace, but by the end it was becoming desperate, hoarse, a dialogue of the deaf. It was as if Europe was pregnant with a war, an inferno that could force its way out of the dark womb at any moment. It had been a close thing during the Sudeten Crisis of the previous autumn. The tension was at breaking-point, but somehow a solution had been found. There were still those who believed that Hitler might also deal with Poland without a bloodbath.

The Führer had come to power with the votes of a minority of the German nation. Unquestionably, however, he had persuaded a majority onto his side during the first six years of his rule. Unemployment had been eliminated, and the lunatic, unjust Treaty of Versailles had been revised, point by point. Instead of paying reparations for the First World War, the German dictator was able to arm for the Second – first secretly, then publicly. Conscription was re-introduced. The Rhineland was re-occupied. There was the invasion of Austria, 'the battle of the flowers'. The Munich Treaty had been the climax, for there the French and the British had sacrificed Czechoslovakia in their eagerness to curry favour with the swastika.

Three million Sudeten Germans – formerly Czechoslovak citizens – were brought back to the Reich. The masses' admiration for their Führer reached a new peak. He was deified, not for playing with fire but because – or so they mistakenly thought – he had prevented war by his diplomatic skill. The fact that the Allies who had won the First War allowed Hitler to break agreement after agreement seemed astonishing. In contrast, they had refused to make even the slightest concession or alleviation to his democratic predecessors, the so-called 'fulfilment politicians'. Later generations would see in this madness the French and British part of responsibility for the Second World War.

Hitler, gambler and liar, had already made his plans. On November 5th, 1937 he had announced to his gloomy generals that German 'living-space' could only be extended by a determined policy of military conquest, and this meant that a war in the East was unavoidable. Publicly, however, he played the statesman, pretended to be making super-human efforts to preserve the peace of Europe. The generals were forced to swallow their doubts, and the German people fell completely for the Führer's protestations of peaceful intent.

In contrast with 1914, there was no enthusiasm for war in Germany. A mere quarter of a century later, the First World War was still too painful a memory. Hitler was forced to prepare his compatriots slowly for the coming cataclysm.

The British Prime Minister, Neville Chamberlain, had excused his humiliation at Munich with the phrase 'Peace for Our Time', but the Führer's reaction had been quite different. After his return to Berlin on that occasion, Hitler had remarked to his SS bodyguards, 'That fellow robbed me of my entry into Prague'. Six months later, however, the 'man with the umbrella and the long, scrawny neck' (Cartier) was forced to admit that his famous 'peace' was a myth. Hitler, who had claimed that Munich sealed his 'last territorial demand in Europe', broke yet another agreement by smashing the last remnants of the Czechoslovak republic.

'The British and French concessions to him at Munich,' writes the author Len Deighton in his book *Blitzkrieg*, 'convinced Hitler that he could screw a few more territorial demands from the men he scoffed at as "old coffee aunties" without much risk of war.'

Nevertheless, there were signs that Hitler had finally gone too far, and that the policy of Appeasement had finally come to an end. Great Britain had introduced conscription, and for the first time she had undertaken to guarantee the existence of the Polish state. The British General Staff had reckoned that the war now looming over Europe would last three years. While in Paris defeatism was the order of the day, the island nation was preparing for a deadly reckoning: shelters were distributed to those who lived in houses without cellars; two-metre-high steel containers, proof against splinters and shrapnel, were dug down into gardens and backyards. At the same time, the government ordered the production of masses of cardboard coffins for the casualties of a coming air war. The bureaucracy, as thorough as it was heartless, had a million emergency death certificates printed in anticipation of losses among the civilian population.

The French, old allies of the Poles, now began to recognise their commitments. Reservists were called up. A new subject was taught in schools: air defence. Squadrons of British bombers appeared in the skies over France to show the strength of the alliance.

The government-directed press in Germany expressed its outrage over these 'provocations' with one voice. Germany's own steps towards the abyss were played down or concealed by the media. Preparations for war became protestations of peace, the piecemeal mobilisation was described as 'training of reservists', and the move towards the Polish border was 'summer manoeuvres'. Under the Propaganda Minister, Dr Josef Goebbels, journalists were mere tools of the state.

While Herman Göring, commander-in-chief of the German Luftwaffe, declared, 'If any enemy aircraft succeed in flying across the borders of the German Reich, I'll change my name to Herman Maier', thirteen and fourteen year old Hitler Youth boys were being secretly trained as messengers for the air defence organisation, to keep up communications during enemy air raids. Gauleiters* inspected the hurriedly-constructed 'West Wall'; 22,000 concrete bunkers, each one fifty metres deep had been built along the borders from Aachen to Lorrach. The 'Siegfried Line' - as the English called it - was celebrated in the German press as an unconquerable barrier, although in truth the Reich's military experts saw it far more as a bulwark of Goebbels' propaganda.

On May 22nd, 1939 Germany and Italy had signed a military agreement, the so-called 'Pact of Steel'. While Hitler continued to declare his love of peace - like a snake-charmer mesmerising his snake - the Wehrmacht's strength was increased to 102 divisions, where six years before the old Reichwehr had possessed only ten. In 1914 the German Empire had been able to call on 25 years' worth of trained reservists; in 1939 it was only five, and only about half of the paper strength of the forces was fully combat-ready. But the new Wehrmacht had gained combat experience in the Spanish Civil War as the 'Condor Legion' and had tried out its weapons, with particular emphasis on tactical co-operation between tanks and aircraft - the basis of what was to become known as the *'Blitzkrieg'* technique.

Germany's generals had been almost unanimous in declaring their opposition to the very war that they were making possible. A few had been sacked or retired in the meantime. The majority were in fact opposed not so much to the idea of a bloody conflict as such, but to the premature timing. Hitler did not allow himself to be deflected from his goal, and the preparations for war continued, openly or in

*A provisional governor in Germany under Hitler.

secrecy, perilously and sometimes with absurd results.

Headlong rearmament and the conscription of civilians had caused a shortage of labour in Germany: a government regulation formally abolished the professions of hotel page, doorman, street-pedlar and professional dancing-partner. The 'Reich Office for German Gardeners' issued an appeal to flower-growers to lay down kitchen gardens to ensure that the population would be supplied with potatoes, vegetables and other necessities. Groups of households had to provide proof that they possessed a dozen anti-air-raid devices; air defence officials were to check everyone had gas-masks. Less obvious preparations for war were the immediate creation of the 'Mother's Cross' – a medal awarded after the birth of a fourth child – and the establishment of the Lebensborn organisation, which encouraged the birth of illegitimate children in huge numbers. Both these Nazi 'achievements' were intended to compensate for the expected war losses.

In August, the hate-campaign against Poland reached a new peak of hysteria. The war of nerves threatened to turn into a shooting war.

On August 19th, Germany's neighbour halted all routine border crossings. Poland had long been in a state of partial mobilisation in the Corridor, the strip of its territory that separated East Prussia from the rest of the Reich. Threats, counter-threats, stories of atrocities by the Poles against the one million ethnic Germans in their country had been the chief content of the news bulletins on the Reich Radio for weeks now. Day after day, they declared, children were being ill-treated with a sadistic thoroughness, women were being raped and men beaten. And not all the stories were lies. The Poles – who had helped to sell out the Czechoslovak Republic the previous year and had acquired a slice of Czech territory – exhibited a keen national pride which could sometimes spill over into chauvinistic excesses. Thus acts of violence and outburts against the German minority were not uncommon. But Goebbels' Propaganda Ministry exaggerated these acts out of all proportion. What may have been 6,000 deaths became 60,000, and in its accounts of the anti-German pogroms, every fist in the face became a murder, every kick up the backside an atrocity.

Night after night there were clashes between Germans and Poles and exchanges of fire in the Corridor and the border districts. All along the 2,000 kilometre border the sparks were flying, ready to drop into the powder-keg. Astonishingly, Hitler had signed a Non-Aggression Pact with his neighbour in 1934. Göring, who valued his hunting trips to Poland, had been in the habit of toasting German-Polish friendship after each stag that fell to his gun. As late as January 1939, during the visit of Reich Foreign Minister, Joachim von Ribbentrop, Warsaw had been a sea of welcoming flags, including many swastika banners. During the Sudeten Crisis, Poland had openly sided with Hitler – the same man who now, just a short time afterwards, was demanding the return of the city of Danzig, which had been granted international status in 1919, and special, sovereign rights for German traffic in the Corridor.

The propaganda turnaround was dramatic. Diplomatic circles buzzed with the planted rumour that Hitler had declared, 'With my motorised units I shall conquer Poland in three weeks'. The Poles found the remark ridiculous, and for their part they spoke of a battle around Berlin, mounted by their own cavalry units when they had broken out of the Corridor. Even their western allies did not take that too seriously, but the French and British general staffs were of the opinion that the Polish army could hold its own against the German invaders for six months.

Meanwhile, fifty-seven divisions, almost the entire active strength of the Wehrmacht, had been brought up to the Polish border in what both sides hoped would be a huge bluff. Hitler had promised his Luftwaffe commanders that there would be no war until 1943, and to the navy he had said 1944. The West Wall was still no more than a huge building-site, and the stocks of bombs maintained by the Luftwaffe would suffice for exactly thirty days.

The raw materials situation was no less alarming. The armaments industry relied on imports for 25% of its zinc, 50% of its lead, 70% of its copper, 90% of its tin, 95% of its nickel, 99% of its bauxite, 65% of its oil, and 80% of its rubber. Storage dumps had been hastily organised. So far as natural rubber was concerned, the dumps were sufficient for two months' use; in the case of magnesium the figure was four months, for copper seven, for aluminium and manganese nineteen. Everyone asked how Hitler could hope to wage a war under these circumstances. On August 23rd, 1939 the answer came, and it sent a shiver through the civilised world.

Nazi Germany and the Soviet Union had become allies. The world had been turned upside down.

Hitler and Stalin the arch-enemies, arm in arm!

On April 18th, Russia had offered Great Britain and France her participation in a Triple Alliance against Hitler, and on July 24th a Mutual Assistance Pact was signed. It was, however, never ratified, because the Western Allies would not allow the Reds the right to take their troops through Poland and Rumania.

While Stalin, Chamberlain, and the French leader, Daladier, continued their desultory talks, the Russians were quietly changing sides. Suddenly the Nazis and the Communists, who had hitherto been poison to each other, stood shoulder to shoulder.

Horror in Poland, confusion in Paris, gloom in London, and relief in Germany. Poland now stood alone. The danger of a two-front war seemed to have been averted, and in future the Russians would supply 52% of their total exports direct to Germany: every month they would provide 58,545 tons of oil, 10,625 tons of phosphate, 6,900 tons of manganese, 700 tons of copper, 88,877 tons of grain, 6,104 tons of cotton, 2,624 tons of oil-cake, and almost 100,000 tons of timber. It was tit for tat: the Soviet Union, who were thereby granting Hitler the means for his war, received in return German weapons, which less than two years later would be turned against the German invaders.

The Nazi dictator hurried to exploit the stunned confusion among the Western Allies by attacking Poland.

'By now Hitler did not want a *Blumenkrieg*,' states the British writer Len Deighton. 'He wanted a real war, and military victory in Poland, but he did not want France and Britain involved in the conflict.'

On the afternoon of August 25th, 1939, he crossed his

Rubicon: the Wehrmacht High Command was given the order to attack at 04.30 hours on the following day.

Within hours the move to the border was in full swing. Göring had issued the codeword 'Eastern Excursion' to his Luftwaffe, and his units were taking over airstrips close to the front. Confirmation reports came in from five German Armies, divided up into Army Groups North and South.

Then came Mussolini's intervention, followed by Hitler's postponement of the attack. He still refused to believe that the French or the British would be prepared to risk war after his conclusion of a Non-Aggression Pact with Russia; he saw a chance to keep them out of the conflict by the usual recipe of meaningless promises and protracted negotiations, and so he rescinded the order to attack even as the preparations were reaching the point of no return.

Europe had one last breathing-space. The next six days were days of frantic activity, panic, fear and hope. In Paris, army reservists gathered and sat in the street cafés drinking noisy toasts to peace. 'Those fools,' said the French Prime Minister, Edouard Daladier, when he heard about the demonstrations. 'If only they knew what they were toasting!'

On August 26th, the French leader sent a personal message to Hitler in the form of a letter. Daladier swore to the Führer, 'as one frontline soldier to another', that he would fight for the maintenance of peace, and indicated that, though France was willing to talk, she would also have to honour her commitments to Poland in the event of war.

On the same day, the ships of the German Merchant Marine received official instructions to proceed back to their home ports or remain in harbour. Simultaneously, civil air traffic over Germany was banned. The next day, the German State Railway introduced cutbacks in its passenger services. From August 28th trains ceased running from France to Germany. Anyone who desired to travel – legally or otherwise – was turned back at the border.

Paris began to evacuate school children. Switzerland, Belgium and the Netherlands ordered partial mobilisations to protect their neutrality. Germany introduced ration cards.

On August 28th the British Ambassador, Neville Henderson, was granted an interview with Hitler and for the last time, Great Britain offered her good offices and declared herself prepared to help with the establishment of direct talks between Germany and Poland. Hitler's answer came a day later and consisted of new demands and repeated protestations of peaceful intent. Once again, he described Danzig and the Corridor as his 'last territorial demands'. But his opponents were no longer willing to fall for his old tricks.

Chamberlain, described by the former Prime Minister, Lloyd George, as a 'fool', and by Len Deighton as a 'dry, honest and very hardworking man with the mentality of an office clerk', had proved himself as a local politician in his office as Mayor of Birmingham and had drifted more or less by chance into national politics, gaining some popularity with the British public by cutting the military budget. The old gentleman, who had never flown in an aeroplane until he went to Munich, was now embittered by the German dictator's broken promises. And he was even angrier with himself, for having been duped by a consummate political confidence trickster. Under pressure from figures in his own party such as Winston Churchill, he was determined not to settle for verbal assurances this time.

Hitler, meanwhile, was being egged on by Ribbentrop, whom he considered to be a 'second Bismarck' – praise indeed for a former champagne salesman whose main strength was arrogance. Accordingly, he judged that the British premier would not, in a crisis, take a hard line. The Führer continued to play his habitual game, declared himself ready to receive a Polish plenipotentiary, then refused to meet him, claiming that the Pole had put obstacles in the way of talks.

'When the sun went down on August 31st, there still seemed to be a small chance of a negotiated settlement,' writes Raymond Cartier of that fateful day when peace lay in the balance. 'Hitler declared himself ready to meet a Polish representative, following Mussolini's suggestion for a conference to settle all outstanding problems in Europe. Europe slept easier that night than it had for many a night.

People were convinced that the crucial stage of the crisis was over and that peace would be preserved yet again.'

But the self-proclaimed commander-in-chief of the Wehrmacht had already unleashed 'Case White' for the second time. The order to attack Poland had been issued to the nation's military commanders at 17.00 hours. The wording of Directive No. 1, the first of seventy-five that he was to issue during the Second World War, ran, 'The attack against Poland is to be conducted according to the preparations for "Case White", except for any alterations that may become necessary as a result of the army's deployment of forces, which is now almost complete. Tactical objectives and operational goal remain unchanged. Day of Attack: 1.9.39.'

While Europe dreamed of peace, the terror-squads of the SS security service had already been unleashed, to provide the *casus belli*. It was a silent battle in which the roles were reversed: Hitler's murderers wore Polish uniforms that were unwittingly supplied by Canaris's Military Intelligence Branch. The victims dumped at the scenes of slaughter were all carefully selected concentration camp inmates, who had been put into German uniforms. The dead cannot talk, and so the international press fell in with Hitler's perverted masquerade. This atrocity went under the name of 'Operation Himmler', and the corpses were known as the 'canned goods'.

On the evening before September 1st, the then SS Untersturmführer, Alfred Naujocks, and a party of heavily-armed SS security men in Polish uniforms broke into the building that housed the Reich Radio Station at Gleiwitz near the Polish border. The raiders were under orders to shoot their way in without regard to casualties and then to broadcast a short proclamation in Polish over the air. Employees of the radio station had not been warned, and they took Himmler's gorillas for Polish soldiers. They defended themselves as best they could. One was left dead, several injured. This criminal farce gave Hitler his final pretext for his Polish campaign, which in its initial stages – true to his hypocritical nature – he declared to be a simple 'police action'.

That action was to end five and a half years later at the cost of fifty-five million dead.

The piercing shriek of whistles suddenly converges from all sides, just as private Kudritzki, crouched in the cramped attack position of the 4th Panzer Division, is about to play out a sure-fire Grand with Three and scoop the *skat* pool.

'Shit,' he says. 'There you see it, boys – three Jacks.'

But neither Unteroffizier Meersmann nor his mate Wicht, nor fat Rambold and skinny Lochner, nor Kiebitz, are interested in the win he has had to forego. Long before the order, most of the young Panzer troops have realised that War will be shuffling the cards in future.

'Here we go,' says Rambold, who always has the greatest difficulty in forcing his stately behind into his Panzer. 'Anything's better than sitting around like this.'

'We'll see about that,' mutters Lochner cynically. 'It's a pity that Feldwebel Sagorski's been transferred.'

'I didn't know you needed a nursemaid,' Rambold mocks. 'Got the wind up, little 'un?'

'Kiss my arse!' The boy is angry, but no one, least of all his sergeant, picks him up on it. Who hasn't got mixed feelings? They have been here, within hailing distance of the border, for six days now. For six days Kudritzki, the one they sent back, has heard no news of Sagorski, Kienbaum and freckle-faced Haselmann. On one hand he is envious, because they will certainly have had some great experiences, but he is also glad to have been shunted off from the special mission at the last moment. There will be other chances to gain glory in this war– and maybe at a time when a soldier knows what he is doing, because in war you don't buy a pig in a poke if you can help it.

The men have drawn rations for three days, army-issue cigarettes, schnapps and plenty of food. Now that the officers have been summoned to the Regimental HQ and the NCOs are holding themselves ready for the subsequent conference with their company commander, the time for uncertainty is over.

They will have all the certainties they need come the dawn.

This evening is cooler than previous ones, but the night, which they are spending in a woodshed, will put fire in their bellies. Fifteen minutes later comes the order to stretch themselves out on their mattresses and snatch some sleep. No chance. They keep thinking of things that had caused them little worry before: letters unwritten, words unsaid. Suddenly mothers are more important than girlfriends. The soldiers make bets on how long it will be until they march into Warsaw: Rambold reckons three days, Kudritzki two months. They try desperately to infect each other with a little courage, but in more than one case it's the man with the biggest mouth who's most frightened. Nerves show themselves in many ways: some of them can't use the latrine for love or money, while others can't get away from the place.

The night is noisy and busy. On the airstrips the mechanics are putting the machines through their paces, hours before they are due to take off. Bluish flames spark from the engines. The propellers are raising dust, but even the 2,000 aircraft of Air Fleets 1 and 4 cannot raise enough dust to strike the Poles blind. They will be the first to hit the enemy in the morning, and they are the most vulnerable. The ammunition carriers are grateful that they don't have to unload the bombs and store them overnight, as they have to in peacetime.

The great awakening is due at 03.30 hours, but hardly anyone sleeps. They watch the infantry moving forward in ordered ranks towards the border. The footsloggers have been trained to cover thirty-five to forty kilometres in a day. Before they reach their jumping-off point they will have walked fifty kilometres, carrying full combat pack. Then they won't have the strength to keep singing, 'Infantry, You're the Tops ...'

'Poor bastards,' says Kudritzki. 'Blisters on their feet, brains cooking, arses raw as hell.'

'"And the first shall be last."' Meersmann recites with a grin. 'At least none of us have to hoof it, not even the mess-sergeant ...'

'In our outfit, only the lice take a walk,' says Wicht happily. Usually he never utters a word before midday.

'All hands on deck,' says the sergeant, reacting to the private's remark. 'I wouldn't mind having your problems.'

The 35th Regiment has a nominal strength of 164 combat vehicles, most of them 'sardine tins', Panzer Is. However, it also possesses some Panzer IIs with two-centimetre cannon, and – pride of the regiment – three Panzer IVs, 22.3-ton giants with 7.5 centimetre cannon and a four-man crew: driver, radio operator, commander and gunner. Its armour can withstand most Polish anti-tank weapons. Though the engines use a lot of fuel, in theory at least they can be filled up at any petrol station, and the Panzer IVs, the ultimate in armoured weaponry, also have emergency exits. Not that anyone is considering that fact at the moment – forty per cent of the armoured branch's officers are former cavalrymen, with all that suggests in the way of dash and spirit – but soon the men in black will realise how important it is. Then the Panzer Is and IIs will be called 'steel incinerators' or 'widow-makers'.

All the Panzers are fitted with up-to-date radio systems. The commander travels in his command-vehicle at the head of his men. While almost all other armies in 1939 use tanks as an auxiliary to infantry, things in the Wehrmacht are quite different. In accordance with the will of its creator and taskmaster, General Heinz Guderian – he commands the XIX Corps of the Army Group North, complete with 278 very serviceable Panzers stolen from the Czechs – the armoured branch functions as an autonomous entity, which can call on the infantry to plug any gaps in its plans. It's an army within an army, with its own artillery, its own Panzer troops, its own sappers, an Intelligence battalion and a reconnaissance section.

Well before time, they are standing about among their vehicles, dragging on cigarettes.

'Sleep well?' asks the company commander – formally a well-known competition rider – companionably, and adds comfortingly, 'You'll soon wake up when the shit hits the fan.' He exudes good nature, real or feigned. 'And I don't want any of you going into this war unshaven, all right?'

*

There's little of that good humour among Luftwaffe commanders, particularly in the northern section, where the ground is shrouded in thick mist. 'Operation Water-Jug', a massive air raid on Warsaw that is supposed to mark the opening of hostilities, has had to be cancelled, for today at least.

It is true that sunshine has been forecast for September 1st and that the ground-fog is supposed to be lifting at some stage, but the weather boys are not infallible and forecasting involves a good deal of chance. There is doubt as to whether the aircraft that are standing ready – 648 combat planes, 219 dive-bombers, 210 fighters, and thirty heavy bombers – will be used at all during this first day of the war. An Oberfeldwebel in the ground crew at the air base near Elbing quips, 'In case of bad weather, the war will take place indoors.' He sees a flight commander march up to him and reports that the three Ju 87s which are to undertake the first mission of the war, a quarter of an hour before it begins, are ready for takeoff, 'Everything in order, Herr Oberleutnant.'

Bruno Dilley nods, knowing that nothing is in order, because if this thick fog had not come, paratroopers would have taken that damned bridge near Dirschau. The bridge is essential if they are to get German reinforcements into East Prussia.

From the border where the 3rd Army is standing ready, it is only 200 kilometres to Warsaw, but that would be a long trip if all the ammunition and fuel had to be brought in over the Baltic by sea. For this reason, the 4th Army, due to launch its attack from Pomerania and join up with the 3rd as quickly as possible, is trying to prevent the Poles from blowing up the bridge over the Vistula. At all costs.

The paratroopers cannot undertake any surprise attack, because – if they are not to risk being smashed to a pulp – they need a minimum height from which to jump. The dive-bombers also usually attack from 10,000 feet. This mission is an exception. On this mission, Oberleutnant Dilley's ungainly birds with their gull wings, tough fuselages, their sharp noses and screaming sirens, have been ordered to make a very low-level attack on the Polish detonation squads to the left and right of the Vistula bridge and blow them to pieces. Disguised as a civilian, Dilley has already been sent into the Corridor on two occasions to make an on-the-spot reconnaissance of the bridge. He is aware that the explosive compartments are located among the undergrowth to the south of the railway embankment. He can see it now in his head, but then a birds'-eye view can look very different from the view from a passing train ...

04.25 hours. The Oberleutnant takes another swallow from his mug of black coffee and nods to his men. The weather will get no better. They will simply have to try to find their way and fly by the seat of their pants.

Once airborne, he guns his plane high up above the treetops into the sheet of fog, turns southwards until he sees the Vistula beneath him, and then banks and turns. The aircraft behind him is piloted by a Leutnant and the third by a Unteroffizier.

Expected flight time: eight minutes. A sheet of mist surrounds the glass cockpit in which the pilot and the gunner sit back to back, as if keeping each other warm. At times, as they fly, they are close to the ground, then soar a couple of hundred feet to safety. If the attack is to succeed, they will have to zero in on their target, the three planes together, by sight alone, and that means keeping under the cloud cover. Six men, dispersed among the three aircraft, ten minutes before 'X-Time', fly hesitantly and cautiously towards the enemy.

Ernst Udet, General Inspector of Aircraft, had imported the idea of the dive-bomber from the USA in 1933, when he was able to observe the way in which the American 'Helldiver' could hit targets accurately to within thirty metres. He acquired two machines from the Curteis-Wright Works, shipped them over to Germany and had them examined by Junkers, where the firm's experts carried out tests and after some years produced the Ju 87, based on the US model. The dive-bombers had their baptism of fire in Spain, as a result of which their engine power was doubled to 1,150 h.p.

The ugly, cheap planes turned into the terror-weapon of

the German Luftwaffe, and were soon known as 'Stukas' – a name that in this war will strike fear into everyone who hears it. Its long approach begins from 12,000 feet, usually under fighter protection. Then comes the fix on the target. The radiator-flaps close; the elevators open; the dive-brakes slam into action; and the single-engined aircraft flips over, often at 200, 250, even 300 m.p.h., and begins to drop at a seventy-degree angle, screaming, screaming, screaming ... Closer, louder, more terrifying all the time ...

The final test fourteen days previously at Neuhammer near Cottbus had been a bloody failure. The first group of Dive-Bomber Squadron 76 had been supposed to take up twenty-seven planes and show the full, horrific capability of these steel birds of prey. Suddenly there was ground-fog, which the planes plunged into at something like 300 feet per second. Their commander, Walter Siegel, was able to pull up his aircraft only a few yards from the ground and warn the other crews over the radio link.

The warning came too late for eleven of the aircraft. They smashed straight into the dry brushwood on the airfield, exploding on impact. Two further Ju 87s overflew and hit the tree line. The area was littered with burning wrecks that reduced precious machinery and human beings alike to cinders. Twenty-six pilots and gunners died that day – but young Flight-Commander Dilley is able to comfort himself with the thought, or rather the actor's superstition, that when the dress-rehearsal is a disaster, the main performance will be all right ...

Fog is still the worst enemy of the new miracle-weapon, but Oberleutnant Dilley and his men are not on a dive-bombing mission today. Nevertheless, the approach to the railway bridge is perilous in the extreme: a mere thirty feet above the ground, right down in the basement, then maybe 300 feet visibility for two or three seconds, when they have to get their sight of the objective. The three attacking aircraft are sometimes so close that a collision seems inevitable, but somehow they avoid each other and disappear from view in the formless swathes of fog.

Two minutes flying-time to go. Nothing moving. As they fly over the heavily-wooded border area, gaze down at the roads, it is still eerily quiet. The three crews stare into the wall of mist until their eyes burn. For the most part they see nothing, nothing at all. But at least there are no Polish fighters. The three Jus come in low over the river Vistula – any moment now they will catch their first sight of the unmistakable steel bridge through the morning mist. No anti-aircraft fire yet. The massive metal vultures seem to be leading a charmed life, but that situation can change from one moment to the next.

04.35 hours. The Stukas have reached their objective. Thirty feet below them is the railway embankment that leads to the bridge. Oberleutnant Dilley presses the button and releases his lethal load – one 250-kilo bomb in the Stuka's arse-end and four 50-kilo bombs under the wings. A fraction of a second and he is forcing his aircraft into a climb, heading away from the railway line, hearing explosions behind him. To his left and right the two other Stukas are attacking.

Their bombs also hit the target.

The Stukas climb sharply, bank and head for home. Behind them, billowing columns of smoke burst towards the sky. The pilots keep skilfully to the basement without incident and land at Elbing to a storm of welcoming applause from the ground crew.

'Mission accomplished,' says the Oberleutnant tersely.

The Poles, of course, now know what is happening. They will try to blow the bridge as quickly as they can. Dornier seventeen bombers – known by their crews as 'flying pencils' – are under orders to go in in waves after an hour for a second attack. And Colonel Medem's task-force is due to head straight over the border from its base at Dirschau to take the bridge intact by the land-route.

It is 04.45 hours. The moment of the attack. It begins rather undramatically: no big artillery bombardment as in the battles of the First War; just the growl of engines and sporadic machine-gun fire. The sole hindrance to the advance of the 35th Regiment's spearheads are the propaganda photographers from Goebbels' ministry, who insist on getting impact-filled snaps of the ritual tearing-down of the border barriers.

No time for that kind of pantomime. The Panzers roll forward. Supply-units will pose for the cameras, but then who cares? The war that the weekly newsreel shows is a prettified version, or maybe even faked.

Brave Kudritzki sits in his Panzer I over his machine-gun and can't believe his eyes. No enemy soldiers, no machine-gun nests, no anti-tank positions. 'Those damned Poles must have overslept,' he says to Lochner; the driver nods, though he can't understand a word above the din of the engines.

Suddenly all hell breaks loose.

Machine-gun fire from their left.

It sounds as if a shower of pebbles are breaking against the turret. For a moment Kudritzki finds himself amazed that the thin armour-plate is really deflecting the bullets. Then he makes his report to his company commander and is ordered to deal with the thinly-held infantry position,

The Panzer I rolls towards it. Sixty metres to go. The Poles use their grenades far too early. Another ten metres. Five. Kudritzki fires both barrels of his machine-gun. One of the defenders loses his nerve, jumps up.

He is the first to be caught by the Panzer's tracks. The six-ton monster rumbles forward over the machine-gun position, turns on its tracks, stops for an instant, turns again. Anything underneath will have been pulverised by the weight of the vehicle.

Then Lochner steps on the accelerator, lurches back to the road, edges his way back into the strung-out column. 'Instructions carried out, Herr Leutnant,' Kudritzki bellows into his microphone. 'Enemy machine-gun nest eliminated.'

His voice may sound fine, but he is less than happy. He can feel vomit rising in his gorge. He can still see the face of the poor swine who tried to get away and was squelched by the Panzer's tracks.

He bites his lip, takes aim at invisible enemies. Gradually

the tension subsides, though his nerves are still jangling in time with the engines. The armoured column is making decent progress. The sun-baked ground is hard, ideal for tracked vehicles. The Narew, Bug and Vistula rivers are low; even if the bridges have been blown, the spearhead of the 10th Army will have no trouble in crossing them.

The sound of the motors is monotonous, almost soporific. A relieved Kudritzki tells himself that this is just like outdoor manoeuvres at home, when he's rolling over the roads around Bamberg and counting the girls: always too few girls and too many soldiers. But many of them have more than one. Kudritzki, for example, has a second girl in Kamenz, where he used to be stationed, and he splits his leaves between her and her rival in Bamberg.

Now leave seems a long way away. The column is rolling forward with the armoured reconnaissance vehicles at its head, straight along the road in the direction of Lublinitz. A village is in flames on the horizon. The armoured spearhead divides. The first Panzers turn north towards Wielun, twenty kilometres from the border, while the second bunch deal with the Polish defensive positions. Civilians are dodging in and out of the fighting in blind panic.

As the day grows lighter, the sun is blocked out by German aircraft. Short-distance commuting to Poland and back, not even elbow-room up there at 12,000 feet. The groups of planes are heading for Lodz, Kattowitz, Krosno. There was no chance for a mass take-off, as planned – the last aircraft could only be mobilised during the late morning – but now they are working overtime, as if making up for lost opportunities.

Their objectives are threefold: first they are to deal with their immediate opponents, the Polish Airforce, if possible destroying it on the ground; second, they will wage a strategic battle against the enemy hinterland, hitting railway junctions, ammunition dumps and troop-concentrations; and thirdly they will play a ground-support role.

Drawing on his experiences in Spain, Luftwaffe commander Major-General von Richthofen has formed special close-combat squadrons composed of light bombers and Stukas – albeit against opposition within his own branch. These are the first to close with the enemy, flying along the main line of fighting, giving tactical support to the Panzer formations. Returning Heinkel-111 crews report that they have destroyed hundreds of Polish aircraft on the ground. But the general belief that air superiority has been seized on this first day will soon be revealed as erroneous: the Poles had removed most of their battleworthy planes to rear areas and left only training aircraft, dummies and unusable machines behind as targets. The active air force units will, however, not be used against the Nazi aggressors, because their superiors in the Polish Army High Command have no idea what to do with them. In any case, they are hopelessly outclassed by the speed, weaponry and manoeuvrability of the German Me 109.

Fuel runs low, but the 35th Panzer Regiment keeps rolling on. Kudritzki doesn't care where they're going; the main thing is that they're moving forwards. He knows the old army saying that it's best to leave thinking to horses – they've got bigger heads. It never occurred to him to object when he, a protestant, was ordered to attend a military communion at the catholic Bamberg Cathedral. The local commander, a craggy General – who would insist on appearing in full uniform every year at the Corpus Christi procession, right behind the canopy, to the fury of the local Nazi boss – had ordered ten men from each company to the service. The sharp lad from Essen would rather be a catholic for an hour than end up in the glass-house.

Suddenly, it's all happening. The Poles are dug in on the edge of the forest. The German artillery gives all it's got – but the gunners haven't reckoned with the speed of the Panzers, and so the shells explode among their own combat vehicles.

An explosion in front and a little to the left. Then one right behind Kudritzki's Panzer. A direct-hit on one ahead. A Panzer I goes up in a sheet of flame. Death is riding on wings of fire. A funeral pyre for Unteroffizer Meersmann, who had been so proud that no one in his division had to walk, and for his driver, Pauli.

*

The invaders have launched an inexorable attack on a front 280 kilometres long, from Slovakia, from Silesia, from Pomerania and from East Prussia. 'Western Poland had become a huge Salient that projected between Germany's jaws,' wrote the British military expert Liddell Hart in his *History of the Second World War*.

In the north, the planes have to wait until midday before they can take off. The first, bloody battles come in the southern sector.

The Poles have over forty divisions and eleven cavalry brigades, divided into seven Armies and for the most part concentrated in the border areas around Posen, Lodz and Cracow. Twelve reserve divisions are ready in the Random area. They are poorly equipped and, as the American author Kenneth Macksey states in his book on the Panzer General, *Guderian*, 'The Poles' strength in defending their country stemmed principally from their grim determination to defend their newly-won independence.'

In fact, they have no chance of doing so. The core of their army is the cavalry. Mounted units are everywhere, horses wherever one looks, and their riders are waiting for the chance to attack the invaders. They have been told that the German Panzers are made of cardboard and canvas, and so, as they clash, two worlds meet: squadrons of cavalrymen engaged in a hopeless conflict, attacking twentieth-century armoured monsters with lances straight out of the Middle Ages. The blood-letting is horrific, and the Panzers move forward, sweeping them out of their path like troublesome insects. If they get stuck, they call on the artillery. If they are beyond the range of the German guns, they summon the Stukas as 'airborne artillery'. There are Luftwaffe officers riding along with Panzer columns, in constant radio contact with their ground-attack squadrons, ready to conjure up air support within minutes.

Anything that resists is crushed, pulverised, shot to pieces, liquidated. The concrete bunkers defending Lublinitz are smashed during the first assault. The Wehrmacht unleashes a whirlwind to conquer Poland, and the world learns a new concept: *Blitzkrieg*.

It is a whole new dimension of slaughter.

The crews of the 35th Panzer Regiment experience war as triumph and terror. At the same time as their machine-guns and turret-mounted cannon are taking aim against Polish cavalry units, they are eye-witnesses to an unimaginable horror near Wielun as Stukas attack a two-mile-long cavalry column. After hours of constant bombing and machine-gun strafing the entire brigade is wiped out.

The leading vehicles of the 35th Panzer Regiment have now halted, not because of the Polish cavalry brigade but because of shortage of fuel. The soldiers will have to wait for supplies to be brought up. Kudritzki climbs out of his Panzer to relieve himself, has to wade through shattered animals, screaming wounded and maimed corpses.

A horse is grazing peacefully in the meadow near Kudritzki. A bomb-splinter has torn open its body; its entrails are hanging down to the ground. The animal obviously feels no pain, simply stares at Kudritzki through great, sad eyes. He snaps the safety-catch off his 0.8, strokes the horse's neck with his left hand. The creature turns towards him and licks his hand with its long tongue.

The shot rings out.

The horse jerks its legs, falls beside a dying Pole.

The man grimaces painfully. 'Th-th-thank you.'

'What's that?' said Kudritzki, bending over the man with tears glistening in his eyes.

'Thank you,' the dying man repeats a second time.

'How did you get to speak German like that?' the private shouts at him in horror, and then he realises that the man is one of the many ethnic Germans who have donned Polish uniform to fight the invaders.

On the morning of September 1st, there were repeated announcements on German radio stations to the effect that the Reichstag had been summoned for an extraordinary session and that Adolf Hitler would be making an important statement. As the dictator swept along the narrow, crowded street towards the Kroll Opera House with his motorcade, his fanatical, applauding supporters could see that for the first time he had exchanged his brown Nazi uniform for one of army field-grey.

The gloomy tones of the Badenweiler March resounded in the parliament building. Then, on this Black Friday in the world's history, Hitler strode to the speaker's rostrum and began his address with the words, 'Deputies, men of the German Reichstag!'

In Greater Germany alone, where schools, factories, offices and garrisons had organised him a radio audience, he could rely on the spellbound attention of some fifty million human beings, who did not yet know that a few hours previously the bloodiest massacre in history had begun to the east.

Hitler, the skilled rabble-rouser, spoke of the 'throttling' of the free city of Danzig, the war unleashed by the Poles against the Germans there – perhaps, he hinted, with the co-operation of 'barbaric, savage soldiery'. He proclaimed his 'limitless patience' and asserted, with reference to the attacks on the Gleiwitz radio transmitter and elsewhere in the border area stage-managed by Himmler, that, 'Poland tonight fired on our own territory for the first time, using regular soldiers. Since 5.45 a.m., we have been returning fire! From now on, bomb will be answered with bomb! . . . I intend to conduct this struggle – against whomsoever it is necessary – until the security and rights of the Reich are assured! . . . I demand nothing from any German man that I was not prepared to give for four years. There will be no deprivations that I will not immediately also take upon myself! From this moment, my entire life belongs wholly to the German people! From now on, my only wish is to be the first soldier of the German Reich. For this reason I have put on once more the uniform that was always my holiest and dearest possession. I shall take it off only after the victory or, – I shall not live to see the end! . . . I should, however, like to assure the rest of the world: there will never be another November 1918 in German history. Just as I am prepared to give my life for my people and for Germany, so I demand the same thing from everyone else! Anyone who believes that they can oppose this national imperative, directly or indirectly, will be crushed. We shall have no truck with traitors! We recognise only our ancient principle: it is completely unimportant whether we survive, but it is essential that our people, our Germany, lives!'

Hysterical applause from his followers obscured the notes of the national anthem, and also the knowledge that the apostle of force had finally destroyed peace – an hour earlier than he cared to admit. A nation that at the last count totalled eighty-six million souls stood between euphoria and despair. While the radio newsreaders announced that the Iron Cross would be re-instituted for the third time – the first German soldier to receive it had already fallen in action – the public asked themselves whether Hitler would succeed in keeping the Western Allies at least out of the war with Poland.

If the French, with their two million men and their heavy tank forces, were to attack the West Wall, Hitler's unfinished brainchild, Germany would not be able to put up a single motorised force in its defence. Six and a half German Panzer divisions and all the Wehrmacht's motorised units were involved, along with most of the country's combat-ready infantry regiments in Poland. The 'Watch on the Rhine' was being maintained by 216 fighter aircraft and a few hastily-formed, scantily-trained and below-strength reserve divisions and soldiers of the Home Guard.

'The thought of what would happen in the case of a French attack immediately after the outbreak of war was enough to make the hair of the experts serving with the Army of the West stand on end,' admitted General Siegfried Westphal, Chief-of-Staff of the Army of the West.

The gambler in the Reich Chancellery was in fine fettle on the evening of September 1st. His forces had smashed their way into Poland without a declaration of war, and so far the French and the English had not lifted a finger. Hitler loudly read the victory reports from all sectors to his cronies: in the north the German forces were pushing forward from East Prussia towards the defensive ring around Mlava which was supposed to protect the Polish capital. In the corridor, the spearheads of the 3rd and 4th Armies were getting closer to each other. The advance was proceeding with a speed never before witnessed, though the enemy was defending bitterly and with a near-insane courage.

A typical example of the Poles' bravery was the battle for the Vistula bridge at Dirschau. Despite the swashbuckling raid by Oberleutnant Dilley and his Stukas, despite devastating follow-up attacks, despite the Panzers of Medem's task force, which were supposed to seize a bridgehead and secure the Vistula crossing, the decimated Polish sappers succeeded in repairing the shattered explosive charges and blew the mighty bridge sky-high at the last moment.

It was not the only débâcle suffered by the invaders on this first day. The new methods of waging war were still unfamiliar. Aircraft festooned with swastikas were repeatedly fired upon from their own infantry positions. Again and again, He 111s and Ju 87s dropped bombs on their own lines. On more than one occasion, the 'slaughtermen' – as the troops called the HS-123 formations, approvingly or angrily, depending on the situation – mounted savage low-level attacks on German ground units which had failed to show the spread-out recognition tarpaulin soon enough or clearly enough. Occasionally, the German infantry, not yet battle-hardened, retreated in the face of the headlong courage of the Polish cavalry.

But on the whole, the war they had unleashed on the country ran with clockwork precision. The Polish Commander-in-Chief, Edward Rydz-Smigly, had reckoned that things would begin at a more leisurely pace, and now he was being literally crushed by the speed of the German advance. The Generalissimo, a handsome story-book hero, cut a great figure in a drawing-room but was indecisive in the front line, and he had failed to draw up an effective plan of defence. He relied totally on improvised counter-attacks and was guilty of self-deception regarding the extent to which the Allies would give immediate support to Poland. The main part of his forces lay west of the Vistula, and thus were lost if the German Army Group South succeeded in its encircling manoeuvre. Its fate would have been avoidable if the defenders had been placed beyond the Vistula and San rivers – which admittedly would have meant sacrificing the industrial areas west of the river barriers.

The Poles were not the only people to ask themselves whether the English and the French would keep to their commitments. The telephone lines between London and Paris glowed red-hot. On the second day of the war, the Allies almost came to blows: the French were inclined to accept Mussolini's mediatory suggestion of a four-power conference. The English rejected this solution. The American President, Franklin D. Roosevelt, declared the USA's strict neutrality and forbade the export of any war supplies.

Hitler was overjoyed. Despite all the doomsayers, he had judged the 'aunts' correctly yet again. He would overrun Poland before his opponents reached agreement on what they would or would not do.

On the radio, special announcement succeeded special announcement. The two Panzer Divisions attached to the 10th Army had reached the Warthe, advancing eighty kilometres in thirty-six hours. The Jablunka Pass in the extreme south of the front, which had seen bloody fighting in the First War, was captured by subterfuge by soldiers of the 'Special Unit Brandenburg', Admiral Canaris's private army, with the support of Slovakian troops. It was not a fighter pilot but a Stuka gunner, Unteroffizier Frank Neubert, who gained the first aerial victory of the Second World War. He declared in a radio interview, 'I came across a single Ju 87 that was being attacked by two Polish fighters. I immediately took a firm decision to help this comrade and then attempt to close on the Polish fighters and achieve a kill-position. When I had succeeded in this, I fired off one burst without visible success. After another burst, I saw the tracer from my guns disappear into the cockpit of the Polish aircraft. But at first there was no further reaction. As I prepared to attack for a third time, the plane suddenly exploded in mid-air; it flared up into a great ball of fire; the fragments literally flew around our ears ...'

The previously-unused Polish bombers and fighters intervened in the fighting for the first time. There was a fifty-minute aerial battle at 6,000 feet north of Warsaw between 100 German aircraft – mostly Me 110s – and sixty-four Polish fighters of the P 11 type, high-winged monoplanes whose manufacture dated back to 1931. Their top speed at sea level was about 160 m.p.h., and though at 6,000 feet they could reach 225 m.p.h., they were still far too slow to match the He 111s, which usually attacked from 12,000 feet.

There could be no question of pursuit under these circumstances. The pilots could only fly straight at their opponents, try to get within their line of flight, and then attempt to bring them down with what guns they had.

September 3rd was a pleasant autumn day. The morning brought more sunshine and more reports of victories. At nine o'clock the British Ambassador, Henderson, presented himself at the Foreign Office in Berlin in an attempt to secure an urgent meeting with the Foreign Minister. The Wilhelmstrasse seemed to be still asleep. Neither Ribbentrop nor any of the Foreign Office's top officials were available. The English diplomat was admitted to see the interpreter Paul Schmidt, who took delivery of a note. It contained an ultimatum: unless Hitler did not order his troops out of Poland, unconditionally, before 11 a.m. – two hours' time – then Great Britain would regard herself as in a state of war with Greater Germany.

At 17.00 hours the French Ambassador presented a declaration of war in which the actual word 'war' was avoided. The spectre that had always haunted Germany's generals, the prospect of a two-front war, had become a reality. It meant that the elite forces would have to be withdrawn from the East as quickly as possible and transferred westwards.

Field Marshal Rydz-Smigly hoped that these moves on the Allies' part signalled relief for Poland. He had been promised that the French would launch an offensive against Germany as soon as war started. However it wasn't until September 7th that a mere nine divisions of the French army moved into the Saar and after five days they had gained only five miles of ground against practically no opposition. After two weeks the French were ordered back to the Maginot Line. Nothing had been achieved.

The British were further from the action and thus distanced from direct involvement in the war. Even before the Expeditionary Force landed in France, the British Air Force had been forced to cut back on its activities. The RAF's strength was theoretically equal to that of the Luftwaffe, but many of its planes were obsolete and fit only for scrap. They had no self-sealing fuel tanks and thus were liable to be easy prey for the Messerschmitts that had been left in the West. Besides Wellingtons, the British still used the veteran Hampden and Whitley bombers, but the only things that they dropped were leaflets. These – according to a later Air Marshal – could serve no other purpose than to provide German households with extra supplies of toilet paper.

They sneaked in at night at very high altitude. 'Things were such for the observer and radio-operator at this time that they had to lie down and rest every few minutes,' said a report from a Whitley crew responsible for dropping leaflets over Frankfurt and Düsseldorf. 'The heating in the cockpit proved useless. We were terribly cold and possessed no means of doing anything about the fact. The commander and the observer used to bang their heads against the floor and the map-table, deliberately creating another pain to distract themselves from the agony of oxygen starvation and extreme cold.'

This war got underway with extreme slowness so far as the Allies were concerned. By the time that the French and the British finally engaged Hitler militarily, the Corridor had already been taken by German troops. In the north, armoured spearheads were pushing forward towards the positions on the Narew. The 10th Army had already crossed the Warthe. The ideal flying and tank weather held. There were no autumn rainstorms.

German air superiority was already beyond question. When individual Polish planes dared to show themselves, they were chased out of the sky. It was common for pilots to return to base and find it destroyed or occupied by German forces. The horse-drawn Polish artillery – they possessed no motorised units at all – was put out of action by German fighter aircraft, which shot away the horses from their gun-carriages.

On September 5th, Rydz-Smigly finally ordered his troops to pull back behind the Vistula. Apart from the fact that the message did not get through in many areas because communications had been destroyed, the order came too late for many units. The Germans pushed on and on without ceasing, with the Panzers always in the vanguard, regardless of the situation on their flanks.

In Lodz, the army under the Polish General Juliusz Rommel, the defender of Warsaw, found itself bypassed, while the army of General Tadeusz Kytrzeba was left behind in Posen.

In the north, Guderian's Panzer Corps had crossed the Narew and was attacked along the Bug behind Warsaw. The spearhead of the 10th Army exploited a gap between Lodz and the Piliza and as early as September 8th had made an epic march of 200 kilometres to push forward into the heavily-defended outskirts of Warsaw.

The speed of its advance had meant losing touch with the 8th Army which was fighting further to the north. Its four infantry divisions suddenly found themselves cut off on the south side of the Bzura, which snakes around the countryside 100 kilometres west of Warsaw. The invaders faced a grave crisis. Kutrzeba, whose forces had been hiding in the forests by day, began a series of forced marches under cover of darkness which took him eastwards. In the process, the Army of Posen was swollen by stragglers from other units. By the time that it reached Kutno, it had grown to 170,000 men, and the Polish General saw the opportunity for which he had been waiting so long.

In a basin formed by wide plains, a lake and thick forests, the cavalry squadrons formed up for their attack. They forced their way across the Bzura by dint of superior numbers, and for the first time the cavalry and the few Polish tanks were able to break through the invaders' lines. The 30th Infantry Division, finding itself in a desperate situation, turned to the commander of the Army Group

South, Colonel-General Gerd von Rundstedt, and he in turn requested help from air force commander, von Richthofen. While the 35th Panzer Division sat at the gates of Warsaw waiting for fuel and ammunition, the Poles were driving a huge wedge that threatened to smash the German armies apart.

The German Panzers keep on rolling, without bothering to secure their flanks, relying on their own invincibility and the power of their air support. They halt only when they run out of fuel, and then they must wait impatiently for the supply lines to catch up with them.

After an astonishing breakthrough, the 10th Army reaches the suburbs of Warsaw as early as September 8th. In the vanguard is the 35th, under the swashbuckling command of the later General of Panzer Troops Heinrich Eberbach. It is a regiment driven by the Devil himself, and it is prepared to try to take the enemy's capital alone, if necessary. Anything on wheels or two legs is pushed forward, through glum working-class districts, on along the main highway, past the park, in the direction of the main station.

The crazy Panzer men are greeted with withering defensive fire from cellars and open spaces, high-rise buildings and storage sheds. The Poles try to disable the Panzers by placing explosive charges under their tracks, defend their positions with grenades and cleverly-camouflaged anti-tank dugouts.

Leutnant Class's Panzer – the lead vehicle of the First Company – is set on fire by a direct hit but keeps rolling. The next hit blows the driver to bits. The young Leutnant and his radio operator stumble from the sea of flames, lie still, are recovered – dead.

The old fortifications are overrun, but the casualties are becoming intolerable. When the smoke clears, for a moment war shows its true face and talk of a 'stroll to Warsaw' seems hollow: of an entire squadron of tanks sent to clear the park, only three come back. Another casualty is the commander of No. 8 Company, Oberleutnant Morgenrot. Disabled

Panzers are towed away under enemy fire.

The attempt to storm Warsaw fails. The men of the 35th are forced to retreat. They care for their wounded, bury their dead. Then they stand around, twiddling their thumbs, telling bad jokes, taking a quick nap in the shade, peering at the western horizon from where the trucks full of supplies must appear at some stage. In an hour, in a day, or maybe never. And that will mean no fuel, no ammunition, and no mail. And without fuel their Panzers are as helpless as turtles turned on their backs.

They have placed sentries. Since fat Rambold was skewered by a cavalry patrol that burst suddenly out of the woods while he was taking a leak, they have become damned careful and follow orders with painful precision.

The men are scarred by their exertions. Contrary to the Old Man's orders, they have long since been fighting the war unshaven. They have been driving on and ever on, to hell or high water, sweaty and filthy but nevertheless halfways content, because, so they say, the sooner they get to Warsaw the sooner the war will be over. And that will mean a wash, some sleep, furlough, perhaps even home leave.

'I've got three cigarettes left,' says Kudritzki. 'If those friggin' trucks don't arrive soon, I shall have to start sucking my thumb.'

'You could have a long wait,' grumbles Lochner. His face had gained lines in the past days, and his hair seems permanently on end. One of his eyelids twitches nervously like a faulty connection. 'The Poles are smoking the bastards,' the driver mutters acidly. 'They've had your ciggies in their pockets long since.'

'Miserable sod!' growls Kudritzki. 'You get more bitter and twisted all the time. Not surprising ... ' Then he adds bitingly, so that everyone can hear, 'Your sour arse-hole couldn't manage a cheerful fart.'

The rest of them laugh. Then immediately their eyes go skywards. The 'slaughtermen' are back, the planes that have trailed in their wake all through Poland like vultures following a caravan in the desert. The Luftwaffe had only been able to put thirty-six into service on the entire front. Six of the HS 123s have gone out of action in the meantime, but the remaining thirty give an impression of permanent presence by flying constantly – up to ten missions a day each. The bases from which these durable aircraft operate have, like the Stuka airstrips, been switched to Polish soil. Since they need less than two hundred metres clearance to take off, they can use practically any cornfield, engage the enemy at low altitude, and then fly straight back to refuel.

'They've got it made,' Kudritzki says. 'When it gets dark, they grab themselves a bath, drink a nice cold beer and go to sleep in a freshly-made bed.'

'Green-eyed monster,' says Lochner, getting his own back.

Seven, eight, nine, twelve aircraft. The terrible din of their engines tears at the nerves. With the aid of its 660 h.p. BMW engines, the 'One-Two-Three', built at the locomotive factory in Kassel, can reach a speed of 300 kilometres per hour. They are not good climbers, but in a permanent ground-support role the pilots rarely need to get above 800 feet. They often fly so low over the front that the troops they are attacking believe that they can throw stones at them and shoot at them with all they have. But the planes are tough. The pilots are protected by the big radial engine and an armoured plate behind their seats. Of all German aircraft, the 'One-Two-Three' is the one most capable of taking punishment.

The formation turns north, takes a fix on the cavalry units of the Army of Posen, then dive. At the same moment, Lochner yells, 'The trucks! The trucks are here!'

While the men of the 35th Panzers refuel their vehicles and stock up on ammunition, ready to go back to the war, the 'slaughtermen' attack the forward units of General Kutrzeba's army. The planes' strength is in their armaments. They carry two machine-guns mounted in their propellors, each possesses two fifty-kilo bombs and ninety-four two-kilo explosive charges. There is an auxiliary tank in their tailplane which they can drop among the enemy with something like the effect of a napalm bomb.

Major-General von Richthofen has sent thirty HS 112s from the second Wing of Air Group 2 to deal with the crisis affecting the 30th Infantry Division.

'To Kutrzeba's men, almost none of whom had been under air attack before, the next twenty minutes were like a nightmare in hell. The machine guns cut swathes in the ranks of men and horses; hundreds of the lightweight scatter bombs flamed and exploded; the heavier detonations of the 110-pounders tore gouts out of the earth, ripped through trees and flung jagged metal shards thudding into men and animals.' So Herbert Molloy Mason describes the scene in his book, *The Luftwaffe*. The attack lasted all day with Henschels being followed by Stukas, which were followed by Dorniers and Heinkels and a final assault made by Me 110s. The attack was renewed the next day until the Army of Posen was forced back into a twenty-by-thirty-mile enclave.

The crisis was over. The 10th, 8th and 4th Armies surrounded Kutrzeba's forces to the north, east and south, and in a battle that cost many lives they forced them into a narrow area between the Bzura and the Vistula. The Poles continued to fight with desperate courage, though they had no chance: only a handful of Polish soldiers succeeded in escaping through the German lines by using little-known tracks under cover of darkness.

And the German air formations continued to pound them. 'A furious air assault was made on the river crossings near Witkovice which, for the number of aircraft engaged, the violence of their attack and the acrobatic daring of their pilots, must have been unprecedented. Every movement, every troop concentration, every line of advance came under pulverising bombardment from the air ...' said General Kutrzeba afterwards. 'The bridges were destroyed, the fords blocked, the waiting columns of men decimated ... Three of us found some sort of cover in a grove of birch trees outside the village of Myszory. There we remained, unable to stir, until about noon when the air raids stopped. We knew it was only for a moment, but had we stayed there the chances of any of us surviving would have been slight.'

The 'Battle of Kutno', fought around the great bend in the Vistula, ended on September 17th. 170,000 Polish soldiers became prisoners of the Germans. The first great 'cauldron battle' of the Second World War had been won. It is true that a few fortresses and strongpoints continued to hold out with desperate courage – such as Warsaw, the Polish capital, and Hela, the Westerplatte and Modlin – but the Germans had broken the back of the seven Polish armies.

But it was not the Germans who delivered the *coup de grâce*. It came from a totally unexpected quarter. On September 17th, the day of the surrender on the Bzura, Soviet divisions crossed the eastern border in a wide front. The Red Army fought its way towards Narew, the Vistula and the San. The defenders, finished in any case, were now forced to fight a two-front war. They put up fanatical resistance against the Soviet aggressors between Bialystok and Kowel. 737 Russians died in the fighting.

German and Soviet troops met in friendship at the 'Demarcation Line'. The invaders from the West pulled back; the men from the East moved forward. The city of Lvov, recently beseiged by German forces, was now overrun by the Red Army. The Poles only surrendered to the Red Army when they were guaranteed free passage to Rumania. The Soviets broke their promise and 217,000 Polish soldiers became prisoners of the Russians.

Warsaw had been encircled by German forces and was to be forced into surrender by a blockade. Hitler insisted that it be brought to its knees by a bombardment. From morning until night, German aircraft filled the skies over the near-defenceless city. Stuka bombs destroyed the water supplies. The artillery rained down death on residential districts. The horizon was filled with billowing smoke from the inferno that was Warsaw. Finally, even Ju 52 transport aircraft were brought in. Since they had no bomb bays, they simply sowed death through their open doors. The gunners used coal-shovels to drop tons of small incendiary bombs on the city. Women and children made desperate attempts to quench the sea of flames with water that was fast running out.

Even before the fall of Warsaw, Hitler had ordered an offensive in the West for the autumn of 1939. On September 27th the Polish capital capitulated. The next day, Germany and the Soviet Union sealed the fourth partition of Poland with a 'Border and Friendship Treaty'. Only now did the world learn of the secret pact between the two totalitarian states, under which Hitler also granted Lithuania to the Russians.

The co-operation between the two savage brothers, Hitler and Stalin, paved the way for such horrors as Auschwitz, Treblinka, Maidenek and Bergen-Belsen. And also Katyn. There, in the midst of dense pine forests, the mass-graves of 4,100 Polish officers were later discovered, all killed by the Soviets through pistol-shots in the back of the neck. Historians estimate that a total of 10,000 members of the Polish officer corps were liquidated in this way.

The Soviets had signed a non-aggression pact with the Poles which was still valid and which they ignored. The British and the French had a treaty with the Poles that committed them to make war on any power that attacked their country. In direct contravention of that agreement, they refused to declare war on Stalin. The Border and Friendship Pact between Greater Germany and the Soviet Union, supposed to last ten years, was to remain in force for a mere nineteen months. It was irrelevant who signed them. In that year of 1939, treaties were not worth the paper they were printed on.

The nineteen-day campaign in the East is over. 700,000 Poles have become prisoners of the Germans. 160,000 have succeeded in reaching neighbouring countries and later continuing the struggle. On the German side, 10,572 soldiers have been killed, 3,409 are missing, and 30,322 have been wounded. 285 German aircraft have been lost.

Long before the end of the Polish Campaign, half of the German air strength had been transferred to the West. In the same way, the Panzer units, which had suffered losses but had performed brilliantly, were pulled out of the fight before the end. They are to be repaired at their bases in Germany, their engines overhauled, and personnel losses made up.

So the 35th Panzers, on its way back home by rail, is

missing from the big victory parade in Warsaw. 'They had forgotten to invite the 4th Panzer Division,' according to Hans Schäufler's chronicle, *So They Lived, So They Died*. 'But the bullet-riddled and partly burned-out thirty Panzers from our regiment that lined the route from the edge of the city to the main station were sufficient to remind the men who took part in the parade that it was we who were the first unit to penetrate deep into the city during those bloody battles of September 8th and September 9th.'

Kudritzki, Seelman and Gütler find themselves kept in Poland on a mission that has nothing to do with army regulations. Travelling from unit to unit, they finally end up in the vicinity of Wielun, under orders to report to a German commission investigating cases of missing men. It is a time-comsuming job, but it enables them to be their own bosses, and the three Panzer soldiers have learned the value of that.

They fill themselves up with food, and then they end up guzzling schnapps first thing in the morning, as if they are trying to put some courage in their own bellies. They have been told to stand ready, but it is not long until they are fetched.

A fresh mass-grave, just excavated, filled with semi-decomposed corpses wearing a sort of civilian garb. Reserve troops, who have piled up their rifles in a pyramid, are recovering the horrific finds. It is a slow process. From time to time a man breaks down and has to be replaced, because both the stench and the sight of those bodies is intolerable.

While they are hauling these products of German heroism out of the hole in the ground, it so happens that a propaganda unit are parked nearby, engaged in repairing the loudspeaker on one of their trucks. It is their job to travel from unit to unit, strengthening the martial spirit. Their main standby is a collection of the Führer's speeches on records.

'Come here, Kudritzki,' says a medical officer.

The boy from Essen finds himself looking down at Sagorski's shattered corpse and the almost unrecognisable face of Kienbaum. He can feel his stomach starting to heave, the schnapps rising slowly but inexorably into his gullet. He nods and makes to leave.

'Don't be so lily-livered!' bellows the M.O. 'You'll see enough stiffs in future.' He notices that his chiding has failed to affect the boy, who seems totally distracted, and adds a little more gently: 'It's not much fun for any of us, but we have to have the names, for their families.'

Kudritzki is standing staring at a corpse that he can no longer identify. At that moment, the broadcasting truck bursts into life with Hitler's voice intoning the words, 'We recognise only our ancient principle ...'

'Leimer,' Kudritzki says dully. 'That must be Leutnant Leimer.'

The M.O. nods. 'And who is the one with the burned-up face?' he asks.

The Private shakes his head. The other two cannot name a name either.

'It is completely unimportant whether we survive,' the loudspeaker drones on. 'But it is essential that our people, our Germany lives!'

Kudritzki leans against a tree and throws up. Then he pulls himself together and searches among the dead for his friend Haselmann. Only later will he learn that the boy with the freckles was hidden by sympathetic civilians, concealed from their own soldiers and looked after. After the German advance, Haselmann had to have his right leg amputated at the knee. For him the war is over, or for the moment, at least. No one can imagine the war going on for so long, and turning into such a desperate struggle, that they will stoop to using one-legged men as supply drivers.

For the moment, the German public demands its heroes, the men who have achieved the first 'lightning victory' in history. On the streets of Bamberg, too, crowds line the route between the station and the barracks, and Hitler Youth and civilians alike cheer their returning heroes home. The Panzers have been cleaned, the soldiers have shaved, and for the most part they have medals on their chests. The Panzer commanders stand in their open turrets in their black uniforms with the death's head on their caps and wave casually.

None of the onlookers watching this triumphal procession is aware that there are forty-five Panzers missing, or that sixty-four soldiers died and fifty-eight were wounded, in the 'stroll to Warsaw'.

Special Operation 'P'

Huge swarms of shrieking gulls circle around the lithe steel shark. Yet again, the captain of U-47 is with Kommodore Dönitz, commander of U-boats, on board the cruiser *Weichsel*. They are in permanent conference in the officer's mess, the second session in two days. And the whole crew knows full well that Kapitänleutnant Günther Prien – a slight, wiry man who can smile like a boy and curse like a drayman – would far rather be with his pretty wife and their sweet daughter at their home in the naval quarter of Kiel-Wik.

'Wouldn't mind knowing what they're jawing about over there,' says Corporal-Radio Operator Steinhagen.

'There's something cooking, you can bet on it, mate,' answers Able Seaman Thewes, the mechanic. 'The old man wants to earn himself a tin necktie,' he adds, stroking his throat where the Knight's Cross would sit if he had one.

'Why not?' chips in Hötzer, the Engineer. 'We'll sure as hell do well out of it, too.'

'Iron Cross Second Class at least,' Thewes agrees. 'And maybe a home leave on top of that.'

'Yeah. So's you can pull the girls, eh?' says Steinhagen, with a grin that splits his face from ear to ear. 'The hero of the Seven Seas, eh?'

The rest of them laugh, and then they start wondering again whether this time it will be the North Sea, or the Atlantic, or back to the Bay of Biscay. The guesses are getting pretty wild, turning into barefaced lies, when young Oberleutnant Varendorff butts into the discussion. 'And what's all this arse and wind, men?' he asks. 'Got a clairvoyant here, have we?'

'No, Herr Oberleutnant,' answers Engineer Petty Officer Werder. 'Not a chance.'

'Right, then kindly keep your traps shut,' the Second Mate retorts.

Hötzer grimaces insolently. 'Plenty of chance for that when we're in action,' he says. 'Where to this time, Herr Oberleutnant?'

'How should I know?' Varendorff lets the mild insubordination pass. 'But if I did, I wouldn't go telling you lot. You're as nosey as old women.'

'Very matey of you,' mutters someone at the back, so quietly that there is no chance of the officer hearing him.

U-47 has already made one successful sortie and has been back from the refitting dock for some time now, overhauled and ready for the next mission. All the crew members have reported back, they are fully up to strength, the sub has been recharged and packed to the gunwales with provisions. Now the crewmen are hanging around the dockyard, first on board the barracks-ship *Hamburg* and now on U-47 itself, with their eyes on the joys of the water-front dives but their feet firmly planted on board ship.

All leave has been forbidden, though they're rolling in backpay. At night all they have to dream of are the tonnages they will sink and the special leave that will follow their mission. Their ghostly-pale faces will sprout beards on the homeward voyage - providing there is one.

By the sixth week of the war, all U-boats except three had reached their home bases safely. U-35 is still operating in the English Channel, but at an early stage radio contact was lost with two further boats, and everyone feared the worse. It was not long before the British confirmed German fears by announcing that U-39 had been sunk after an attempted attack on the *Ark Royal* on September 14th and that six days later U-27 was hunted down and sent to the bottom by a combined task force of destroyers and bombers. The crews of the two U-boats, the first of many lost, were fished out of the water, down to the last man, by the British.

The double fiasco has been known to the men aboard U-

47 for some days now. Scarcely any of them feel any unease. More a vague sympathy for comrades who had to swim for it and will have to sit out the war without the benefit of decorations and medals, special rations and special leave, not to mention the submariners' special pay allowance.

The men of U-47 play *skat*, tell jokes, or recount for the hundredth time all those things they did with the girls they met on their last leave. Their imaginary playmates seem to get more beautiful, more spectacularly built, with each telling, with tits you wouldn't dare dream of and glorious, firm buttocks. They share their fantasy-girls with each other, offer them freely.

The verbal battle of the bedrooms is in full swing when Oberleutnant Endrass, the First Mate, breaks up the game.

His orders plunge the crew into utter confusion; they are brief and unambiguous, but nevertheless incomprehensible, because it is either crazy or criminal to pack the tub chock-full of rations and then unload half of them and put them back ashore. They obey in silence, but at mess-break they notice that there are butterflies in their stomachs, fluttering on leaden wings.

First there is the business with the torpedoes: the ones that work on air-pressure are all taken out and replaced with electrically-powered missiles. That can be at least partially explained, because the compressed-air torpedoes pack 180 kilos less in explosive power and tend to leave a trail of foam that can betray the boat. Maybe this time the Old Man's going after big game.

But then things get really weird: the fuel tanks – and fuel is always short on any overseas trip – are being pumped half-empty. Their precious drinking-water supply is also being reduced, and the waterproof sacks of rations are going in the wrong direction. Their treasured special rations, which would usually dangle picturesquely from the mast in the form of rows of sausages and hams – a little bit of paradise in the midst of a seaborne hell – are also taken away. A sailor in the U-boat branch often has to eat standing, or at a crouch, or lying down, and often with his hands filthy, but he only eats the best. He has his pockets full of cigarettes, despite a pemanent ban on smoking. And usually it's forty men to one toilet, but now Leading Engineer Biermann looks on in astonishment as the second of the boat's closets – until now crammed with goodies, because food comes before hygiene – is emptied. 'Jesus,' he says. 'Two shit-houses. This is gonna be a ruddy luxury cruise!'

'Don't you believe it,' murmurs Werder. 'Either we'll be put on half rations, or we'll be back in Kiel within three weeks.'

'Or helping with the potato harvest this autumn in Scotland,' gripes Thewes.

'Watch your mouth,' Werder growls angrily.

No one is interested in putting a bad face on things, and in any case their commander's return an hour later puts an end to the arguments. The crew line up on deck to greet him. Kapitänleutnant Prien clambers out of the launch, recognisable from afar by his white cap; a brand-new ribbon to go with his Iron Cross Class II glistens crimson on his uniform tunic like a fresh cut. The Old Man is only thirty-one which makes him a Methuselah among U-boat captains. Born in Lübeck and raised in Leipzig, he had served in peacetime as an officer in the Merchant Marine, with a full captain's certificate.

The Kapitänleutnant acknowledges his crew with a brisk nod and says a few words, but they fail to get the explanation they long for. They hide their disappointment as best they can. The crew of U-47 – average age twenty – know that their commander is a man with brains and guts, a trained sailor, almost more at home at sea than on land. That's half their life insurance and the rest is up to them.

But even before Prien can give the order to weigh anchor, there comes a chance encounter that sends shivers down his spine for one brief moment. U-40, returning from collecting torpedoes from the naval arsenal at Kiel-Gaarden, comes sailing into the harbour. As she passes, there is the usual good-natured exchange between the men on the bridges. 'Hey, Günther,' yells Leutnant Barten through his loud-hailer. 'Anything special on?'

'We're off,' Prien answers.

'Well, the boss won't be so crazy as to send you into the lion's den,' Barten shouts with a laugh, and the commander of U-47 freezes for a moment.

Kommodore Dönitz is exactly that crazy, and Prien is even crazier, because he has taken on the lunatic job that Dönitz offered him. Only Oberleutnant Endrass and Obersteuermann Spahr, both sworn to secrecy, know the objective of Special Operation P, which the American Rear-Admiral, Dan Gallery, will later evaluate as 'the greatest individual deed of heroism in the war at sea, which will keep its position for long years to come'.

The commander of U-40, shooting blind, has hit a chance bull's-eye. Prien and Barten, two friends, wave to each other once more; they do not know that they will never meet again. On the same day that Prien penetrates the home base of the British Fleet, U-40 will strike a mine in the channel, explode and sink immediately with no survivors.

Electric motors haul the two hundred foot long boat away from the mooring pier. U-47 turns to go with the current. The diesel motors are switched on. The submarine with its complement of four officers and thirty-six crew chugs through the Kaiser-Wilhelm Canal to the North Sea. Soon German sailors will dub it 'Murder Sea'*. U-47, her keel laid in 1937 at the Germania Yard, a Krupp offshoot, and launched early in 1939, already has her baptism of fire behind her. Three Allied freighters, the steamships *Bosnia*, *Rio Claro* and *Gartavon*, lie at the bottom of the sea, a total of 10,113 registered tons.

Their crews were for the most part saved, Prien insisted, though it cost him valuable time and wear on his nerves. The war at sea is still mostly a chivalrous affair; both sides put on velvet gloves before they slaughter each other.

The two 'jumbos', the powerful 1,400 h.p. motors, push the boat through the night; for the observers on the conning-tower the horizon ends in swirling mist and water, the proper scenario for a covert mission. It has been planned for the thirteenth, which happens also to be a Friday.

Seven hours later the U-47 reaches open sea and steers a course north-north-west. A direct run. A few freighters, unwieldy tubs, cross the U-boat's torpedo-sights, but Prien

*A grim pun on the German words *nord* north and *Mord* murder.

– usually after tonnage like a dog after a bone – resists the temptation. An outsider watching him on this voyage, seeing how he dives to periscope depth at the merest whisp of smoke on the horizon, would think that U-47 was commanded by the biggest coward in the German navy.

Prien continues to keep his secret. He is a friendly man, filled with optimism and good nature, though to tell the truth he longs for a more civilised life than this one. Today the calming effect that he usually has on his men is less pronounced than before. The boat has acquired a stowaway, and his name is fear.

U-47 reaches Helgoland. Emergency dive. The four men on watch above plunge down through the hatchway into the bowels of the boat like ripe fruit tumbling from a tree. If the boat is to be under the surface within twenty seconds, they have 1.25 seconds for this operation – measured in practice exercises with a stopwatch – and on active service time can make the difference between life and death.

The off-duty members of the crew shoot out of their bunks and hurry to action-stations. Three men from the technical section are hard at work in the control centre, nine in the engine rooms, seven on the electric motors, and four more are making ready to carry out the filthy task of priming the torpedo tubes.

'At it again, are we?' says Petty Officer Bleek to Able Seaman Herrmann with a grin – at nineteen, Herrmann is the baby of U-47, and maybe it's the lighting, but the boy seems to have gone a little green. Green with fear, not of the Tommies, but because of the seasickness that he still can't shake off. As soon as they leave port, it is there. His mates give him a hard time, but they support him under the arms until he feels better, offer him rough comfort.

A practice-alarm.

U-47 surfaces again. The dive is switched from the electric motors to the diesels, so as to save power. When submerged the boat can cover no more than sixty miles in twenty-four hours, and then the batteries are exhausted and the boat must surface to allow the generators to be recharged by the 'jumbos'. Every commander is therefore very eager to conserve electricity. But not the Old Man. Not this time.

From now on he goes over completely to a system of staying submerged all day and only surfacing under cover of darkness.

True, below decks it is always night, but now everyone notices that time has been turned on its head. They sleep by day; breakfast is at midnight and lunch is at dawn.

Everyone breathes the same foul air, which is bad from the outset and gets steadily worse. They piss in the same empty tin can, because the shit-house is occupied again by the deck lookouts, who have priority. They share their fear and their dirty jokes. They sleep two to a bed, not together but one after another. Everyone belongs to everyone else. They all know if their bunk-mate sweats or beats his meat, farts or has the runs, whether he sleeps or prays, belches, has wet dreams. And there can be no prima donnas when you live cheek-by-jowl with high explosive torpedoes.

'When words or information come down from the bridge, the men accept it like blind men being told what light is like,' writes Hans Herlin in his book *Damned Atlantic*. 'Everyone was stuck at his post in front of his instruments. Each knew only his own job. They were the modern galley-slaves, 40 men in a narrow, steel dungeon. Their lungs were filled with fumes from the engines, and they carried with them the stench of their uniforms, which they never removed or changed in all the time they were at sea. They heard noises. They heard orders. They tried to put together a picture from it all. They could only hope. They could fear. They could listen with drooping mouths. Often they didn't even know when death was coming near ...'

When U-47 surfaces in the twilight south of the Dogger Bank, it has its trimming tests and the German mine barrier, known as the 'West Wall', behind it. The weather is stormy. The skies are grey, and the men on the conning-tower have to lash themselves to the rails to avoid being swept overboard by the big breakers. The boat, with its emblem of a steer painted on its side, keeps to a north-easterly course.

The next day it stays submerged during daylight and surfaces only as evening falls. The sea is boiling. Able Seaman Hermann, of all people, has been detailed to wait tables in the officer's mess. He snaps out the collapsible tables, fetches the food from the warmer, fights his way back to the control room.

'Herr Kapitanleutnant,' he shouts up to the bridge. 'Your meal.'

The boat pitches, rolls to one side. The tray falls to the ground, and the mess-tin full of cocoa goes all over the Chief Engineer's trousers just as the commander clambers down from above.

'Doesn't matter, Herrmann,' he says comfortingly. 'Tell the cook to make me a sandwich.'

The boy, who had been told by his comrades to keep his ears open, can only report his own personal disaster, nothing about where they are heading.

On Friday the 13th, U-47 has almost reached its objective and at 04.37 hours she dives again. The commander orders all available men into the torpedo chamber. They will need time and patience. So that the boat can be kept upright, each individual crew member has to be careful where he puts himself. But finally most of the crew is assembled in the narrow, dimly-lit room. All topsy-turvy: standing, lying, crammed side by side and on top of each other – even though half the rations have been left at home, life on board a U-boat is still like living in a sardine-can.

'Thank you. Remain seated,' says Prien when someone tries to salute. He gazes at his men, smiles at them encouragingly. He had thought up a few clever words, but now he has neither the time nor the desire to make a big speech. 'I won't beat about the bush,' the commander begins laconically. 'We are going to try to penetrate the harbour at Scapa Flow. Air reconnaissance has shown that the British Home Fleet is at anchor there.' He realises that his crewmen are surprised but not terrified. 'We shall sink whatever crosses our path. Now get some sleep. We wake at 16.00 hours.' Before returning to the control room, he turns round once more and adds, 'I promise you that I shall do all I can to get you safely out of Scapa Flow again.'

The electric motors hum gently. All inessential lighting is switched off to save electricity. They are only allowed to whisper on U-47 now, but they do it with style.

'Scared?' Biermann asks his mate Thewes.

'Rubbish,' Thewes snaps back. 'But I'll be glad when it's over.'

'Me too. And when we get home they'll get out the champagne eh?'

'When –' the torpedo mechanic reminds Biermann, and stares moodily at the bulkhead.

They shut their eyes, but anyone who afterwards claims to have got any sleep is a liar. Scapa Flow? England's legendary naval port, where the wrecks of the German Fleet from the First War lie rusting on the sea bed? The ban on talking breeds compliance, but it also breeds fear. The men think of the mesh nets under the water. The listening devices. The guard ships. The coast patrols. The mines – and the deadly pursuit that the British will mount if U-47 actually succeeds in turning the harbour into a killing-ground.

The attempt to penetrate the lion's den is suicidal but not new: in November 1914, Kapitänleutnant von Hennig and his U-18 tried to slip into the Hoxa Sound in the lee of a freighter. He was spotted by a patrol boat and rammed. There was one survivor.

In 1918, shortly before the end of the war, UB-116, commanded by Oberleutnant Emsmann, attempted the breakthrough once more. Listening devices detected the steel intruder. The U-boat hit a string of mines and was blown to pieces. British divers found the shattered corpses of three sailors on the bridge. They climbed down into the bowels of the boat, and fought their way past hideously-mutilated bodies to the control room. The hatchway was jammed. But through a gap they could see a pair of hands grabbing frantically in death, as if in life they had been reaching out into nothingness to seize an impossible goal. It was not possible to prove that they belonged to the commander of UB-116, since the hatchway could no longer be opened. And in the final analysis it was irrelevant, since all the men of UB-116 had died together at the same moment that they had tried to enter Scapa Flow.

'Dammit. Against England again,' the Commander of

Submarine Vessels had said on Sunday September 3rd 1939, when the news of Britain's entry into the war was brought to him at his command post on the Toter Weg in Wilhelmshaven. 'For the second time in my life.'

Karl Dönitz was surrounded by naval officers, who watched his outburst dumbly; the First World War U-boat commander and U-boat C-in-C of the second, Kommodore and Kapitän zur See in an Admiral's chair, who in a few years would make it to Grand Admiral, left the map room without another word and lurked in his office for some tea.

His distaste for a new duel with the strongest sea power in the world had not prevented the man who commanded Germany's U-boats from preparing the war at sea with all the energy at his disposal. Since August 19th, four-fifths of his small U-boat force had been lying in concealment around the great sea-lanes, including twenty-one 'frontline boats', as they called the grey wolves intended for the Atlantic war, the type VIIs. They were 500-ton vessels, equipped with a special 8.8 centimetre cannon and five torpedo tubes – four in the bows, one to stern – and capable of an active service tour of more than 6,000 sea miles; they could travel on the surface at a speed of 16.8 knots, and underwater at eight knots.

Half of the U-boat Fleet, however, consisted of 250-ton Type II boats, which – in contravention of the Versailles Treaty – had been built to German designs at shipyards in Finland, Holland and Spain. They had a crew of only twenty-five and only three torpedo-tubes. Their limited operational range allowed their use, to all practical purposes, only in coastal waters and in the North Sea. They were soon withdrawn from active service and used exclusively as training vessels, to bring on new crews.

With a mere twenty-six 'frontline boats' instead of the required 300, the war at sea could hardly be waged effectively. The twenty-one that Dönitz had in action on 'X-Day' were a kind of 'bulk special offer'. It was a saying in the U-boat branch that for every boat on active service there was a second sailing to or from the area of operations, and you could reckon on a third being laid up for repairs and re-equipment; at the beginning all the boats were usable, but once the overture was over the usual rhythm would be established.

As a determined lobbyist for his U-boats, Dönitz had always pointed to the under-representation of his branch, but with re-armament going ahead at full tilt there were too many spoons in a relatively small honey-pot: Göring was demanding his planes, while Guderian agitated for Panzers, and the navy was not at all clear whether it should prepare for a war of conventional surface battles or a submarine conflict.

Their potential enemies, the British, considered the U-boat to be an outmoded weapon, and for this reason they had made concession when a Naval Agreement was signed with Germany in 1936. The rest of the German Fleet was allowed, under its carefully-documented terms, only to reach thirty-five per cent of the English strength, but in the case of the U-boats they made an exception with forty-five per cent.

And the British were not alone in writing off the importance of submarine war. The German Naval High Command shared their views. What use would these slow U-boats be in the age of the aircraft? Even before the theory of *Blitzkrieg* was evolved, most military authorities shared the opinion of the Italian Air Force general and theoretician, Giulio Douhet (died 1930), to the effect that any future war should be decided from the air. Dönitz remained a lonely voice in the wilderness, a nuisance not only to rival branches of the armed forces but also to his own High Command. If the Kommodore was to expand his fleet to the point where he could use the planned 'wolf-pack' technique, he would have to show evidence of spectacular successes, and quickly. He had already made this quite clear to the commanders of his steel sharks, and for their part they were passionately eager to show the lethal potential of a method of warfare that had been all but buried by the 'experts'.

The twenty-five year old Oberleutnant zur See, Fritz Julius Lemp, was one of those commanders with a burning desire to show what his boat could do. Ten hours after the outbreak of war, his U-30 lay in waiting some 250 sea miles west of Ireland, observing enemy merchant vessels and warships. At about 21.00 hours a fat prize crossed his path with its deck lights still blazing: it was the liner *Athenia* (13,581 registered tons), on its way from England to New York with 1,400 passengers on board.

Observing the luxury liner, which was moving on a zig-zag course, Lemp assumed it to be an auxiliary cruiser. Without warning she fired one torpedo straight at the vessel. Two more followed. In the end, three exploded in the target and tore open the ship's stern. While the *Athenia* sent out frantic SOS calls and finally, south of Rockall, began to evacuate its panic-stricken passengers, U–30 slipped away from the scene, maintaining total radio silence.

The British destroyers *Electra* and *Escort*, the Norwegian ship *Knut Nelson*, the American steamer *City of Flint*, and the Swedish yacht *Southern Cross* came to the aid of the shipwrecked victims. Some 1,300 were fished out of the water. 112 passengers including twenty-eight Americans, lost their lives. The Second World War had its *Lusitania* case – the sinking that in 1915 had played a major role in preparing American opinion for entry into the war.

The Allied propagandists created an atrocity out of a case of over-eagerness. The British Admiralty decided that its opponents would conduct a totally ruthless U–boat war from now on, and it prepared for this eventuality.

The sinking of the *Athenia* did not suit Hitler's purposes at all. He still hoped to make a quick peace with the British and French after the conclusion of the campaign in Poland. The dictator had therefore instructed his warships to keep so punctiliously to the rules of the blockade-war that they were virtually aiding the enemy. Lemp's action – a mistake, but also an example of inhumanity – was substantiated by hundreds of eye-witness accounts and photographs and allowed the 'hun' atrocity-legends of the First War to be resurrected.

Propaganda Minister Dr Joseph Goebbels knew what he had to do: he twisted the *Athenia* facts and asserted that Churchill had put a bomb on board the ship, hoping by the slaughter of American passengers – among them women and children – to goad the USA into a declaration of war.

Churchill, then First Lord of the Admiralty, rejected this

version and raised the most vigorous protest, but not everyone believed him. The whole truth was only established after the war, when it turned out that Kommodore Dönitz had sworn the crew of the U-30 to silence and had forced Lemp, their commander, to tear out the offending page in his log. Dönitz's order showed clearly that the notion of honour held by naval officers otherwise well-known for their conservatism was becoming shockingly elastic.

The next act in the developing drama at sea was also a tragic mistake, this time on the part of the English. At night and in difficult conditions, the English submarine *Triton* was cruising the Norwegian coast near Obrestad when it happened on what it believed to be a German U-boat. The *Triton* immediately attacked with its torpedoes – and sank a sister-ship, the *Oxley*. Only the captain and one crew member survived the destruction of the submarine.

Meanwhile, the Führer had issued orders to German U-boats not to attack passenger ships even when they were sailing in convoy. The only exceptions were troopships. The U-boat commanders kept precisely to these instructions, but the bloody battle to sink tonnage escalated quickly. U-48 encountered the *Royal Spectre.* Her commander, Leutnant Herbert Schulze, sunk the freighter and radioed Winston Churchill in person with the request to 'please pick up the crew'.

On September 17th, 1939, U-29 under its commander, Kapitänleutnant Schuhart, came across the 22,500-ton aircraft carrier *Courageous* in the Bristol Channel. The big ship was engaged in a cumbersome manoeuvre, turning against a strong wind in an attempt to enable its aircraft to land. The *Courageous* went down with 500 crewmen.

The SOS calls of stricken, burning and sinking merchant ships turned the Atlantic into a bloody inferno. The English quickly realised that they had discounted the U-boat danger too readily. In the first six weeks of the war, the boats the British called the 'monsters of the deep' sank as much tonnage as their predecessors had during the entire war year of 1916.

'In the first week we lost 65,000 tons to U-boats,'

Churchill admitted to the House of Commons. 'In the second the figure was 46,000, and in the third 20,000 tons. During the past six days we have lost another 9,000 tons.' The future war leader had no intention of admitting losses, but was trying to juggle the figures to prove that preventative methods were proving effective.

But the victory reports continued to come thick and fast in the German press and radio, while British shipowners had great difficulty in hiring hands to serve on their big, vulnerable freighters, or even on tankers. London put the ships into convoys, guarded by fast warships that dashed and snapped around the convoys' flanks like sheepdogs minding their flocks. The Royal Navy possessed a new piece of locating equipment, the Asdic device, a predecessor of radar, which was supposed to be able to ferret out the position and depth of a submerged U-boat with pinpoint accuracy. The German Naval High Command had no precise information on the real value of this equipment. But the first boats returning from active service had already been unlucky enough to make the acquaintance of Asdic. When they were caught by the locating beam, a hideous clicking noise went through the entire boat, as if small stones were being thrown against the steel shell of the vessel. What they feared were, of course, not stones but the new British underwater bombs (depth-charges), which could be set to explode at a precisely-calculated depth.

The German Navy also possessed a 'miracle weapon': TMB-mines filled with 400-500 kilos of explosives which went off whenever a passing ship strayed within their magnetic field. The mines, laid sixty to eighty feet below the surface, could also be adjusted so that they reacted to propellor-noise or water pressure from the ships. The British could do nothing about the repeated and inexplicable explosions that damaged so many ships. It took some time until they discovered the secret of the lethal eggs laid beneath the sea by U-boats and destroyers, and they then took steps to demagnetise the keels of their ships.

The 'grey wolves' had provided swift and unexpected evidence to disprove the theory that 'this particularly treacherous weapon' (Lothar Günther Buchheim, author of the world bestseller, *The Boat*) belonged in a naval museum. Its resurgence showed all the more clearly that of the three branches of the Wehrmacht, the Navy was by far the least well prepared for war. Hitler had repeatedly assured the Navy's commander-in-chief, Grand Admiral Erich Raeder, that a war against England was out of the question, and his guarantee had not been qualified until 1938, when he had added, 'In any case, not until 1944.'

Hitler, a total landlubber, had no feeling for naval warfare. Born in land-locked Austria, he regarded big battleships as a bad investment and, recalling the mutiny of the Fleet's sailors at Kiel in 1918, as breeding-grounds for defeatism. At first his decisions were either non-existent or naïve, such as his order to rename the *Deutschland* the *Lützow* for symbolic reasons - he wanted to prevent the possibility of a ship named after the nation being sunk in any future war.

As his version of power-politics dragged him into international confrontation, Hitler suddenly changed his opinions. Now he considered that the construction of a 60,000-ton, H-class monster was vital to his dream of world power.

This brought him closer to the views of most veteran naval officers - though for different reasons. The Navy's commanders still imagined conflicts along the lines of the Battle of Jutland in the First War, while a small minority held the view that the advent of air power would totally transform war at sea.

There were debates, arguments, resignations, until seven months before the outbreak of war they agreed on the so-called 'Z-Plan', which was to be carried out over the next seven or eight years. While Kommodore Dönitz, still making a nuisance of himself by his demands for 300 'frontline boats', was to be granted 229 by that time, the emphasis of the plan was on the construction of destroyers and torpedo-boats, and most importantly on six super-battleships, two aircraft carriers, and five heavy cruisers.

'The early declaration of war affected the Z-Plan in the initial stages of its realisation,' writes Gajus Becker in his *Illustrated Book of the German Navy*. 'The keels had been laid for only two of the projected H-class ships, and materials were quickly cannibalised. The stuggle for resources and priorities had been joined all along the line . . .'

While Grand Admiral Raeder, a schoolmaster's son and himself not free of schoolmasterly rectitude, continued to defend the now moribund idea of big battleships, it immediately became apparent that the German Navy had been equipped too late and incorrectly for the conflict with England.

War forced a rethink of the Navy's armament. Debates that had been going on for years all ceased in the face of one overwhelming priority: to build U-boats. On average, each worker in the ship-building industry could make one ton's worth of battleship in a year. A monster of the H-class type would therefore keep 60,000 skilled workers busy for a year. For the same outlay, Germany could build 120 Type VII U-boats – in theory, at least. The Naval High Command could no longer ignore such facts, but while Dönitz saw the priority in building medium-sized U-boats, the High Command insisted on constructing cumbersome 'U-cruisers' of some 4,000 tons, which the Kommodore considered absurd. He intended to keep his entire U-boat Fleet worrying at the British convoys and use the 'wolf-pack' technique – already tried and tested in the Baltic – to torpedo them to pieces. Because of lack of numbers, however, once the initial strike at the outbreak of war was over he had hardly more than three or four U-boats operating in the Atlantic simultaneously.

Even the Naval High Command recognised the absurdity of the situation, but if U-boats were to become the main weapon of the blockade, the expansion of production would have to reach an unheard-of level – particularly as it would also be necessary to find ways of dealing with the increasingly effective British counter-measures

The piercing notes of the so-called 'England Fanfare' which preceded the announcement of each victory at sea ensured Dönitz an audience, but he was also working to carry out a sensational coup that would grab the attention of the entire world. Immediately after the outbreak of war, he had begun to prepare the penetration of Scapa Flow in conditions of the strictest secrecy. As commander of UB-68 during the First World War he had found his way through the underwater netting protecting the Sicilian port of Augusta, had evaded all the security devices and sailed right through the harbour basin before getting his boat out again unscathed. The plan to carry out a similar act of bravado, this time in Britain's most important naval base, had become an obsession with him. The Kommodore gathered Intelligence, had the base in the far north of Scotland inspected by long-range reconnaissance flights, and then looked through his U-boat commanders for an officer who was both cool-headed and courageous. He plumped for Günther Prien and his U-47. Dönitz revealed his secret plan to Prien, advised him of the extreme risk while at the same time tempting him with the rewards that would follow if the crazy mission were to be carried out successfully.

The Kapitänleutnant had no intention of going into the mission blind. He consulted his First Mate and Chief Navigation Officer. All three of them studied the documents separately, and all came to the same conclusion: that such an action, if it could succeed at all, could only be mounted on the night of October 13th/14th, when there was a new moon and both high tides occurred during the hours of darkness.

U-47's commander was given two days to think it over, but Prien would not have been Prien if he had not accepted this hazardous mission. Not simply for Führer, *Volk*, and Fatherland - at the contemporary jargon had it - but also, perhaps principally, to persuade the outside world that the U-boat arm had a crucial, lethal role to play in this war.

The unreal calm that reigns aboard U-47 is valueless. Certainly it does nothing to calm the men's nerves. Even though the man who wakes Cook-Private Walz at 14.00 hours wears rags round his shoes to deaden the sound and moves like a sneak-thief, everyone can hear him just as clearly as they can hear Leutnant Varendorff, who is wandering around the boat with two men, placing charges in case they are forced to scuttle themselves.

There is no need to wake the crew. They are out of their damp, tiny bunks at 16.00 hours like clockwork men. 'A hearty breakfast, eh?' Thewes says, prodding his mate. They nod and grin as they set up the collapsible tables. There is soup, rib of bacon in gravy, potatoes, cabbage, and afterwards real, strong coffee. No one wants to admit they have lost their appetites; they set to with a will, though they know a fighter doesn't go into battle on a full stomach.

Then they hang up their waterproof bags containing emergency rations and slip on their life-savers and breathing apparatus, just in case they have to abandon ship in a hurry. But this is only possible at a moderate depth; if the boat is deeper than that, the water pressure will squeeze its steel skin and the men inside will be squashed to pulp, like swatted flies.

They are aware of the fact, but their minds suppress the knowledge; in any case, the target will have to be fixed from the surface, since U-47 will be attacking at night. The volunteer observers climb silently, moving their lips without speaking, listening to the sound of their own hearts beating and wondering stupidly if the English listening devices can pick up a man's pulse.

The commander withdraws to his miniscule cabin, the only place on board where he can be alone. It is some two metres square and contains a bed that folds into the wall, with a curtain for purposes of privacy. He is pretending to a calm that he does not feel, cannot feel. He keeps going over the route again and again, though he knows it by heart and keeps thinking of all the things that can go wrong.

He does not have long to wait. His Chief Engineer brings the first bad news, pushing aside his curtain and sticking his head cautiously into the cabin.

'What's up?' asks Prien.

'Salt water in the lubrication oil,' answers Oberleutnant Wessels.

'Shit in the goddamn works,' the commander curses.

'At top speed, the bearings in the diesels will not be lubricated, and then –'

'Can't we repair the jumbos once we're back in port?'

'We won't get that far, Herr Kapitänleutnant.'

'Then we shall have to repair them here and now.'

A thorough investigation reveals that the cylinder casing on the rear engine is not watertight. Salt water is running through the hole into the crankshaft.

'How long will you need to replace the cylinder casing?' Prien asks his Chief.

'Hours –'

'Any other ways round the problem?'

'I'll have a try, Herr Kapitänleutnant.'

The Chief Engineer conjures up some materials from somewhere, improvises a device not unlike a gutter to drain the water away from the defective casing.

This simple, clever emergency measure overcomes their first problem, but there is nothing they can do about the next disaster. When U–47 surfaces, aiming to exploit the tidal currents to make its way through the moonless night into the narrow Kirk Sound and the enemy naval base, the sky is brilliantly lit. They stare at the horizon in horrified astonishment. But the light is neither a burning tanker nor a full moon.

'The Northern Lights!' Prien growls.

The sea is pitch-dark, but above them hangs a shining halo of light, picking out the contours of the highland terrain all round the bay. It is as if there is a huge, eerie searchlight pointing straight down at them. For a moment Prien considers calling off his special operation, but for a second attempt he will have to wait until the next full moon, which will mean trying again in a few weeks' time – and by then half the Navy will be aware that Dönitz's prestige project had to be postponed.

All other routes into the strongly-defended harbour seem impossible. Prien considers the barriers across the Hoxa Sound well-nigh impregnable, but an approach through the Switha and Clestrum Sounds would be bound to fail. The only, slim chance would be via the Holm Sound, between three wrecks that lie bang in the middle of the channel. To the south of the wrecks there is – according to the reconnaissance photographs – a gap twenty-five feet deep and about six feet wide. Notwithstanding the strings of mines protecting the approach, U–47 would have to squeeze its way through this narrow entrance.

On the surface.

On the way in and on the way out.

Close to the surface, the commander stares through his periscope. Above him it is too bright, below him too dark. Thick clouds pack the horizon like bulging bags of grain. The shadows seem to be moving all the time; maybe just an illusion. But they could be patrol boats that may sound the alarm at any moment.

U–47 rises fully to the surface. The diesels start up with a roar; they are so noisy that it seems to everyone on board that they will wake every Englishman for miles.

The strong current takes the boat. Prien has to use his rudders to try to keep her on course, bring his propellers into action. If he brings her about too sharply, the boat will end up spinning like a top and drift helplessly until she hits one of the wrecks blocking the passage; if he is too timid, the current will take her wherever it wants.

'Visibility is appalling,' as the Navy's War Diary relates. 'On the surface it is pitch-dark, but the skies are filled with the flickering halo of the Northern Lights, so that the bay, which is surounded by high hills, is illuminated directly from above. The wrecks litter the sea passages, ghostly in the strange light.'

As U-47 makes course for them, her commander glimpses the steel cables that line the wrecks.

'The light shone directly on to the steel hawsers, which drooped from each wreck into the water and emerged from the sea at the next,' Hans Herlin describes the third catastrophe that threatened. 'They resembled nothing so much as sharp, lethal blades. The current was strong, and it pulled the boat with it to starboard, towards the shore. The current pushed U–47 straight for the steel hawsers that trailed from the stern of the northernmost wreck towards the shore. It felt as if the boat was heading for those blades like a candidate for suicide.'

Orders to the helsman. Some desperate manoeuvring avoids the worst threat, a head-on collision with the three half-submerged wrecks. But, driven by the powerful current, the slim steel shark brushes against a steel hawser and loses its mine-repelling paravane.

A jerk, a shudder.

The boat tears itself free.

Forty men breathe a sigh of relief.

'We're through,' Prien announces over the public address.

His whispered report goes through the ship like a clap of thunder.

Entry in the log for October 14th, 1939 reads, 00.27 hours: We are inside Scapa Flow.'

U-47 has also penetrated the second mine barrier and is feeling her way through the lion's den. The boat is travelling slowly, with her jumbos on throttle. It is so quiet that the Second mate climbs down from the conning tower into the control room, but is greeted by a whispered curse from Prien and shooed back above.

The commander peers through his periscope.

Where is the Home Fleet that the German reconnaissance planes claim to have seen at anchor in the harbour?

Where are the battleships *Hood, Repulse, Royal Oak, Nelson,* and *Rodney,* the cruisers *Newcastle, Sheffield,* and *Aurora*, the aircraft carrier *Furious*?

Wherever they are, they are not anchored here.

'Have another look, Endrass,' says the commander.

The First Mate checks the positions where the ships should be. 'Nothing,' he murmurs.

The real catastrophe number three: the Home Fleet is not in Scapa Flow, and the men of U-47 have been through all that fear, expended all that courage, for nothing.

'Over there, Herr Kapitänleutnant,' says the First Mate suddenly, forgetting to keep his voice down. It could be a mirage born of hope, but it could a battleship or at least a cruiser.

Prien looks.

Cautiously, U-47 approaches the shadowy phantom on the far side of the harbour.

Secrecy had bred its own problems. Only very few officers had been informed by Dönitz that Prien was intending to sneak into Scapa Flow. For security reasons, even Grand

Admiral Raeder's agreement to Special Operation P had never been put into writing. Thus on October 8th - at almost exactly the same time as U-47 left port - the *Gneisenau*, with Fleet Commander Admiral Hermann Böhm on board, the cruiser *Köln*, and nine destroyers had sailed north-west in the direction of the Kattegat to set a trap for the British Home Fleet.

The *Gneisenau* and its escort ships were merely acting as decoys to draw the British battleships out of Scapa Flow. Once the Home Fleet had set sail they were to withdraw and leave the work to the Luftwaffe's bomber squadrons.

The English had the same intention, though according to a slightly different plan. The Home Fleet left Scapa Flow and approached the German ships. The weather was appalling, and for this reason alone neither of them fell into the other's trap - aircraft could not operate in the dense sea fog. Admiral Böhm took his *Gneisenau* and her flotilla back to port without engaging the enemy. His opponent, Admiral Forbes, also broke off the search and steamed for home; he decided not to go to Scapa Flow but to take his armada to the base at Loch Ewe. *The Royal Oak*, however, a veteran of the Battle of Jutland, lagged slightly behind the rest of the Fleet. The old battleship - nicknamed the 'Mighty Oak' - was given permission to leave the main group and return alone to the safety of the base at Scapa.

The old-established British naval port of Scapa lay among the Orkney Islands off the northernmost tip of Scotland, where fisherman catch cod of outstanding quality. The area itself was so bleak and remote that ships' crews were more comfortable and at home on board than on shore leave. They had been assured that Scapa Flow was safe from attack by sea, and that they could concentrate solely on countering attacks from the air.

The warning sirens had indeed sounded every time the enemy reconnaissance aircraft flew over the harbour. The Admiralty had moreover commissioned the salvage firm 'Metal Industries' to check the passages and in particular to establish whether the half-submerged wrecks at the entrance to Kirk Sound were in themselves sufficient to keep out German U-boats. When it came to the crunch, however, the Sea Lords had baulked at the cost of further security measures and had sent 'Metal Industries' away with their thanks but little else.

The salvage manager of the firm Thomas Mackenzie disagreed with the decision. He wrote a letter of protest to the Admiralty, in which he admitted that the strong tidal current, the complications of navigation through the Sound, and the wrecks were a strong deterrent. He added, however. that 'one cannot suppose with any certainty that a courageous U-boat commander in wartime would not be prepared to face these risks – though any sensible seaman in peacetime would never contemplate them.'

The British naval bureaucracy could be just as hard of hearing as its German counterpart, but finally, albeit slowly, it dawned that security was more important than money, and it was decided to scuttle a further blockade-ship in the gap through which U–47 was creeping into Scapa Flow. If Prien had decided to postpone the mission a day longer the blockade-ship would have gone down and it is doubtful whether he would have been able to penetrate the Sound.

It was now long after midnight, and almost the entire crew of the *Royal Oak* was sound asleep. Kapitänleutnant Prien recognised the *Royal Oak* as a battleship of the Revenge Class and approached to within 3,000 metres. The board lights had been extinguished, but in the darkness the shapes of a nearby warship and several destroyers were visible.

It was 00.54 hours when Prien gave the order to prepare the forward torpedo tube for firing.

This was the order that thirty-nine men had been waiting for.

'All tubes ready,' the First Mate reports.

Prien takes a deep breath. 'Fire tubes one to three!'

Oberleutnant Endrass makes some final adjustments and turns the firing-lever.

The torpedoes part from the boat with a hard jolt that goes right through the vessel, leaving a heavy, vibrating resonance in its wake. Three torpedoes cut through the water like homing predators.

They gaze from the conning tower until their eyes water.

Below, men wait with bated breath for the explosion. Time seems to stand still.

One minute.

Into the second minute.

The torpedoes are taking an eternity.

Then comes one explosion.

One, not three.

No burning ship on the horizon.

This is catastrophe number four. Two of the launched torpedoes have lost their way, and a third has missed the target and struck an anchor-chain.

The explosion has caused no damage, but must surely wake every Englishman within miles.

Prien pushes the engines into reverse.

He fires his stern torpedo.

They wait for the thunderclap. The burgeoning pillar of water. The fireball that will spread as the ship breaks up.

Three minutes.

Three minutes and fifty seconds.

Coxswain Sahr shuts off his stopwatch after four minutes. Another failure.

By now the harbour should be teeming with launches and destroyers in the hunt for the intruder; there should be searchlights sweeping the waterway, depth-charges falling all around U-47.

But the damned place still seems totally silent, sleeping the sleep of the blessed.

It is inconceivable. In fact the British think that there has been an explosion aboard the *Royal Oak* itself and are scouring the lower decks for the cause. But Prien has no time to mull over the reasons why the English are still abed; he exploits the situation in order to prepare a second attack.

'Reload tubes one to three!' he barks.

It is laborious, dangerous work. The torpedo squad complete it in twelve minutes, a new record for U-47.

Meanwhile, the boat has gone about again and is moving towards the *Royal Oak*. 2,000 metres to go. 1,500. Prien creeps closer and closer to his 29,000-ton victim and its thousand-strong crew.

And still the harbour is deceptively peaceful.

Range: 1,000 metres.

'Closer!' Prien orders, like a man possessed. Neither he nor his First Mate, who is in charge of the torpedoes, are taking any chances this time.

At last he rasps the command, 'Fire torpedoes!'

At 01.23 hours three torpedoes slice through the water towards their targets: two are aimed at the big ship, one for a smaller vessel that Prien wrongly believes to be the *Repulse*.

No dud. All three hit their targets.

A huge wall of flame shoots skywards. Seconds later comes another, and a third.

Prien has no time to observe the death-throes of the *Royal Oak*. By now the British must be well aware that a German U-boat has penetrated their naval stronghold. If they manage to block his exit, then it is all over for U-47 and its crew.

Full speed ahead. The screaming jumbos struggle against the current. The chase is on.

'There was mighty rolling, banging, bumping and crashing,' says the log book of U-47. 'First pillars of water, then pillars of fire, then fragments flying everywhere. It was now that the harbour came alive. Destroyers were lit up, frantic morse signals were exchanged, and on shore some 200 metres from the water there were motor vehicles roaring over the roads.'

Everyone on board knows that they have succeeded, but the men at action stations are uncannily silent; the torrent of joy will follow a while later. At the moment their main concern is not victory but self-preservation.

'Prien pushed his boat at full power in the direction of Kirk Sound,' writes David Mason, describing the hunt for U-47. 'Leaving a tell-tale stream of foam behind him that was certain to be seen by the enemy. And a destroyer was already at his heels, coming perilously close, flashing ominous signals at the fleeing U-boat. Then something incredible happened: the destroyer suddenly turned away and dropped her depth-charges somewhere else entirely. The U-boat hugged the coastline, where her silhouette merged with the rocky cliffs. Then a car came along the coast road from Scapa, and for a moment, as it took a bend in the road, its headlights caught U-47 in their beam. The vehicle turned quickly and raced off back towards Scapa. The fight against the current continued, with the electric motors being coupled together with the diesels to squeeze the last ounce of speed out of the boat.'

As U-47 attempts to escape from Scapa by the same route she had used to get in, the scene aboard the *Royal Oak* is one of unimaginable horror. Her crew, many of them still half-asleep, waste precious time as they stumble around in panic and confusion.

The initial impact against the anchor chain had woken most of the sailors, but during the thirteen wasted minutes that followed, the crew were more inclined to anger at a disturbance to their night's sleep than interested in the cause of the mysterious explosion. While they were still venting their anger, the first of the second batch of torpedoes exploded against the ship's hull, tearing a great hole. For the men in the lower decks, it felt as if a huge fist had punched the ship.

The other explosions followed at intervals of a few seconds.

The hatchways amidships had been sealed for safety reasons. During the decisive seconds and minutes it does not occur to anyone that the men there are condemned to sit helplessly and be eaten alive by fire. From bow to stern, above and below decks, only one law operates: the law of survival.

The *Royal Oak* does not go up in a ball of fire. Her ammunition stores do not explode. Death takes its time, practising new refinements of cruelty. In their frantic attempts to escape the fires below, men rush headlong towards the sea of flames above. They writhe on the red-hot decks, trying to douse the flames in their hair and uniforms. They suffocate and are roasted alive. The emergency power unit proves unreliable, as does the radio link with which they are trying to summon aid from other ships.

'The *Royal Oak* was listing more dramatically with every passing moment,' Gerald S. Snyder describes the scene. 'Everyone ran wildly in all directions, climbing any ladders that came to hand, diving through any available door or hatchway, crawling over the sloping decks, each trusting only his own instincts ... Ribbons of fire twirled and whirled, then rolled through the messes ... Most of the men had no chance to get out, the flames swirling about, back and forth, catching them about waist-high, or before they had time to jump from their hammocks. Those who did make it to their feet had flames clinging to thin undershirts and shorts, some driven so crazed that they ran directly into the flames ... Her death-throes over, Drakes' Drum gone, the *Oak* plunged beneath the water – a tomb for more than eight hundred men and boys, fifteen fathoms down, at Latitude 58° 55' 42" N, Longitude 2° 58' 54" W, to lie with her old adversaries of Jutland. It was about thirty-three minutes past one, twenty-nine minutes after the first explosion, seventeen after the last ...'

At 02.15 hours, U-47 left Scapa Flow unscathed. Prien bellowed into his speaking-tube, 'We're through. Pass the message!'

It was only now that a kind of madness broke out. Men slap each other on the back. The crew cool down with a bottle of beer each, by special permission of their commander. The Navy's War Diary stated, 'The lights of Scapa Flow were visible for a long time. It seemed that they were still dropping depth-charges.'

As the British Admiralty announces the loss of the *Royal Oak*, U-47 has gone to ground. Not until well into October 14th does Prien announce in a specially-coded radio message to Kommodore Dönitz, 'Operation carried out according to plan.'

Once during the trip home U-47 strays among enemy ships and is located: her commander counts thirty-two depth-charges, which explode some distance from the boat's stern. Prien has five torpedoes left on board, but the war needs its heroes – and so U-47 is ordered back to port.

Even the trip through the Kaiser-Wilhelm Canal is turnedanises a massive propaganda beanfeast, and this plays right into Dönitz's hands.

Dispersed in several limousines, the U–boat men are driven through the streets of the Reich capital. The Hitler Youth are given the day off school to line the streets along with the adults who pack the pavements too, cheering and waving. The crew get out of their cars at the Kaiserhof Hotel, and from there they continue on foot to the Reich Chancellery. In front of the whirring cameras of the Weekly Newsreel, Hitler pins the Knight's Cross on the chest of the Kapitänleutnant Günther Prien, now elevated to the status of a national hero. The entire crew has already been awarded the Iron Cross Second Class.

Prien is asked to submit further suggestions for Iron Crosses First Class. The radio stages a veritable propaganda orgy. In honour of Prien's crew, the ban on dancing in Berlin's night-clubs is lifted. The carnival continues for days. Finally the men from U-47 are granted home leave. At the end of it all their commander is glad to return to the boat that has become his destiny.

In Greater Germany the propaganda barrage continues, but Churchill, First Lord of the British Admiralty, is forced to declare to the House of Commons, 'At about 1.30 on the morning of October 14th, while at anchor in Scapa Flow, the battleship *Royal Oak* was sunk by a German U-boat. At this stage we can only speculate as to how the U–boat penetrated the defences of the harbour. When we consider that during the entirety of the last war this anchorage was considered immune to attacks of this kind, due to the natural hindrance of the currents and the extra barrier presented by the underwater nets, then the success of the U–boat must be seen as a remarkably skilful and bold deed ...'

Along with Prien, Dönitz is the man of this glorious hour. He is promoted to Admiral, and his wishes regarding the construction of U-boats become – resources permitting – as good as orders. During the course of the war, 691 of the Type VII boats preferred by Dönitz were built in German shipyards.

There is a rush of volunteers to the recruiting offices, all eager to join a branch of the Navy that will have sunk 2,779 ships by 1945.

Dönitz, dubbed 'the lion' by his crews – though by his own estimation he felt himself to be, compared with the Führer, 'very small fry' – is granted the title 'Commander of U-boats' after the victory of Scapa Flow.

He will lead this force until the last day of the War in ever more desperate situations. His men will suffer the gravest losses of any German servicemen. Three out of four U-boat crewmen will die, and two out of three U-boats will never return from active service.

The men who volunteer for submarine warfare will die in their hundreds, betrayed by the ping-ping of the Asdic, later by sophisticated radar. Perhaps they will survive for one more mission, to be able to make an emergency evacuation, succeed in reaching the surface, to be fished out of the water by the enemy. But the next depth-charge may always be the direct hit that blows them to pieces – to grant them a comparatively merciful death. If the damaged vessel sinks to the bottom, to a depth it is not built to withstand, then it will buckle inwards like a tin can, or the pressure of the water will explode into it and slice the human beings inside like a cutting-torch. Even this death will not be the worst, because if a damaged boat sinks and cannot be raised, the men will have to sit there, thinking of home, slowly losing their reason, while they suffer a cruel, infinitely slow death from suffocation.

Even today, there are regular memorial services for the victims on board the *Royal Oak*. One man who takes part is Herbert Herrmann, once the seasickness-prone baby of the crew of U-47, who spilled cocoa all over his Chief Engineer's trousers shortly before they entered Scapa Flow. Later transferred from U-47 to another boat, he survived the war and afterwards married an Englishwoman, with whom he now lives in Scotland.

The Secret War

The dance begins in March 1940 by the beautiful, blue Danube. But firstly, the river is by no means universally beautiful, secondly, it is never blue, and thirdly, waltz-time has long since given way to a marching step.

The war, now in its seventh month, has found a new theatre of operations: neutral Rumania. When the weather is good, it is carried on in the open air, but its main zone of operation is well behind the scenes. This war is paid for in British pounds, German marks, or French francs. Or with the odd well-placed bullet. Not forgetting the knife in the back that is the tradition of the country itself.

That was how they did for Link during a fight in a bar; the culprit escaped without being identified. Frenssen was found in a barn, dangling from the end of a rope. And Bauer, an excellent swimmer, had ended up drowning in the river at Orsova. Both these cases were filed by the Rumanian police as 'suicide for personal reasons'. Three men of the Intelligence unit 'Brandenburg' joined the list of the lost, murdered by local thugs, probably in the pay of the British or French secret service. Not a single member of the small German special commando infiltrated into the country doubts the fact, because all of them use the same dirty methods and follow the same motto: tit for tat.

Anyone who doesn't take precautions has only himself to blame, or at least that is Unteroffizier Jonas's opinion: at the moment he is calling himself Brändli and is supposed to be a watch salesman from Switzerland. His passport is as phoney as a whore's kiss, but who cares about names in this business? Back at headquarters he is known by the nickname 'the Prophet', and he's reckoned to be the sharpest of a sharp outfit, where privates have been known to bawl out majors and a hero's death can mean the gallows.

Jonas doesn't need to be a prophet at the moment to know what is happening. The list of British agents that the supposed German military attaché slipped to the Rumanians has scored a bull's-eye.

Whereas any Rumanian worth the name usually sleeps until midday, today, at the crack of dawn, there are military columns and police cars roaring through the streets of the city, apparently aimlessly, but Jonas is certain thay they are operating under the orders of the Intelligence chief, Stefanescu, a smart cookie, and that they are at present scooping up Allied agents in the same way that they processed the Germans the week before.

The Intelligence chief in Bucharest is slim and elegant, looks like one of those lounge-lizard hussar officers from a nineteenth-century operetta. But his appearance is deceptive, a façade. He is a tough, cunning operator. And incorruptible. He and his men are desperately determined to keep Rumania out of the Second World War, like non-swimmers trying to keep their heads above water.

Jonas walks further along the street to the Café Dragomir on the Boulevard Elisabeta, where Melchior, one of his agents, is waiting for him. Jonas has to make do with the Swiss cover because a five-day crash course is not enough to learn Rumanian, and so he quite openly speaks German with a slight Zürich accent.

The other thirty-five boys here all have some command of Rumanian. Some of them are ethnic Germans from the Banat, or Transylvanian Germans who grew up bilingual, and they have been pressed into service more or less overnight as links in the hastily-formed German espionage network.

They are soldiers, but operating in secrecy: their uniform in Bucharest is a well-cut suit, off the peg from the tailoring section of the Brandenburg Division. The real elite are the few men from the dirty tricks department who have infiltrated the 'Bavarian Lloyd' shipping company and now work as steamer captains on the Danube, sailing up and down with complete impunity.

Jonas spots the plump figure of Melchior from some distance away. The agent is lurking at a round table at the Dragomir. The fact that he is sitting on a powder-keg doesn't seem to bother him. Since he was sent here as a 'Czech refugee', he has come to the opinion that Paris is nothing compared with Bucharest and its delights. Admiral Canaris pays his expenses, and so even this early in the morning Melchior is hard at work eating and boozing, filling himself up with Ruburet, the fine young Rumanian wine, and ordering his third portion of Pastrama, wind-dried goat's meat, which is his favourite dish.

'Christ, do you have to spend your entire time feeding your face?' says Jonas by way of greeting. 'You'll end up fat as a suckling-pig.'

'You never know when the lean times'll come,' the private croaks. 'The well-padded citizen survives.' He pats his belly. 'All good cover,' he adds and laughs evilly.

Another police car drives past, crammed with suspects. Stefanescu does not do things by halves. He tends to grab anyone he can find, on a pretty indiscriminate basis. Most of his 'guests' will probably be hauled off to the Hungarian border in truckloads and unceremoniously dumped. A few days later, at least half of them will be back in circulation in Bucharest.

They always come back, like boomerangs, Germans and British alike. Or the others. The ones no one knows. They are the dangerous ones, because you have to penetrate their cover.

The farce of the secret war is not the whole story. Rumania is heading for a cataclysm. And the name of the game is blood and oil.

Captain Stefanescu is still wearing kid gloves. He does not want to give either side an excuse to invade, and so he is involved in a permanent tight-rope act, without a safety-net. Acrobatics, Rumanian-style.

The waiter takes his order. 'Hey, William Tell,' he says to Jonas. 'How d'you like it: today they're slinging the Tommies and the French into the caboose.'

'Far as I'm concerned they can have the Germans too,'

Jonas answers loudly. 'I don't give a damn. We Swiss are strictly neutral. Don't forget we're supplying Oerlikons to the Tommies *and* the Germans for their submarines.'

A few customers at nearby tables grin and nod. You can tell a true Swiss by the fact that he slates his own country but immediately gets nasty if a foreigner criticises it.

By eleven o'clock the tension is unbearable. Even the usual fashion-parade along the boulevard has lost its languidness and the passers-by are showing the tension. But the women are just as beautiful as on any other day. Bright-eyed, dark-haired, temperamental and unattainable except to the likes of fat Melchior, who is an expert at undressing them with his eyes.

'Just look at that,' he says, pointing to a newly-arrived couple who have just sat down at a table close to the street. The woman is the Countess Levandovsky, on the arm of a familiar stranger. The countess is, in fact, not a countess at all, but then her companion – broad-shouldered, blond, close-set grey eyes – is also not a Flemish oil-importer but a Leutnant in the German Secret Service.

'Christ, he's a lucky devil,' says Jonas with feeling. 'What a way to go.'

'You're right there, my Swiss friend,' Melchior drools. He stares malevolently, notes the skill with which the countess's boyfriend arranges her cushions for her, fusses around her, billing and cooing as if the war were a thousand miles away. 'Fucking for Germany, eh?' he adds softly.

'For Führer, *Volk* and a few fringe benefits,' Jonas chuckles.

Leutnant Schübler, the man playing court to the countess, is Jonas's long-time comrade and his friend since together they staged the coup from Slovakia that led to the taking of the Jablunka Pass from the Poles. Schübler always liked a nice bit of skirt. At the moment he must be enjoying combining business with pleasure.

His Rumanian lady friend is a well-known – or perhaps notorious – figure on the Bucharest scene. She is rumoured to have a very close relationship with the British Military Attaché, with an important French journalist, and – so they say – to be the mistress of Stefanescu himself. Whether or not she is involved with the Rumanian security boss at the moment, she certainly enjoys his confidence and knows a lot more than most about what is really going on in the Balkans. The countess is, shall we say, available. Not for money, of which she has plenty. But she loves life – perhaps a little too much – and enjoys playing with fire, particularly when there are combustible materials about.

'How's the war?' she asks Schübler baldly.

'I'll have to disappoint you on that score,' says her 'Belgian'. 'You know what I feel: it's just a damned nuisance.'

'You would make a splendid soldier,' Mariu Levandovsky answers with a laugh. 'Speaking of which, I had the British Military Attaché to tea yesterday.' She turns her flashing eyes on him at full power.

'The attaché?' Schübler says a little stiffly.

'Curious?'

'I'm always curious. About everything. And jealous of everyone.'

'Whose side are you really on?' She steers the conversation back to the subject of the war.

'No one's. Maybe my own.'

'Somehow I'm very fond of the Germans,' the countess continues, ignoring his apparent lack of interest. 'On the other hand, I don't dislike the British, either –'

'And who really has your heart at the moment, Mariu?' asks the attentive lover, taking her hand and delivering a delicate kiss on her milk-white fingers.

'Whoever wins,' she answers and stubs out her cigarette. 'Heard anything about Sulina?' she asks suddenly.

'You mean the Black Sea port?'

The countess nods. 'There's a lot going on there,' she says with relish. 'A mass of ships. The *Lord Byron*, for instance, and the *Princess Elizabeth*, the *Thermondt* and the *King George*, and quite a few others whose names I can't remember –'

'Ships at a port are not exactly an unusual phenomenon.'

'And tomorrow the *Mardinian* is due. Three guesses what they are carrying and what's going to happen.'

'How do you know all this?'

'You haven't been listening, René,' the countess chides him. 'I told you: yesterday the British attaché . . .'

'Are the English always so talkative?'

'That,' the woman says meaningfully, 'depends on the situation.'

They exchange a smile, lean back in their chairs, turn to face the sun.

'Christ, he's going at it,' says Jonas, five tables away. 'But he'll have his work cut out to keep his place in that big French bed of hers.'

'How d'you know she's got a big French bed?' asks the fat man.

'Women like her always do.'

'Oh yeah? Got experience, have you?'

'Moron,' Jonas says wolfishly. 'I only go out with virgins, you know that.' He grins, sees Schübler stand up, make his apologies to the countess and go into the café. 'You take over,' he mutters to Melchior.

Jonas follows the Leutnant into the toilet. They wait until they are alone, even though the message that Schübler has to pass on is so urgent that they have no time to lose.

'Emergency,' says Schübler. 'Case *Iron Gate*.'

Jonas is fully prepared.

If Schübler's report is accurate, the major will activate the plans for 'Operation Boudoir.'

The man who arrived in Bucharest on December 8th, 1939 looked slight, almost frail; he stood only five feet three and was only fifty-three years old, but his eyes were weary and his hair grey. He was travelling under a false name, but the Rumanians knew perfectly well whom they were dealing with: one of the most dangerous men in Europe, a strategist of the secret war.

As a human being, he had his quirks, but also his merits. The English admired his abilities no less than the Germans, whose military Intelligence organisation he commanded. He was known behind his back as 'the little Levantine'. He was always afraid of illnesses, even imagined ones, and indeed he had a marked susceptibility to colds. He could not abide big or tall men, and visitors with large ears were not welcome in his empire, along with any men whom his two dachshunds, Seppl and Sabine, took a dislike to. He often took his four-legged friends with him on trips, even on covert missions, and on such occasions he would rent a separate suite in the hotel for the dogs. If he was unable to take them with him, he would conduct hours-long telephone conversations with his wife, enquiring about their welfare, and the enemies tapping his phone would then expend enormous trouble trying to track the code they thought he was using. They were always on his trail – and never successful. Whenever he surfaced in a country, it was never long before the place became a centre of the secret war.

The real name of the mysterious visitor from Berlin was Admiral Franz Wilhelm Canaris, and on that December day in 1939 he was due to meet the head of the Rumanian Secret Police, the *Siguranta*. Very few of Colonel Moruzov's colleagues were aware of their guest's identity, and even fewer knew what their secret discussions were about. Nevertheless, there could be only one subject on the agenda: oil, Rumania's black gold.

During the First World War, Rumania had fought on the Allied side, and its government had co-operated in the destruction of its own production rigs at Ploesti to stop them from falling into the hands of the invading Germans. Not a penny of the compensation that the Rumanians had been promised by the British was paid until 1923, and even then it was calculated so ungenerously that most of the local oil companies were forced to sell out to multinational corporations.

Four of the five centres of production had been owned by British and Dutch firms before the war, and the fifth belonged to the Rumanian royal family. The largest company in the country, 'Astra Romana', was a fully-owned subsidiary of Shell, and – like the rest – it sold the greater part of its refined petroleum to Hungary, Austria and Germany. Low transport costs determined the choice of customers.

When the Second World War broke out, the industry found itself in a grotesque situation, with almost all the oil produced by British-owned companies going directly to fuel Hitler's war machine. The German dictator paid the 'Astra Romana' to enable him to make war against Britain. Admittedly, the big corporations had initially blocked oil exports to Germany, but the Rumanians, who were unwilling to give either side a reason to invade, had insisted that the tankers continue to ply their trade up and down the Danube, just as in peacetime. The firms quietly got rid of many of their staff, so as to reduce production. The Rumanian government intervened and forced the foreign multinationals to maintain pre-war levels of supply.

Germany was dependent on Rumanian oil. Her scientists had discovered a method of making synthetic oil from coal, but it was complex and expensive and would never provide a real substitute. Experts had calculated that without Rumania's oil the Germans would only be able to wage war for a maximum of two years.

It was obvious that the British would do everything they could to prevent the export of oil to the enemy. A part of their staff in Ploesti had been replaced by agents of the secret service. It was only a question of time before they took concrete steps to sabotage the supply of fuel to Germany's war machine.

The minor acts of sabotage that preceeded their big coup were relatively childish and served mostly to arouse the wrath of the German Abwehr. For instance, British agents hired members of a Rumanian gipsy clan to steal all the brass armatures from railway trucks of German origin – items of equipment hard to replace in wartime. It was supposed to appear as if the Rumanians, whose land was short of raw materials, were making up the lack by theft. This organised robbery did not last long, however: Abwehr agents identified two scrap-metal merchants in Bucharest as receivers of the stolen goods. The men were arrested and confessed that their real employers were sitting in Ploesti.

The next attempt to sabotage was also a failure. By law, only Rumanian citizens could act as pilots in the Danube estuary. The British offered enormous sums – up to 20,000 marks – for these pilots to report sick. After a few initial successes, however, the pilots went back to work en masse, even though the British offered even higher bribes. The *Siguranta* had forced them to refuse the money and continue their work. The Rumanians had strong cultural links with France, sympathised politically with England, but were economically dependent on Germany. They had no choice but to keep walking the tightrope for as long as possible.

Canaris, the consummate manipulator, did not come away from Bucharest empty-handed. He had brought Colonel Moruzov a copy of the London *Daily Mail* which contained an article by Gordon Beckles, a journalist who had lived for a long time in Bucharest and possessed detailed first-hand knowledge of the country. The piece contained an enthusiastic account of how it would be possible to cut off Hitler's supply of oil from Rumania.

The eager journalist left strategic considerations to Britain's military planners - there were something like a million British troops under arms in the Middle East, not far from Rumania - and also ruled out the idea of blowing up the oil rigs. He put forward a simple, cheap idea of his own: that of blocking the Danube passage by sinking a number of block-ships packed with concrete at the river's narrowest point. He had even found the right spot: the picturesque Iron Gate with its steep cliffs which, expertly detonated, would slide into the Danube and provide a further barrier, one that would probably block the passage until the war was over. What Beckles did not know was that the British Secret Service already had well-prepared plans along these lines.

The *Siguranta* had, in any case, already read the *Daily Mail* article, and so the German Intelligence chief was pushing at an open door. Canaris demanded that Moruzov allow plain-clothes agents from his 'Brandenburg' special operations outfit to operate freely inside the country to protect the oil shipments and the production centres.

Something had to be done about the British sabotage, and from the *Siguranta*'s point of view Canaris's suggestion was ideal: the Germans would do most of the work, while the Rumanians could appear to be maintaining strict neutrality. Canaris was expert at covering his tracks, if necessary by lethal means.

Moreover, Colonel Moruzov had known since November

10th at the latest of the existence of a second Intelligence organisation in Hitler's Germany. The so-called 'Venlo Incident' had provided the first success for SS leader Reinhard Heydrich's Reich Main Security Service, an outfit which seemed, if anything, to court scandal and international outrage.

The agents of the British Secret Service inside Germany were controlled from the neutral Netherlands by the SIS officers Major S. Payne Best and Captain R.H. Stevens. These agents had happened upon a resistance group centred on one Hauptmann Schemmel, an officer in the Transport Department of the Wehrmacht High Command. True, they had checked that a Hauptmann of that name existed – in fact Schemmel had been granted temporary rank for the purpose of the 'game' that was being played – but otherwise they were acting like amateurs. The men of the world's most experienced and prestigious Intelligence service had begun to stumble, while their opponents, Heydrich's relative newcomers, could apparently do no wrong.

The English had always mistrusted bona fide representatives of the German opposition, who had been trying for years to overthrow Hitler and avoid a war, but they fell completely for this unknown Hauptmann, whose identity was as fake as his monocle. 'Schemmel' was, in fact, none other than SS-Oberführer Walter Schellenberg, who during the course of the war was to rise from failed law student to boss of the entire foreign espionage network.

Schellenberg's chance for glory came after the attempt on Hitler's life at the *Büregerbräukeller* beer hall. Hitler, who had a blind belief in the ubiquity, effectiveness and cunning of the British Secret Service and immediately suspected its hand in the assassination attempt, gave personal orders to the SS Intelligence leaders that the two SIS officers were to be lured to the border and from there, in contravention of Holland's neutrality, forcibly removed to Germany.

Schellenberg sent a radio message to a company named 'N.V. Handelsdienst voor het Continent' at 15 Nieuve Uitleg in Amsterdam. The long-winded name of the firm concealed the headquarters of the British Secret Service in Holland. He made arrangements to meet Best and Stevens at Venlo, close to the border, where he lay in waiting with a squad of fourteen men – the same SS thugs who had unleashed the war by their attack on the Gleiwitz radio station.

'There was a lot of traffic on the road that day, including large numbers of men in civilian clothes with police dogs,' writes Schellenberg in his memoirs in true gangster-film style. 'I was a little nervous and ordered an aperitif in the café where I was waiting in Venlo. Would Best and Stevens come? They were taking their time – it was already 3 p.m., and there was still no sign of them. Suddenly I froze: a grey car was approaching at high speed. I leapt to my feet, but my companion grabbed my arm. "A mistake. It's someone else." I glanced anxiously over towards the German customs post – would the SS squad hidden there make the same mistake? But things remained quiet. Finally I ordered a good, strong cup of coffee, and I had only taken one sip when my companion nudged me, "It's them!" We strolled outside with assumed casualness, with our coats draped over our arms... The Buick turned off the road with a squeal of brakes and headed for the car park behind the café. I was still some ten paces or so from the car when I heard the growl of our squad's car's exhaust. Shooting had already broken out. Then I heard loud shouts, obviously from the Dutch border police, who were dashing to and fro like scared cats. At that moment, Lieutenant Copper leapt out of the Buick, drew a heavy service Colt and took aim at me. I was unarmed and threw myself to one side. Meanwhile, the squad's car came racing around the corner of the café building. Copper turned towards the more immediate threat and fired several times through the windscreen. I saw the windscreen shatter, and for a split second I thought that he had hit the driver, or the squad commander, who was sitting in the passenger seat. But the commander was already bounding out of the car, and now a real gunfight began between him and Copper. Suddenly Lieutenant Copper dropped his pistol, fell onto his knees. I was still standing very close to him. Then I heard the commander's harsh voice bellowing at me, "Now for God's sake get out of here!" I fled round the corner to my car, and in that final moment I saw Best and Stevens being manhandled out of their car like two sacks of potatoes...'

Copper – in reality a Dutch lieutenant named Klop – died on the way to hospital in Düsseldorf; the SIS officers were taken to Sachsenhausen concentration camp near Berlin for 'special treatment'.

The world had witnessed a horrific 'first': a state-sponsored kidnapping across the border of a neutral country. It was a flagrant breach of international law, and also a violation of the unwritten rule of secret intelligence: never make yourself conspicuous. Hitler, however, awarded the Iron Cross to the kidnappers before a full guard of honour in the courtyard of the Reich Chancellery, thus putting thugs on an equal footing with the frontline soldiers. From then on, the neutrals knew that they had good cause to fear Hitler's Fifth Column.

The Abwehr had not been given advance warning of the Venlo coup; Canaris was presented with a *fait accompli* by his rivals, the SS amateurs from the Prinz-Albrecht-Strasse. When two secret services exist side by side in one country, one manned by experienced experts, the other by political adventurers, it is not hard to predict that they will work more against than with each other. The 'little Levantine' was soon engaged in a bitter 'two-front-war', at home as well as abroad. It was true that Canaris was a welcome guest at the home of his neighbour, Heydrich, and that he often listened dutifully to the SS leader's violin recitals, but it was clear that one day there would be a savage reckoning.

The Rumanian *Siguranta* was well aware of the situation in Germany, and Colonel Moruzov knew that if he rejected Canaris's request he would end up saddled with Heydrich's desperadoes. Under these circumstances, he had no choice but to reach agreement quickly with Canaris. The Admiral was able to set off back to Berlin on the same day without the British getting wind of his lightning visit.

The man they called 'the Fox of the Tirpitzufer' – so called after the Berlin street where Abwehr headquarters was situated – did not control a worldwide espionage network established in peacetime, but he did possess his own private army, known as the 'Brandenburgers' after the town in which they were based. By the outbreak of war, the single company had grown to a battalion, and from now on this special operations outfit, whose badge was a sword and serpent, became big business. In later years it would reach division-strength. A division of men who fought alone, whose weapon was deception, whose trademark was audacity, and whose final destination was mostly an unmarked grave. They were examples of a new breed that would arise in this war: commando groups that would operate behind the lines in enemy uniforms and there – protected by no international agreements – create confusion and chaos.

In America, their own patriotic desperadoes were called Rangers, in Britain, the Special Air Service. Whether on the German or Allied side, they were tough individualists whose courage bordered on madness, expert saboteurs, masters of explosives, trained parachutists, and crack shots. Their first commander, Dr von Hippler, gave the Brandenburgers their motto: 'You are to be a bunch of villains, the kind who could kidnap the Devil out of hell'.

A peculiar bunch of men with their own peculiar morality, always on the lookout for people with a talent for subversion, men who had attracted attention as mountain-climbers, long-distance swimmers, glider-pilots, dog-handlers, experts in Sanskrit or top sportsmen. If possible they were to have a command of English, French, Croat, Serb, Slovene, Greek and Rumanian, or to be able to keep their mouths shut convincingly. There were Germans who pretended to be deaf-and-dumb Russians.

Members of this special unit were among the enemy before every offensive – perhaps hours previously – skilfully disguised and dispersed under the motto: 'Brandenburgers are everywhere'. They were indeed everywhere, and everywhere many of them died heroes' deaths.

In neutral Rumania, however, their job was not the seizing of a bridge or the taking of an airfield but the protection of the petrol for Hitler's Panzers and aircraft. At first Canaris sent an advance party of about forty men into the Balkan state. Since he did not entirely trust the

Rumanians, despite Colonel Moruzov's assurances, he advised the government there of the arrival of only some of his agents. The rest were infiltrated over the border from pro-German Bulgaria, disguised as tourists or members of a visiting sports team.

The waterfront dive calls itself the Yellow Cockatoo, but the only yellow items there are the stained table-cloths. The place offers cheap schnapps and willing girls. Money disappears here like rain in the desert. The fat proprietress slips hastily behind the counter, welcomes Jonas like a favourite customer. She knows most of her other customers even better, because her establishment is in the restricted area, where one can only go with a government pass – real or forged.

'Let's talk business,' says the Prophet arrogantly. 'How many girls do you have?'

'You're kidding,' the old woman answers. 'Enough for the likes of you.'

'How many?' he repeats, then shortens the negotiations in the traditional Rumanian fashion by shoving a fat envelope packed with lei notes across the counter. 'How many?'

'Eleven.'

'Can you get reinforcements?' asks Jonas. Both his line of questioning and his manner are, to say the least, unusual for a little Swiss watch salesman.

'As many as you like,' the madam says quickly, then rubs thumb and forefinger together in an unmistakable gesture of greed. 'So long as you can pay, eh?'

'I'll pay whatever it takes,' Jonas grins, playing the big spender. 'Myself and my friends, you understand. I only have one birthday a year, and today's the day. You're invited too, if you like. Brändli will pick up the bill. But it will have to be strictly a private party.'

'And you'll pay for everything in advance?' says the woman, hardly able to believe her luck.

They agree terms quickly, organise a band, vast quantities of schnapps, call-girls of the best quality. The trap has been baited.

Outside at the harbour dam lies the *Mardinian*, with a

small British skeleton crew and a scratch complement of Rumanians, Bulgarians, Yugoslavs and Hungarians hired during the past few days. The captain was forced to take on these none-too-reliable Balkan cut-throats in order to give himself some camouflage. The *Mardinian* has forged cargo documents, but the soldiers also aboard are real enough. These specially-trained sappers are under military discipline and keep to their own quarters. The 'Foreign Legion' of Slavic sailors would, however, be liable to mutiny if they were not allowed ashore. It is on this fact that 'Operation Boudoir' is based.

Jonas pretty soon realises that the bill is going to be a high one.

The first sailors arrive. In hunting-packs. Fat Melchior supports Jonas in his new role of brothel-keeper by standing outside and touting for custom. 'The best-looking girls in Sulina,' he bellows at the sailors. His hands trace seductive shapes in the air. 'Great legs, tits like melons,' he adds, then gets a little carried away with enthusiasm: 'Randy as she-cats, hot as a stoker's arse.'

At first they stare at him mistrustfully, obviously labelling him for a crazy, but men are men, and the prospect of women never fails. Particularly in waterfront districts, where the girls are willing but thin on the ground.

The Brandenburgers' paid helpers are spilling, in a manner of speaking, out of the windows, visible from a way off. And they're not bad looking, at least by night.

The first of them enter the whorehouse, to be greeted by a drunken Swiss who is in the process of inviting everybody to his birthday party. The news that there's a free party happening at the *Cockatoo* spreads like wildfire among the crew of the *Mardinian*. The pianist begins to pound keys that are as stained as a smoker's teeth, hits a few wrong notes, and the Rumanian-Bulgarian-Hungarian-Czech-Yugoslav chorus growls along with him. A mass of lonely sailors, eager to make up for all they have been missing through the wasted weeks aboard ship. They want love, or at least the semblance of it. And tonight they don't have to pay a penny. It's like a seaman's dream come true . . .

The Swiss is paying for everything. And the blonde

Greek girl, star of the evening, has a smile for each of them. It will lead to trouble. She is stoking the fires with cool expertise, tempting one, flirting with a second, dancing with a third, stepping over the prone body of a fourth, who has drunk himself insensible because he couldn't have her.

Things are going swimmingly, but Jonas is still sceptical: no counting chickens. Nevertheless, they begin to chalk up the first victims of excess alcohol shortly before midnight. Melchior and Fiedler help with the processing. They drag the snoring sailors out from under the tables, lure them upstairs to an empty room with the aid of the girls.

In the room the drunks are given a powerful night-cap: a generous shot of a narcotic drug mixed in with their drinks. Some manage a quick paw at the girls who got them up here to the first floor, maybe a single kiss - and then off into the land of nod.

The Brandenburgers' allies against HMS *Mardinian* are the IG Farben drugs company and bought sex.

Jonas looks round the room, counts his haul, proud as the devil counting lost souls. 'Seven,' he says to fat Melchior. 'Much too few.'

They can still hear the noise of the party down below in the bar. The girls' laughter, squeals of faked pleasure, and the rough voices of the sailors. The Brandenburgers are forced to make another sally downstairs. Jonas finds himself staring at the Greek girl more often than he should; he has other business on his mind at the moment, but he can't help wondering whether he might get time for a short interlude with her - without an anaesthetic.

'We must have ten more,' growls Wagenseil to himself. They set to work.

More sailors from the *Mardinian* are pouring in all the time, being given a hearty welcome. Eleven are now safely upstairs, beyond thirst, beyond lust. They won't get back to the *Mardinian* tonight; firstly because they will all have two-day hangovers, and secondly because the boys from the Brandenburg Commando, to be on the safe side, will be shipping them off somewhere else to sleep their fill.

More will be dragged off upstairs, and then the Captain of the British ship will have no crew. He will have to take any replacements that he can get. And they will make sure that the sailors he gets are supplied by the Brandenburg commando unit. Men like Jonas, Wagenseil, Melchior, Dumbrowski and Fiedler. Each one hailing, so far as their potential employer is concerned, from a different Balkan country. From anywhere but Germany.

'Going like clockwork,' grins Melchior. Even Jonas is so optimistic that he forgets his self-imposed ban on alcohol and takes a hearty swig of schnapps.

And then it happens.

An officer from the *Mardinian* enters the brothel, shouts angrily at his sailors, starts ushering them outside.

'Bleeding nerve,' says long, lean Backe.

The angry Englishman manages to haul a couple of Bulgarians out. The others stay put, cursing but hesitant, not daring open revolt.

'What are you doing, breaking up my birthday party?' Jonas says in heavily-accented English, lurching threateningly towards the lean-faced, pale-eyed officer.

The man continues doing his job, ignoring the Prophet. With his carefully-trimmed beard, precisely-parted hair, and his aquiline nose surrounded by freckles, he is a storybook Englishman.

'Birthday?' he asks finally, turning to Jonas. 'And who in God's name are you?'

'My name it is Brändli,' Jonas answers in his best schoolboy English, knowing that his life could depend on it. He grins stupidly. 'I come from Basel.'

'Swiss?' says the naval officer, the flush of anger beginning to disappear from his smooth features.

'And an admirer of your Great Britain,' the German Unteroffizier continues. 'Would you drink a glass with me to your glorious victory?'

The man hesitates. 'O.K. Yes,' says the naval officer, and reaches for the drink that Melchior has already mixed for him. Very thoughtful of the fat man. The Englishman's suspicions are melting like ice cream in the sun – patriotism can make a man stupid.

'Cheers,' Jonas toasts, and the man who had been threatening to wreck his plan swallows the first dose of

Melchior's Mickey Finn. 'And now to His Majesty, the King!' He passes him his second dose.

The man responsible for getting the *Mardinian's* crew back to their ship is already starting to feel the effects. He looks at his men with narrowed eyes, grimaces contemptuously. 'A right bunch, eh? It's a crime, having to work with these Balkan cut-throats.'

'Then why do you not use your own people?' asks Jonas, as if genuinely puzzled.

'We need our boys at the front,' the Englishman answers. He makes to continue rounding up his men, but the phoney Swiss salesman forces him to have another drink. They work their way gradually through the entire royal family, drinking a toast to each: to the Princesses Lillibet and Margaret Rose, to the Queen Mother. To the uncles and nieces, aunts and cousins.

'God bless them!' says Jonas, raising his glass correctly to chest height.

The officer from the *Mardinian* slips slowly to the floor to jeers and laughter from his crew, and finally falls asleep under the table. Fat Melchior and Fiedler carry him out like a stricken wild boar after a hunt.

It is a farce, but a farce that is making history. The Balkans are a powder-keg, but no one wants to be blamed for lighting the match that sets it off. As night clothes the *Mardinian* like a winding-sheet, and closes in on the tugboat *Princess Elizabeth*, the *Lord Byron*, the six Danube barges taking 'exports' to Budapest, the lights at the *Siguranta*'s head-quarters burn through the night.

The Port Commander at Sulina has long since warned the secret police of the goings-on at the *Cockatoo*, but to his amazement Captain Stefanescu, far from sounding the alarm, has simply told him to take things as easy as possible and to turn a blind eye. The Rumanian cooks are helping to thicken the broth. The rest of the country is otherwise engaged. The Bucharest parliament is in recess, and King Carol is in bed with his mistress, Madame Lupescu, telling her – or so the Rumanian wags have it – what a great lover he used to be.

Jonas has had to get his wallet out again. Not that it

matters: Canaris is paying the bill, swapping schnapps for oil, if need be on a one-to-one basis. The lights are flickering, the place is full to bursting-point, and tempers are starting to fray in the crowded bar. A chair for every two drinkers. Eight or ten men grabbing for each girl, all of them full of schnapps. Melchior and Fiedler bring in more bottles.

'Watch out for that damned Hungarian!' Jonas bellows to them.

He has noticed that one particular sailor, a good-looking lad, is getting a little too obsessed with the Greek girl. Staring at her with a pining, doggy adoration that could soon turn nasty. 'Hey you, c'mon,' he says.

'In a minute, Magyar,' she says with a laugh.

The Hungarian finally loses his temper. 'Not in a minute. Now!'

He comes up against a Bulgarian built like a small tree. Soon they have picked sides and are arming themselves with chairlegs and knives.

'Great,' mutters fat Melchior. 'They'll do our job for us.'

'Idiot,' growls the Prophet. 'And bring down the police on us.'

Just as the two groups are about to start trading blows, Hungary against Bulgaria, Jonas leaps between them with a coin in his hand, suddenly fluent in a whole lot of languages. 'Heads or tails?' he grins at the two main participants, hoping grimly that the coin he tosses will fall in favour of Joschi, the Hungarian.

He laughs. It has worked out. Jonas glances at the Greek girl. She answers with a quick nod while Wagenseil takes up position behind her. Joschi, the victor, takes her proudly by the arm, beaming all over his handsome face. The road to paradise leads through the badly-lit corridor to the foot of the stairs. And here Melchior is waiting with a cosh to deal with Joschi. Using just enough force, and gaining a great deal of pleasure from the achievement.

The Hungarian ends up in their private drunkards' Valhalla, as number seventeen or eighteen. And from now on the 'dormitory' fills up quickly. Most of them without the aid of Melchior's cosh. A little Bulgarian spends so long showing off somersaults that he finally crashes over one last time and doesn't move again. Zdenka, the whore with the ginger hair, doses three admirers with sleeping-pills. Her tall, skinny fellow-professional, Nilla, tries the same trick but gets the glasses mixed up. As she fights against sleep, big-breasted Joana does the dance of the seven veils to keep everyone's attention away from her.

The laughter slowly dies. The bar is no longer so crowded. Suddenly there are more girls than sailors. It is still night when the Brandenburgers drag the last drunk off to their special room. Anyone who wakes up yelling for water gets it – liberally spiked with narcotics.

By four in the morning, the battle is over. Jonas says his farewells, distributes a final bonus to the girls. The blonde Greek girl smiles at him invitingly. Quite a mixture. Fair hair and dark, flashing eyes. Smooth, olive skin...

'Come with me,' she says throatily. 'I like you.'

'I like you too,' the Prophet answers, looks at his watch, grimaces. 'Tomorrow...'

But he knows full well that tomorrow there will be no time for the joys of the flesh. Tomorrow is the day of 'Operation Iron Gate'.

The master of the *Mardinian*'s face shows his ill-humour. Thirty-eight men from his crew are missing. Thirty-eight Hungarians, Bulgarians, Rumanians, Yugoslavs, Czechs. And one British officer, sent to round them up, is overdue back from shore. That's the worst thing. 'The fellow's been kidnapped,' he says gloomily.

'Ah. By a woman, perhaps?' the Rumanian harbour master asks, suddenly interested.

'Rubbish,' says the old sea-dog tersely. 'By the Huns.'

'Bring me the criminals responsible, and I shall have them locked up immediately.' Sulina's dockyard boss answers. 'Now, shall we proceed to the question of your cargo. Provisions for Budapest?' He shakes his head in a way that shows his disbelief. Salami for Hungary? It's like the English saying: coals to Newcastle...

The captain hands over a fat envelope filled with lei notes, and the Rumanian officer shoves it into the pocket of his well-cut uniform without batting an eyelid. He is following orders direct from the *Siguranta* today. In fact, the harbour master is not in the habit of taking bribes, and it goes against the grain.

'A whisky?'

The harbour master nods, though his stomach is churning.

'Ah . . . If you wanted to, you could be a rich man, you know,' the British captain begins, trying to approach the subject as diplomatically as possible. 'I'm in a jam, you see. The useless specimens who call themselves my crew have disappeared off the face of the earth.'

'All of them?'

'Two turned up – drunk out of their minds. They didn't get as far as the Yellow Cockatoo. They filled their skins somewhere else.'

'Sailors are thirsty by nature . . .'

'Well,' the commander of the *Mardinian* says quickly. 'For whatever reason, I'm suddenly lacking a crew. I'll pay you a princely commission for each replacement.'

'I'll see what I can do for you,' the Rumanian answers, and says a polite farewell. He now knows the *Siguranta*'s game. The whole business of the 'birthday party' in the brothel stinks to high heaven, of course, but it is even more suspicious that someone arrived in Sulina the previous day and hired all the available sailors in the port for a fat downpayment. The newly-hired men did not, moreover, go on board a Danube barge, but were taken by the truckload inland to a luxury hotel. There they are living with all expenses paid for three days, and on the fourth they will get their final payment for services rendered.

All that is available for the *Mardinian* is a group of fifteen or eighteen men, and they're not proper sailors. Their home port is Brandenburg. The harbour master is well aware of the fact, but he sends the men to the *Mardinian*, whose captain has no choice but to take what he can get. The merchant captain, no veteran of the secret war, starts with fat Melchior, after him Fiedler, and after him Jonas. Just as he is about to start interviewing them, to prevent any German agents finding their way among the British convoy that is heading towards the Iron gate, the Rumanian harbour master, looking pleased as Punch with himself, herds a whole new bunch of replacement sailors on board. The Englishman's ill-humour abates. He gets to his feet and takes a few steps towards his eager helper, who greets him with open arms.

'Bloody hypocrite,' growls fat Melchior.

'Shut your mouth, arsehole,' Jonas hisses.

He has recognised a few familiar faces from the Jablunka Pass along with the strange ones, fresh as newly-minted five-mark pieces. The Prophet has a sixth sense when it comes to recognising his own kind. 'Welcome, mates,' he murmurs to himself, and tries to carry on looking stupid and surprised.

It is only then that Jonas sees the full extent of the pantomime: in the midst of the newcomers stands Leutnant Schübler, talking earnestly to them as if he was trying to sell combs to a convention of bald men.

'Look at that, look at that,' says Fiedler, hazarding a witticism. 'The Trojan Jackass.'

They are so close now that they can understand what Schübler is saying to the 'sailors'. He is playing a German agent and playing it to the hilt, offering tempting sums of money if they will refuse to join the British ship.

'He's blown his cover,' Jonas whispers. 'His days in Rumania are numbered.'

'And his nights,' Melchior answers with a leer.

Coldly but politely, the captain has his unwelcome guest removed from his ship and then turns to view his new crew. So far as appearances are concerned, the men look no worse than the 'foreign legion' that he had lost the previous day. And he has fifty or so to choose from instead of thirty-eight. how is an old and honest captain of the merchant marine to know that the entire collection has been supplied by Admiral Canaris?

The delayed interviews begin.

Jonas and his henchmen take a back seat, for safety's sake, and allow the comrades who were not involved in the Yellow Cockatoo caper to go through their paces. The interviews are swift and superficial. The Tommies do not have much time if their armada is to sail today. And it will have to, for if the Rumanians have time to investigate their cargo thoroughly, the entire plan to block the Iron Gate will be blown.

The first seven pass the captain's test quickly. They have all rehearsed their parts, and where their acting talents fail they can take refuge in language difficulties.

The eighth is deliberately evasive. 'I am a Czech, but –' he stutters in appalling English. 'But my mother –' he suddenly claps his hand across his mouth.

'And what is your mother?' asks the captain harshly.

'Before she married, she was an Austrian,' admits the man, with a hangdog expression.

'Sorry. Very sorry,' the captain says sympathetically. 'Please understand that I shall have to let you go.'

Jonas comes next.

'Swiss, eh?' says the captain. 'Traveller in watches, you say. What are you doing here, then?'

'The watches aren't selling,' the Prophet says. 'The Rumanians are short of cash.'

'You don't look like a Swiss.'

'And you,' Jonas says cheekily, 'don't look much like an Englishman.'

The captain laughs loudly and waves him through. 'All right. Go on, boy.'

Within twenty minutes the entire procedure is over. The commander has taken on forty men as crew to replace the thirty-eight he lost. Not a bad exchange, even though the Rumanian harbour master's palm has to be plentifully greased at the British taxpayer's expense.

Meanwhile, the newly-hired men begin to unload the *Mardinian*'s cargo onto the other ships. Under close guard. Suddenly a squad of well-built, tough-looking characters appear from below decks, part of the British permanent crew, and they don't look as though they are to be messed with. The 'sailors' have no choice but to slave away, sweating and waiting. Four of them get together to haul a heavy crate onto a cargo barge. Most of it has to be shifted by hand, because the few cranes are needed for the really heavy stuff.

They come back from the barge, short of breath and cursing in a variety of languages, and with faces that say: 'What the hell do we do now?'

The stoker who is guarding them is not looking quite so fierce now. He even goes off to get them something to drink – non-alcoholic, admittedly.

AUSTIN CORPORATION is stencilled onto the side of the crate. You would have to be pretty stupid to believe that. As if the British had nothing better to do than supplying the Hungarians with car parts.

By the time they have shifted the fifth crate, the stoker seems to have lost his distrust of them. And that is when it happens: Jonas hauls it up. Melchior pretends to stumble. lets go, taking Ritschel with him as he falls. Fiedler jumps to one side to avoid being squashed. The crate crashes down onto the deck complete with its block and tackle, and breaks open.

The stoker curses to high heaven, blows a whistle.

A few men from the English crew are on the spot within moments – but not quite fast enough. By that time, the Brandenburgers have verified that the crate was full of dismantled machine-guns.

'So,' says Jonas. 'If we now supply proof to the Rumanians, that old sea-dog will be off with his tail between his legs, well away from the Iron gate.'

The loading is over by the afternoon. The 'sailors' are dispersed among the various vessels of the convoy. Jonas and Melchior succeed in staying together on board the *Princess Elizabeth*. The armada of barges weighs anchor. The *Mardinian* leaves at the same time, steaming back into the Black Sea.

The tugboats give all they have, but the barges are sailing against the current in more ways than one. On board, the orders come from officers who could just as well belong to the Brandenburg Division, but in fact are experts from the British Secret Service.

The atmosphere is tense. No one speaks. The men stick together. Everyone senses that the ghostly flotilla is being watched by many eyes from the bank. The scenery on shore changes slowly: now there are vineyards, cliffs, mountains.

The river broadens out, then narrows again as it snakes through the countryside.
The first port of call: Braila.
A Rumanian officer comes aboard, salutes politely, checks their papers, takes some money, wishes them 'bon voyage' and leaves.
Next stop: Harsova. The same performance.
Then Gernavoda. It is turning into a routine.
The commander of the convoy is named Brown, but he could be called Müller for all it matters, because both names would be false. He looks more sure of himself now, more impatient. He has the Rumanians in his pocket, bought and paid for. Money has always called the tune in the Balkans.
What are the Germans up to? Are they asleep?
'All going well, sir,' says one of the officers to Brown.
'I hope you are right,' says the commander of 'Operation Iron Gate.' 'I feel as if it has all been too easy.'
Silistra comes in sight. Even the Rumanians are becoming nervous now, despite their decision to leave the Germans and the British to fight over the oil between themselves.
The boss of the *Siguranta*, Colonel Moruzov, has checked with Major Luca to ask if he is sure that the Germans are doing what they promised. Luca has passed the request on to Captain Stefanescu, who has given an evasive answer, although he knows the truth.
The convoy is now steaming towards Georgiu. The Iron Gate is coming closer and closer. Even a few of the Brandenburgers are starting to feel uneasy.
The waves are getting choppy. There is a distinct swell. A few men climb onto the upper deck of the *Princess Elizabeth* to catch some air. The man on deck watch sees them immediately. What language are they speaking, he wonders. Could it be German?
He is uncertain. But he is certain enough that he sees the torch tracing careful circles in the darkness. He makes his way towards the light. It is quickly extinguished.
'What are you up to?' the Englishman growls at the man responsible.
Temporary crewman Brändli smiles stupidly. 'Nothing.'

Much good it does him. He is frog-marched off towards the bridge.

The waves lap against the ship. Marker lights blink through the darkness. Green, red, and white, like giant glow-worms. At this point, just before Georgiu, the Danube is wide enough to allow two convoys to pass each other: the English one coming up from the Black Sea and the German one travelling from Hungary, which has already passed the notorious bottleneck of the Iron Gate.

'This man was giving signals, sir,' says one of the two Englishmen who caught Jonas.

'Don't believe them, Captain,' the Prophet stutters, turning imploring eyes to Captain Brown. 'I was taking some air.'

'And the torch?'

'I was looking for my cigarette case.' Jonas fumbles, pulls out the case and shows it eagerly to the assembled company.

'You should give up smoking,' the officer retorts sarcastically.

At that moment, on April 4th, 1940 at exactly 23.23 hours, it happens. A shadow. A scream. A tanker comes loose from the approaching German convoy, swings crazily out into midstream, heading straight for the *Princess Elizabeth*. A big, dark portent of disaster that must crash into the middle of the British convoy at any moment.

'Attention!' bellows the man on the bridge watch. 'Attention!'

'Stop engines!' Captain Brown orders, so that at least he will be able to avoid a head-on collision.

The helmsman acts immediately. The ship's propeller turns wildly in the opposite direction, forcing down the prow of the powerful tugboat. The crew are thrown all over the place. For a moment it seems as if the *Princess Elizabeth* is bowing to the intruder. Then the tug's stern comes round and she hits the out-of-control tanker with an almighty crash.

The quiet river is suddenly turned into a broiling witches' cauldron. Searchlights probe the darkness hungrily. Through navigational skill, the *Princess Elizabeth* has avoided a head-on collision, but has got itself entangled in the other vessel's anchor chain. The two end up circling in midstream like scorpions involved in a mating dance.

Jonas, discovered signalling to his own people and immediately sacked by Captain Brown, made himself scarce as soon as the first alarm was sounded. He vaulted over the deck and sprang overboard unnoticed. He was able to watch while the tanker, exactly according to plan, came alongside the barge to starboard. He strikes out towards it, hauls himself on board the barge, still dripping wet from his swim. He arrives just in time to help his comrades in shifting the first crates.

'Just a moment,' Ritschel calls from above. 'Two are better than one.'

God alone knows how they do it. They heave the second crate up out of the hold, heavy work, and no one must see them while they are doing it. They slave away, panting and cursing, but so long as the Tommies don't smell a rat they are happy as pigs in shit.

'My apologies, sir,' calls Captain Weiss of the Bavarian Lloyd - for this read Brandenburg - to the British through his loud hailer. 'Stupid business. The tanker came away from its towline. Our insurance people will, of course, recompense you for all the damage.'

'Damned Jerry,' murmurs his British opponent through gritted teeth. Such disasters happen from time to time in inland waterways. But with a German convoy responsible, he is sure that it can't be an accident. Captain Brown has managed to avoid the worst, and he is now trying to see what can be salvaged from the wreckage of 'Operation Iron Gate'.

His sailors are working like madmen. For a moment, both vessels are heading towards the bank together. *Princess Elizabeth* is still dragging the cargo barges behind her, and the German ship is sticking to one of them like a limpet.

'They must be ruddy-well blind,' shouts fat Melchior delightedly as they off-load the second crate onto the stern of the ship. But he is crowing a few seconds too early.

One of the British spots the boat they are loading the crates into and suddenly understands the game they are playing. They see him too, grab him, send him crashing unconscious to the deck, but not before he has yelled the house down.

'Fuck it!' screams fat Melchior in a different tone.

Long, thin Fiedler is the first to jump overboard. Ritschel, the new man, follows him. It is too late for the others.

The launch shoots off like a bullet from a gun.

A British lieutenant appears on the upper deck of the cargo barge with a machine gun at the ready. 'Stop!' he bellows. 'Come back!'

'Cover!' Jonas roars, but how do you conceal yourself at fifty metres in a tiny boat like this?

The first burst, meant as a warning, whistles over their heads. The launch is travelling on a zig-zag course. The Englishman aims, squeezes the trigger, cuts skinny Fiedler literally in two. Bullets rip into the side of the vessel. The men huddle behind the stolen crates, flattening themselves against the bottom of the boat.

They have no chance of reaching the bank, but just in time some speedboats of the Rumanian River Police put in an appearance. They succeed in getting close to the police craft and force the British to hold their fire.

'Christ,' says Jonas with feeling. 'They damned near did for us.' He notices that Ritschel is still under cover. 'You can stop shitting your trousers, comrade,' he mocks. 'It's over. This is the all-clear.'

But still Ritschel doesn't move. They turn him over. A burst of machine-gun fire took away half his face. And his mates suddenly lose their joy in their coup. War has extracted a straightforward, grim payment: two dead men for two crates.

In order to investigate the incident, the Rumanian police direct all ships into the harbour at Georgiu. It is exactly fifty-six kilometres from the Danube to Bucharest. The Prophet and his hired truck make it in record time. While his explosive booty is on its way through the night, the German Ambassador, Herr Fabrizius, had already made representations to the Rumanian Secret Police.

'Awful, if what you say is true, Excellency,' says Captain

Stefanescu with feigned astonishment. 'If you can supply me with proof, I shall force the British convoy to turn back.'

'Bear with me for another half-hour...'

But Jonas, fat Melchior and a few comrades make it in twenty-eight minutes. They display weapons, ammunition and explosives and swear in oath that they 'secured' it aboard a British cargo barge.

With this German counter-coup, 'Operation Iron Gate' is finished.

The cargo is seized, the crew is interned and later deported. The Danube, the chief route for oil exports to Germany and Central Europe, is kept open. Rumania's black gold continues to flow to Hitler's armies.

But it is clear that the English will try again, notwithstanding their failures. In Bucharest the whisper is still: Will the British parachutists come or not?

The English also lose the second round in the struggle for oil. They try to smuggle the plans of the oilfields, the production complexes and rigs out of Rumania, a move that can only mean that they are plotting large-scale sabotage.

Warned by the Brandenburgers, the *Siguranta* intervenes and captures the truck in which the blueprints had been concealed for their trip across the border and into the British hands.

Then comes the third, decisive round. A secret conference is summoned at the *Astra Romana*'s private rest home on the coast near Snagov, on the edge of the Restricted Zone and some forty-five kilometres from Bucharest.

The British Secret Service has thrown a security blanket over the entire meeting. No enemy agents, no listening devices. No one allowed within miles. Only a few selected oilmen, such as Mr Miller, managing director of the *Astra Romana*, his technical manager, Mr Page, and some specialists from London. All of them have entered Rumania under conditions of total secrecy, as has Colonel Smith of the SIS, who is in charge of the meeting and is well-known as an expert in 'scorched earth' withdrawals.

'Gentlemen,' he begins. 'We have only one problem. Once I have issued my orders, we shall need seventy-two hours. Three full days. Not a moment more or less.'

His eyes flicker from one tense face to another. These businessmen are having to destroy their lives' work. For twenty, thirty years they have invested the sweat of their brow and their money and skill, and now they must choose to blow up installations that are the property of their shareholders - or continue to supply oil to the blasted Germans.

'We shall bluff things out, come what may,' the colonel continues. 'As a temporary measure, we shall even increase production, and we shall forcibly arrest anyone who comes near Ploesti.'

'Rumanians as well?' asks Mr Miller carefully.

'We shall dissuade them,' the colonel says. 'It should be easy to manage.'

'And if the non-British workers smell a rat before time?'

'We shall deal with them. We don't intend to take any risks, though I will not pretend that we shan't suffer losses during the withdrawal. Ploesti will immediately be placed under martial law.'

The colonel is known for waging war by his own rules - if necessary, against the Rumanians in their own country. The managers of the *Astra Romana* will do their duty, even though it sickens them. The tension has become intolerable. It has begun to gnaw at the nerves of innocent civilians as well, for somehow everyone knows that the underground war will soon become open conflict.

Someone has tried to kill Major Luca. A hand-grenade thrown through the window of his bedroom. The *Siguranta* officer survived the attempt, but even he does not know who was responsible. It looks like a British-inspired dirty trick. The security arrangements are tightened up yet again.

There are danger signals as the Calea Rahovei, the huge cluster of buildings where the German Abwehr have set up their headquarters. One Brandenburger warns his closest comrade, and the alarms snowball.

Leutnant Schübler, back with his mistress, the confidante of Captain Stefanescu, comes out of her door, still warm, so to speak, from the battle of the sheets. He pauses in the porch for a moment before approaching his Bugatti, which is parked close to the countess's house. His colleagues have been maintaining a round-the-clock watch on him for some time now, but his motto is: safety first.

While Schübler is still looking around, trying to see who is shadowing him today, his pride and joy goes up in a pillar of flame.

'Dry your tears, Leutnant,' says Jonas. 'The Abwehr will buy you a new toy.'

They hurry away, eager to make themselves scarce before the police arrive.

'And you watched while they wired up my precious car?' says Schübler as they scuttle through the streets.

'I wouldn't have let you get into the thing, Leutnant,' the Prophet pants, then grins. 'Those fellows were careless. You saw what happened.'

They arrive at the square, low building with its underground entrances. The blinds on all the windows are pulled down; no lights showing outside. Even the shots fired in the shooting range in the cellar cannot be heard on the street.

'There you are,' says the major to his men by way of a welcome. He looks at Melchior. 'You've put on weight, for God's sake...' Then he gets back to the subject. 'Gentlemen, the name of the game is: out of the closet.'

'How's that?' Schübler asks.

'I believe that we have solved our problem,' says the man who is supposed to be Germany's military attaché.

Something is brewing at Ploesti. Where before it had been a struggle to squeeze a drop of oil out of the English firms, now there are no production difficulties. The roads leading out of the oil-producing area are full. Day and night, tanker trucks roll towards the Danube ports, but there are also trucks coming in the opposite direction, filled with sand and stones.

Where men are drilling for oil, there are always building sites. But what is the point of these astonishing quantities of builders' materials? 200 truckloads of stones and 400 of sand in Boldesti, 100 truckloads of stones and 200 of sand for Moreni, 75 of stones and 150 of sand for Ochinri.

The Abwehr major who is the Brandenburgers' contact man in Rumania is beginning to become uneasy. He puts in a scrambler call to an expert in Berlin, tells him the details of consignments. 'Tell me, for God's sweet sake, what they can possibly do with the filthy stuff?'

'Come, come,' the specialist says. He stares at a map of the area on the wall in front of him, compares the destinations and the quantities. 'Tell me, Herr Major. Just sand and stones? Are you sure there was no cement included?'

'A lot of grey sacks were sent, too,' says the Abwehr major.

'Then it's a clearcut case. When sand, stones and cement are mixed with water, you have concrete. And if, to speculate for a moment, you were to fill the oil drillings with the stuff, they would be out of action for the duration of the war, even if it were to last five years...'

'Holy mackerel,' the major howls. 'How long does it need to turn into concrete?'

'Unless the English have discovered a method of hurrying up the process, about three days.'

The major puts out an alarm, level three, which means that every last man they have on the job in Rumania will be involved. It means that a long-prepared plan will go into action, and that for once speed is more important than maintenance of cover.

The major takes Schübler on one side. 'I've got a special job for you,' he says temptingly, and pats him on the shoulder.

'Very well, Herr Major,' the Leutnant answers proudly, glad to be back in proper action again. He has nothing against the pleasures of love, but when it comes down to it, a fellow can't spend the whole war in a big French bed.

'Getting our boys into the border district is no problem,' the Abwehr major continues. 'But we need to have explosives. Not much. Say, a suitcase-full.'

'It will be arranged, Herr Major,' Schübler says quickly.

'But not by you, Leutnant,' grins his boss. 'Do you think that your friend Mariu could be persuaded to take a trip into the border district, perhaps along with Captain Stefanescu.'

'That could also be arranged, Herr Major.'

'And that while they are at it they could carry our goodies for us in their car?'

Schübler looks shocked. 'But this is men's work, Herr Major.'

'What we do with the explosives afterwards is men's work,' the major retorts with an edge of steel. 'That's an order, Leutnant Schübler.'

The men of the Brandenburg Division assemble from all corners of Rumania and from neighbouring countries. They travel on forged papers, or sneak over unguarded stretches of border, and filter skilfully through the military cordon that the Rumanians and the British have established around the oilfields. A guide brings them to their destination.

'Look after yourself,' Schübler tells the Countess Levandowsky.

She nods and smiles. 'So this is goodbye,' she says.

'No. Never.'

'I can help you to get out of the country,' she says. 'Once this business at Ploesti is over, surely you will have to leave?'

'I don't know where they'll send me,' the Leutnant answers. 'But things haven't yet reached that stage. Just look after yourself,' he repeats. 'Keep Captain Stefanescu happy and let someone steal your car in Ploesti. But don't forget: leave the boot unlocked.'

'Fine.'

The plan goes into action on the following morning: Rumanian tank units occupy the offices of the oil companies, despite British protests. 'Sorry,' Stefanescu assures them. 'I have been ordered to search the fields.'

'But surely not here?' says Colonel Smith.

'Including your's and Mr Page's private apartments.'

'For what reasons?'

'Suspicion of smuggling explosives.'

The Englishman shrugs his shoulders. But he has underestimated his enemies for the last time. He informs his ambassador, Sir Reginald Hoare, and while he is still speaking to him on the telephone they find a suitcase in the cupboard containing dynamite, a substance strictly forbidden inside the Restricted Zone.

'The damned Germans,' the colonel curses.

And it is the final word in the battle for Rumanian oil. Before the English can block a single drill with concrete, the entire area comes under military occupation, and Rumania's oil is secured for the Greater German Wehrmacht. A Greater German Wehrmacht that will soon move through the Balkans like a whirlwind...

Operation *Weserübung*

It is a grey spring day. A biting wind chills the harbour installations at the port of Wesermünde. An April without sun, without a hint of the year's renewal to come. It is the kind of day that a dog wouldn't venture out into, but there are hundreds of mountain troops moving at the double along the pier, their spiked mountain boots striking sparks as they go. With their heavy rucksacks and their outlandish dialect, the soldiers with their Edelweiss badges are something of an exotic phenomenon here in the flat, sober plain of North Germany.

The men of Mountain Regiment 139, under the command of Lieutenant-General Edouard Dietl, have come from their temporary base in Bremerhaven, and they have no idea where they are going. They have been told that they will play a key role in the glorious times that are coming, which means that they will be shoved about like pawns on a chess-board.

'Fancy being on that thing?' asks Private Geiger, pointing to the trim destroyer onto which the First Company is being embarked, 200 mountain troops with grinning, or grimacing faces.

'Think I'm stupid?' Pirmoser answers gruffly. 'Water. I bloody hate it!'

'Ah, but once we're on board that tub, we'll be all right,' says Geiger comfortingly. He has his army-issue LMG spread across his shoulders, like the Last of the Mohicans carrying his flintlock. 'At least we'll be able to play a decent hand or two, eh?'

The men of the Advance Section of the Third Mountain

Division are strapping lads from Upper Bavaria, from the Tyrol and the Allgäu, used to climbing up steep mountain tracks with a heavy trench mortar on their back, grooming their mules, or tearing down into a valley on their skis in the terrifying attack manoeuvre known as the 'bear' – but not to being tossed about on the foaming sea. They are about to be shoved on board and packed in like sheep in a fold. They are all volunteers who joined this specialist unit of their own free will, because its garrison towns are in their own area, which allows for easy weekend passes home, and because even as soldiers they have their beloved mountains and their skis. All in all, this is an outfit they feel at home in. 'Also because,' as Private Bachmaier always points out with great passion, 'there's not a damned Prussian in sight here.'

Most of the mountain troops are going to sea for the first time, and very few of them can even swim. Their mules have been left at home, rations have been shortened, and their heavy weapons – guns, anti-aircraft cannon and shells – have long since been sent on to their secret objective by supply ship. If that lethal cargo fails to arrive, they will be right in it.

A destroyer is not a cruise-ship. The mountain troops board her in groups of 200-250 to be interred below decks. The general is already aboard the commanding destroyer, the *Wilhelm Heidkamp*, and at 23.00 hours a total of ten warships weigh anchor and steam off through the pitch darkness, move through the Weser estuary and enter the North Sea with their lights covered for protection against British spotter vessels.

The sea is a boiling mass of foam. Breakers as high as houses roll over the decks. Fog banks swirl around the ships like ghosts. The spring storm seems to have been going on for ever, and the slim destroyer suddenly feels like a child's toy that is being played with out of its depth. Ice gleams on the barrels of the ship's guns.

A destroyer is not even a troop-transporter, and so the wretched mountain troops are forced to bed down on straw, not the feather mattresses they are used to at home. It is damned crowded and sweaty. Any careless movement and you get your skull cracked or bruise a comrade's ribs. This, however, does nothing to prevent the permanent game of *skat* in the corner. The rest of them wait, curse and suffer; at regular intervals they stumble over to the buckets placed around the edge of the hold to throw up.

'We look bloody marvellous, don't we?' oaths Bachmaier from Münich in his thick dialect. 'If we'd of been meant to go to sea, we'd have fins, and that's the bleedin' truth.'

By his side, Private Foigele is trying to put on his life-saver by following the instructions. And failing. Because he comes from Augsburg, he is really almost a flatlander and is only in this outfit on sufferance.

'Sweet God and Biberach,' he growls in Swabian singsong. 'I reckon growin' fins'd be easier.'

The men have travelled a thousand kilometres by train to get here from Southern Germany. Sealed carriages. Confined to barracks when they arrived. No trips to the *Reeperbahn*. No strolls past the famous red lights. Just out of barracks and into these ships, 2,000 men dispersed among ten destroyers.

Since then they have been swimming around the ocean. Sealed off again. No one is allowed on the upper deck. No one wants to go there. And so they lurch on. Where, only the Devil knows. Greenland? Iceland?

They don't give a damn. The main thing is to get safely out of this floating sardine-can and back onto dry land.

The company commander forces his way into the hold.

'Attention!' bawls an NCO.

'Well, men of the Mountain Navy,' says Oberleutant Sedelmeier by way of greeting. He laughs. 'Carry on!' He wrinkles his nostrils. 'To be honest, you stink like skunks.' He pushes his way slowly through to the middle of the hold. 'Now listen!' he bellows, suddenly serious. 'Our objective is Narvik, Norway's northernmost port. We have the job of taking it and holding it. And there are supposed to be mountains there, so I'm told.'

'Wassa name of the dump?' asks Geiger, whose geography was never strong.

'Narvik,' the Oberleutnant repeats, realising that for these boys a port 1,200 sea miles away is about as significant as a Chinese village. But then they have other worries. It is amazing how sick a man can be, even on half-rations.

The Old Man distributes a wad of brochures. 'Here,' he says. 'Keep you amused.'

Private Pirmoser opens the slim booklet and leafs through it. '*Hvor er kassen*?' he reads aloud haltingly.

'Hey, is that Prussian?' Geiger grins.

'Na, Norwegian,' Pirmoser answers, proud of his new vocabulary, and continues, '*Jeg beslaglegger pengene*.'

'And what does that mean?'

'I requisition this money,' says the Swabian.

'Great language,' Geiger mutters approvingly. 'And with this money I buy mesself a barrel of beer.'

While the Edelweiss boys are coming close to suffocating below deck, all hell has broken loose on the bridge. The night is dark as death. The convoy cannot keep course by sight, but radio communication is forbidden. You can hardly see your hand in front of your face. A whole armada of German ships is creeping through the night. Troop-transporters flying the Union Jack for deception purposes. Every shape looming out of the night could be part of the British Home Fleet. The British don't know what the Germans are up to, and the Germans are completely in the dark. In fact, both have reached the area at the same time: the British to mine the Norwegian coast as a prelude to their own planned invasion.

Radio communication is allowed only in English.

So far, the silent aproach has been successful. The only chance for the crazy gamble they call 'Operation Weserübung' is for the German Navy to sneak through the British-dominated seas like a convoy of ghosts. If the 200 transport ships are spotted, most will end up on the bottom of the sea, sent there by the Tommies. But the weather has proved itself a friend of the Germans, at least until now. And the deception has worked. The *Köln* has been pretending to be HMS *Cairo*, the *Königsberg* HMS *Calcutta*. No soldier is allowed up on deck. Even for internal communications, English must be spoken.

Suddenly the wind whips up to Force Eight, lashes the

sea and drives the breakers even higher. The strength of the sea reduces the planned speed of twenty-six knots. The storm-tossed convoy is torn apart in the pitch-dark night. Each of the ten destroyers is constantly in danger of ramming its neighbour, or being rammed itself.

To add to their anxiety, the destroyers' commander, Kommodore Friedrich Bonte, has just received news that the British have located him and that two British battleships, a heavy cruiser and six destroyers have set course northwards from the Orkneys. The *Scharnhorst* and the *Gneisenau*, which were to have turned back at this point, have stayed with the destroyers. The smaller warships are listing to an angle of up to fifty degrees. The storm is pounding the deck fittings, sweeping away motor cycles lashed to the deck, crates of ammunition, machine-guns – and the men who are fighting to prevent a disaster.

Private Pirmoser, a much-acclaimed mountaineer in Civvy Street, is at the end of his tether. He feels as if the ship is permanently tipping. Though the men below decks are packed like sardines, the storm is throwing them all over the place, all over each other. They are green-faced, certain as only real landlubbers can be that the end of the world has come. They throw up and piss over each other, feel as if their bowels are about to burst, or that they must suffocate, or that the next lurch will finally stave their skulls in.

'I can't stand it any more!' pants Pirmoser. 'I've gotta have air.' He staggers to his feet, avoiding all attempts to hold him back.

'Stay here, you silly sod!' yells his mate, Geiger.

No chance, Pirmoser is running amok, stumbling and lurching but heading grimly onward. He hears nothing, sees nothing. He has only one urge, one dream: to have light and air and get out of this rat-trap before he drowns or suffocates.

Geiger lunges and grabs him. 'Stand still, you idiot!' he screams, and tries to haul Pirmoser back, but fails. Geiger watches as his friend crawls through the hatchway, squeezes out, staggers around the upper deck, falls and slides around like a sack of potatoes. He follows, tries to grab hold of Pirmoser, but finds his hands clutching at emptiness.

The ship pitches upwards violently. Geiger slides towards Pirmoser on the sloping deck, grasps him firmly. Then a huge wave rolls over them and drags them off the deck, arm-in-arm into the night and the endless sea.

There were several eye-witnesses, but they are under orders not to attempt life-saving procedures. Keeping to the timetable is more important than human life, and so Pirmoser and Geiger become the storm's ninth and tenth victims that night from this ship alone – two among 2,375 soldiers and sailors lost during the voyage.

Day comes, the voyage goes on. The storm is still raging. Suddenly, the destroyer *Bernd von Arnim* makes contact with the enemy and is involved in a battle with the British ship *Gloworm.* The *Admiral Hipper* comes to her assistance and sinks the attacking English destroyer, but from now on the convoy has the whole British fleet breathing down its neck.

On the evening of April 8th, the convoy reaches the West Fjord. The escort ships turn back. For its reluctant passengers, the torment reaches new heights.

'The third night at sea, the most severe, began,' writes Alex Buchner in his study, *Narvik*. 'The weather worsened further, the storm gathered strength and changed direction. Where previously it had lashed at the ships from the south-west, they now had to combat a savage north-westerly of Force Ten to Eleven. It was hard work for the slim, agile destroyers in those heaving seas; they pitched and rolled, heaved, at times invisible amidst the seething spray. The sea seemed like a single mass of pale-green, boiling soup. The storm rocked the destroyers from side to side, shook them like a cat shakes a mouse. The ships pitched violently in the swell, heavy breakers rolled at the ships again and again, hurling great floods of salt-water over their decks, damaging fittings and tearing vehicles loose from their chains. But the convoy steamed ahead at full speed despite everything, at times reaching 30 knots and turning the voyage into a wild race – a race run in fog, rain and snow squalls through the starless night.'

*

Operation *Weserübung*, the attack on Denmark and Norway, had not at first been included in Hitler's plans. The Führer, otherwise eager for new conquests, had shown reluctance even when on December 14th, 1939 Grand Admiral Raeder introduced him to the former Norwegian Minister of War and leader of the Nazi-style *Nasjonal Samling* party, one Vidkun Quisling. Quisling, whose name – like that of Judas – was to become a synonym for traitor, insisted that the Norwegian government was secretly co-operating with the British and that the country would be occupied by British troops in the near future.

Raeder pointed out that transports of Swedish iron ore – more than half of the German war effort's requirements for iron came from Sweden – passed through the arctic port of Narvik, in Norwegian waters. Even as Hitler's then ally, Stalin, launched his brutal attack on little Finland and suffered repeated humiliations in his 'Winter War'; even while the Allies procrastinated on the question of aid for Finland, or intervention; even then, Hitler refused to become involved in war in Scandinavia, not because of any moral qualms about attacking neutral countries, but because he was totally obsessed with the planned *Blitzkrieg* in the West, which for him overrode all other considerations.

On September 27th, 1939, the day of the fall of Warsaw, the dictator told his gloomy generals that he intended to launch an offensive in the West during the late autumn or early winter. He gave orders for the working-out of detailed plans for the attack, paying as little heed to the unanimous opposition of his generals as he did to the weather forecasts. Until a few days before, he had been assuring them that with Poland defeated, England and France would be on their knees, begging for peace. While in his public statements he made 'peace offers' to the western Allies, he was demanding that his commanders fulfill an order that bordered on madness.

The offensive against France was to roll as early as November 12th.

A week before this, the self-created military genius met with the commander-in-chief of the army, who had just returned from a tour of inspection in the West, at the New

Reich Chancellery. Walter von Brauchitsch – *de facto* successor of sacked War Minister Werner von Blomberg, the man they called the 'rubber lion' – had been briefed by army and divisional commanders and had drafted a memorandum in which he pointed to shortages of equipment, weather problems, and also the determined opposition of the army's leadership.

Hitler tore the paper out of his hand, trampled on it, lectured the general as if he were a naughty schoolboy. Brauchitsch offered his resignation, but Hitler refused it, saying that the 'little infantryman can't just go home'. After the chastened general had left, Hitler wrote a letter stripping Brauchitsch of all his offices. He left the letter in a drawer and tore it up three days later, but the order for an attack on November 12th remained in force, though it was now too late to make the necessary preparations.

General, later Field Marshal, Ritter von Leeb suggested a 'generals' strike', but the terrified commanders were not prepared to go that far. They made preparations for the senseless offensive, hesitantly and with bad grace, until the weather proved rather less compliant with the wishes of the Führer than the commander-in-chief.

Suddenly rain set in. The Panzers were stuck fast in the mud, most aircraft could not even get off the ground and those that did found it impossible to navigate. The autumn of 1939 was miserable. Constant rain-storms led to high water everywhere, a further hindrance for the Panzers. The Luftwaffe's weathermen asserted that conditions would get even worse, helped by an area of low pressure approaching from the Atlantic.

Hitler postponed the offensive. First for three days, later until the 20th and then the 27th, and then, for the fourth time, until December 12th. The dictator may have ordered a *Blitzkrieg*, but lightning did not strike that winter. The English called it the 'phoney war', and the French dubbed it '*drôle de guerre*', the 'joke of a war'.

On the West Wall and the Maginot Line the opposing sides sat watching each other, doing nothing. Meanwhile, the British Expeditionary Force under Sir John Gort had grown to 161,423 men, with over 23,000 vehicles, 36,000 tons of ammunition, 25,000 tons of fuel, and 60,000 tons of provisions.

The English were arming at full speed. The French, however, relied on their Maginot Line, on their cumbersome tanks, their superior artillery, and on the advice of their ageing General Staff, who failed to draw any conclusions from the success of Hitler's first *Blitzkrieg* in Poland. So far as France's military leaders were concerned, Poland was a small country, poorly-armed and with more pride than solid military power. A combined advance by Panzers and Luftwaffe could not be repeated in the West.

The war spread over to the minor theatres, took place at sea or in the air. The German Luftwaffe showed its growing strength by shooting down twelve of twenty-four British aircraft that attacked Wilhelmshaven on December 18th. Kapitänleutnant Lemp torpedoed the British battleship *Barham* at the mouth of the River Clyde. The 'grey wolves' operating in the North Sea and the Atlantic sank 100,000 registered tons of shipping during December 1939, a total of thirty-seven merchant ships. The U-boat arm's spectacular successes continued, but on December 17th the *Admiral Graf Spee* met its fate at the mouth of the River Plate.

She was one of the famous 'pocket battleships', with armour ten centimetres thick, provided with 28-cm guns and a top speed of twenty-eight knots. Her commander was Captain Hans Langsdorff, a fair-minded, extremely chivalrous officer who had scored some great successes against merchant shipping overseas and was chased by the British for his pains. 150 sea miles from the coast of Uruguay, the 10,000-ton ship was engaged in battle by three British cruisers. At 6.14 she opened fire from a distance of nineteen kilometres, and after ninety minutes the *Exeter* was so badly damaged that she had to steam away from the fighting. Her escort ship, the *Ajax*, also suffered considerably. Their fast, thinly-armoured opponent, however, was able to make good her escape, though also damaged. Langsdorff headed for the port of Montevideo, to get his wounded ashore and his ship repaired.

During the three days that the government of Uruguay allowed him for these purposes, British naval forces, led by the *Cumberland*, lay in wait just outside the three-mile zone. The *Graf Spee* was trapped; as soon as she left port, the British would sink her.

For three whole days the entire world waited, laying bets on how long the pocket battleship would hold out. The German ambassador delivered orders from Hitler to the effect that the ship was to go down fighting. For safety's sake, a Gestapo agent also appeared, to ensure that the force of this order was properly understood.

The *Graf Spee* sailed slowly out of the port. The captain had left the greater part of his crew ashore; he had kept only as many men as he needed to scuttle the ship. Several explosions blew the stern to pieces. Langsdorff, who had spared his crew a futile death, was the last to leave the sinking ship. He went ashore and shot himself. Hitler, robbed of his heroic battle to the death, was beside himself with rage.

For the first Christmas of the war, female citizens received a special issue of a pair of stockings, while each man got a tie. But immediately the holiday was over, Hitler had plans to use the first glimmer of decent weather to attack. Finally, the date of the offensive was fixed for January 17th, no matter the weather, but a week beforehand a series of coincidences occurred, the kind that can change the history of the world: an Me 108 flying on a courier mission and crewed by Luftwaffe majors Reinberger and Hoenmanns became lost in fog and was forced to make an emergency landing in the vicinity of the Belgian town of Mecheln. In the process, it hit a group of trees, a branch tore off both the wings, and the Me landed nose-down in a thicket. A farmer watching from close-by saw two German officers crawl from the wreckage.

They were carrying documents – in fact, German plans for an offensive in the West – and within seconds they were hard at work throwing them into the burning remnants of their aircraft. Almost immediately, however, a military patrol arrived. The Belgian soldiers arrested the two men and retrieved the papers from the flames almost intact.

At the guardhouse, Major Reinberger surprised his Belgian interrogator and put the officer's gun to his own head. But his guards were swift to react, and they wrestled the gun away from the German. The captured Luftwaffe major smashed his head repeatedly against the door of his cell, shouting 'I am dishonoured', until his captors managed to restrain him by force.

The Belgians evaluated the captured plans; they now knew that in the course of his offensive in the West, Hitler would attack Belgium, Holland and Luxembourg as well as France. They passed on their prize to the British, who spent a long while trying to puzzle out whether these were genuine documents or part of a deception plan.

When word of the Mecheln fiasco reached Germany, it became clear that it would be impossible to proceed according to the old plans. Within a week, the General Staff had produced new plans. The *Blitzkrieg* in the West was also finally postponed until the spring, to the intense relief of the generals.

Hitler had the families of the two Luftwaffe majors taken into custody and interrogated. He sacked the Luftwaffe General Helmuth Felmy and threatened that heads would roll; at the same time, however, he issued orders that all concentration of troops was to be halted.

Meanwhile, he and the rest of the world were transfixed by what was happening in another war: the Finnish Army – 33,000 professionals and seven divisions of reservists, armed with sixty out-of-date tanks and 100 ancient aircraft – had achieved miracles of courage under the leadership of Field Marshal Carl Gustav von Mannerheim. Incredibly, the Finns had stopped the Russian 'steamroller' that had already crushed Lithuania, Estonia and Latvia, and had delivered a crushing blow to Stalin's prestige as well as his imperialistic ambitions. Companies of Finns defeated divisions of Russians. When the defenders realised that after running for lengthy periods the armoured skins of the Russian tanks grew red-hot, they threw containerfuls of petrol at the vehicles and thus invented the 'Molotov Cocktail'.

Stalin sent in 3,000 tanks, of which the Finns destroyed

1,000. The Red Army lost 900 aircraft. They dominated the roads, of course, 'but the impenetrable forests to the left and right of the highways belonged to the Finns,' writes American author Richard Condon in his book *The Winter War*. 'The Russian sentries could stare until their eyes watered, but they could not catch a glimpse of the enemy. Only the forests: snow-covered, silent walls to either side of the road. And somewhere close was the enemy, lurking in the undergrowth, waiting to strike suddenly. They would appear as unexpectedly as white wraiths and fall upon the Russians whenever it suited them. And they would disappear as suddenly as they had come, back into the forests, where no Russian dared follow them... Since the ground was already frozen solid, the Russians were unable to bring up tanks and heavy guns. The Finns possessed neither of these. They fought where they stood, dug themselves into the snow and the frozen earth. And held their ground...'

Despite being hopelessly out-manned and out-gunned, the 9th Finnish Division beat the 44th Russian Infantry Division east of Suomussalmi. In the two battles, the Red Army lost 27,500 men and had 1,300 taken prisoner, as well as more than 50 combat vehicles. The Finns fought on a 1,600 kilometre long front between the Arctic Sea and Lake Ladoga with such verve that the Russians, under the command of the recently-appointed Marshal Semion Timoshenko, were forced to call on élite units from as far away as the Ukraine and even the Caucasus.

The 'heroes of the arctic' (Raymond Cartier) faced an enemy whose strength was a hundred times their own. It was clear that by the spring at the latest, David would have to surrender to Goliath. The sympathy of the entire world – including Hitler's Germany, whose hands were tied by its Pact of Friendship with the Soviets – was with the Finns. Concrete help, though often promised, was pathetic: 8,000 Swedish volunteers, 200 Norwegians and 800 Danes joined Mannerheim's forces. The French supplied 5,000 machine-guns dating from 1915 which they no longer used because of the number of accidents they had caused.

Churchill, who had quickly become the heart and soul of

the British war effort, saw his hour come: if Britain went in to aid the Finns, then she could also ensure that the Germans would never be able to seize the iron ore port of Narvik. The First Lord of the Admiralty – soon to be Prime Minister – drafted two memoranda in which he suggested that Norway's neutrality should be ignored. But one of the advantages of Parliamentary rule is that even in wartime a country cannot put aside her scruples without some thought. Not until February 5th, 1940 did the English and French agree to send an expeditionary force of three or four divisions to Scandinavia. The French gathered together their own mountain troops and units from the Foreign Legion for the adventure, but planning proceeded slowly.

On February 16th a bloody encounter off the Norwegian coast underlined an already dangerous situation. On personal orders from Churchill, the British destroyer *Cossack* entered Norwegian sovereign waters in clear contravention of international law and boarded the *Altmark*, formerly supply-ship to the scuttled *Graf Spee*, in order to free 303 British prisoners. Seven members of the German vessel's crew were killed during an exchange of gunfire. Neutral Norway had not approved the operation, but she had tolerated it.

Hitler now knew that he had to reckon with Franco-British intervention in Norway. He reluctantly handed over the draft plan of 'Weserübung' to the Army High Command for activation, under constant pressure from Raeder to secure northern bases for the German Navy. It was obviously going to be much more than a pleasure-cruise across the Skaggerak. The Grand Admiral's men would have to carry the main burden of the operation, and every available ship would have to be pressed into service. Though the commander of Naval Group East, Admiral Rolf Carls, had worked out a casualty figure of more than fifty per cent, the Naval High Command was determined not to shrink from the consequences. They simply began to calculate how quickly the losses in ships could be made good. Blood is always expendable.

By March 1st an improvised plan of campaign was in existence. Hitler put General von Falkenhorst in command of the invasion of Norway. The old soldier, rather surprised by it all, left his meeting with the Führer and immediately walked into a bookshop to buy a Baedeker guide to the country he had just been told to conquer.

'Weserübung' was ready to roll; but now the man who had always demanded it, Grand Admiral Raeder, began to get cold feet. He suddenly swung in favour of postponing the northern campaign until after the offensive against France. Hitler rejected his advice. The die was cast.

The German navy would have to do battle with the British, who were far superior in ships and men and operating from nearby home bases, at a time when the weather would make the participation of the Luftwaffe uncertain. Whether conditions improved or not, Raeder's sailors would carry the major part of the burden, and every ship that was at all seaworthy was commandeered for the operation.

The Germans had still only just reached the point where the French and the British had been some weeks previously, but nevertheless the Allies' raid on Norway was postponed for quite a different reason. The Finns – having lost 60,000 dead, wounded and missing – signed an armistice with the Russians which was quickly followed by an unfavourable peace treaty signed in Moscow on March 12th, 1940. It was clear that the Finns had come to an agreement with the invaders only under duress, but for the moment the Allies had lost their excuse for their northern adventure.

The fact that ships were massing in North German harbours was not lost on the British. Although it was clear that they were intended for a Scandinavian operation, the Allies assumed that the Germans were simply making preparations for a counter-move in the event of a British landing.

This landing, codenamed 'Operation Wilfred', had now been set for April 4th. There were discussions between the Prime Ministers in Paris, after which it was postponed for a further four days until April 8th. The mining of the coast would begin on April 5th. The troops intended for Trondheim, Bergen Stavanger and Narvik embarked in the Firth of Clyde. At Scapa Flow the Home Fleet set sail, though under orders to take no risks.

The explosion in the far north was a long time in coming. Then, overnight, the peaceful countries of Norway and Denmark found themselves involved in a *Blitzkrieg*. They were concerned but not yet forewarned, although 'Wesurübung' was already in full swing: two battlecruisers, three heavy and four light cruisers, fourteen destroyers, eight torpedo-boats and all seaworthy U-boats were in action, to escort six invasion groups due to land at Narvik, Trondheim, Bergen, Kristiansand, Arendal, Oslo, Egersund, Nyborg, Korsør, Copenhagen, Middelfahrt, Beltbrucke, Esbjerg, Nordby, Fanø and Tyborøn.

The German invaders had a few hours' advantage over the Allies, who were planning the same thing. It was as if two rival gangs of thugs had chanced to break into the same bank at the same time.

While Dietl's mountain troops are being transported to the most northerly landing-point and undergoing the longest, most pitiless torment of all the invading units, the North Sea is ablaze. On the storm-tossed, snow-driven seas off Norway, behind a curtain of secrecy, a catch-as-catch-can game of pursuit and deception, death and destruction, bravery and incompetence, luck and ill-fortune, is being played out.

On April 8th, the Polish submarine *Orzel* sinks a German troopship, the *Rio de Janeiro*, twenty-four hours before 'X-Day'. Norwegian fishermen rescue uniformed soldiers and recognise them as German sevicemen; the soldiers explain that they have been sent to protect Norway from a British invasion. That same evening, a report is sent from Oslo to London, but the officer on duty there simply consigns it to the in-tray for attention the following morning.

The next day is April 9th, and as dawn breaks the force of ten German destroyers is nearing the port of Narvik. Soon the ships are slipping along the Ofoten Fjord, past the sleeping town nestling in its cradle of mountains, and it is then that the wind picks up and blows away the cloud cover.

05.00 hours, April 9th. The German ambassadors in

neutral Copenhagen and Oslo fetch the Prime Ministers of the two countries from their beds, to tell them officially what the survivors from the *Rio de Janeiro* had already revealed to their rescuers the previous day.

At the same time, the Gericke Company of the 1st Parachute Regiment seizes the bridge between the islands of Falster and Funen and opens the way to Copenhagen.

The Danes, without a chance, capitulate within hours.

The Norwegians bravely refuse to surrender to Hitler's invasion forces, because he demands that the traitor Quisling be installed as head of the government. Even the roar of German aircraft overhead does not deter them from making energetic preparations for the defence of their country. The planes are flying above the cloud-level; they can be heard but not seen. More than 500 transport aircraft, mostly three-engined Ju 52s, are in the air, carrying parachute troops to the war's flashpoints. The first mass airlift in history.

Their commander, Major-General Kurt Student, had opposed the use of his men for this operation. He had wanted to give them their first airing in a major theatre of war. These soldiers dropped from the sky have one big advantage: surprise. Their trademark is the sudden coup from the air. Student had no desire to play that trump prematurely, and his reluctance proves justified. In the general confusion of these days, such exceptional deeds of bravado as the conquest of the Western Norwegian Airfield at Stavanger-Sola by the 3rd Parachute Company under Oberleutnant Brandis, remain ill-reported.

As in Poland, planes are used as 'vertical artillery'. As soon as there is a gap in the cloud the crews of the 'Lion Squadron', KG 26, or the 'Eagle Squadron', K 30, appear and swoop down on the English ships. The picture is the same everywhere: swift attack, ruthless prosecution of the attack, everything in its place.

But there are disasters, such as occurs at the Fornebu Airfield near Oslo, which the paras are unable to take quickly because of bad weather. They are forced to withdraw to North Jutland. The Norwegians are organising their defences. The King and the government exploit the delay to flee into the forest around the capital. The coastal batteries are put on alert, German ships come under fire. Norway is fighting back.

The heavy cruiser *Blücher* sinks in Oslo Fjord after direct hits by Norwegian torpedoes and artillery at the Dröbak Narrows. The cruiser *Lützow* staggers back to port in Kiel, seriously damaged, and is out of action for a year. In Bergen, fifteen British aircraft attack the light cruiser *Königsberg* and sink her. In the Vest-Fjord there is a brief battle between the British battlecruiser *Renown* and the *Gniesenau* and the *Scharnhorst*. Two unexploded German shells lodge in the superstructure of the *Renown*. The *Gneisenau* suffers three direct hits and is forced to withdraw.

The worst fiasco suffered in the sea war is, however, the failure of the U-boats: thirty-one torpedoes, including all those fired from close distance, fail to explode. Dönitz has realised long before the end of the Norwegian adventure that he faces a serious crisis: Prien's dud torpedoes at Scapa Flow were no unique event.

Only a change of wind-direction, pulling the storm round from the south-west to the north-west, enables the destroyers bound for Narvik to reach their goal, operating on their last dregs of fuel. They sail cautiously past the critical point, the narrows between Hemnes and Ramnes. Great walls of rock rise sheer off the water to either side of them, reminding the men aboard of the Königsee lake in Bavaria. But this is no tourists' idyll. Here the soldiers who wear the Edelweiss badge will have to contend with the Norwegian coastal batteries and put them out of action, by force if necessary.

The soldiers crammed below decks hear the order they have been longing for: 'Make ready for landing!' They pour up onto the decks like a mass of mushrooms seeking the light. Light, air, mountains, snow; no one needs to tell them to get busy.

On shore, no movement. The fjord is filled with a ghostly silence. The 'coastal batteries' are – as they will learn later – the product of some idle Intelligence officer's fertile imagination.

During the run into Narvik, the destroyer *Wilhelm*

Heidkamp sinks the Norwegian coastguard boat *Eidsvold* (eight survivors), and the *Bernd von Arnim* the coastguard boat *Norge* (ninety-seven survivors). The way to Narvik is open.

Shortly afterwards, the mountain troops launch their assault on the town and the harbour. They have been weakened by seasickness, but now that they have firm ground under their feet they are back in their element. Weary, pallid figures dash from the ships like sprinters, ski slalom-like through the exploding Norwegian artillery shells.

The fire from the courageous Norwegian defenders is feeble, but it will certainly warn the English ships lurking in the vicinity of the town. The Edelweiss boys get their first proper view of Narvik from a lying position, bellies in the dirt. As soon as they raise their heads, bullets fired by Norwegian army snipers scream past.

This is rough country, extremely bare and cold. Wolves howl at night. Daylight refuses to come. Here in Norway's far north, where the borders between Sweden, Norway and Finland converge, the sun comes up as rarely as a ticket of leave.

General Dietl's men gain ground quickly, taking house after house, street after street, with Sedelmeier's company on the right flank of the bridgehead.

The sky is on fire. The air stinks of cordite. Aircraft will be arriving soon. Or the Allies' counter-strike from the sea.

As their neighbouring companies reach the foot of the mountain and prepare to consolidate and snatch some rest, Sedelmeier's boys draw the short straw and come under fire from a Norwegian artillery emplacement.

'Give cover!' bawls the Oberleutnant, then grabs a few men. 'I'll attack from the side!'

Two platoons move forward slowly. Several casualties. The enemy position is extracting a price in blood and lost time. Regimental HQ is demanding action.

At first Sedelmeier's chosen few are delayed by civilians blocking the road, then they run into a unit of Norwegian infantrymen. The Oberleutnant fires one burst from his machine-pistol and they raise their hands in surrender. One tries to escape in a jeep. A hand-grenade puts a stop to his game but the vehicle's engine keeps running.

The officer has an idea. 'Men!' he yells. 'Get in!' He sees the hesitant looks on his men's faces, grins and adds, 'We're going by limo, boys.'

The officer gestures for Foigele to get behind the wheel. At first the Augsburger stalls the engine, but after a moment he manages to engage gear.

Sedelmeier wrenches Bachmaier's machine-gun out of his hands. As the jeep crashes and kangaroos its way up the road, he smashes the front windscreen with the butt. 'Broken glass is lucky,' he screams delightedly, an excited schoolboy. 'Come on, Foigele, faster! Step on it!'

Two or three soldiers have leapt onto the vehicle and are crouched behind him.

'Hey!' yells the Oberleutnant. 'Now we're playing at Panzers!'

The Norwegian gunners have seen their target. Their guns are moving round on their turntables. Explosion to the Germans' right. A crater in front of the jeep. Foigele swerves, riding on two wheels, manages to avoid the pitfall.

Sedelmeier fires like a lunatic into the Norwegian position. Fifteen metres to go. Ten. As they drive, Huber hurls a grenade into the middle of the Norwegian guns.

Explosion. Any of the defenders who still have hands to raise, raise them high.

By midday, the town, the harbour and the approaches to the surrounding mountains are all firmly in German hands. But the supply ship carrying the heavy equipment is sunk by the British. The destroyers become involved in a battle with the Royal Navy and are soundly beaten. Ten of the twenty-four destroyers available to the German Navy are sunk in one day, an irreplaceable loss.

Ammunition begins to run low. No German vessels are able to get through by the sea route. And the weather, which has suddenly begun to deteriorate again, allows little hope of their being supplied from the air. Worse than anything, the airborne troops promised as reinforcements do not arrive.

The conquerors become defenders. They take refuge among terrain that is more stone than earth. They have nothing to eat, nothing more to hit the enemy with. The barren heights where they have decided to take their stand are a place where nothing grows. Digging trenches is impossible.

At Führer Headquarters they have already given the Edelweiss boys up for lost. General Dietl has been given permission to lead his men into neutral Sweden.

'Good night... Now it's off with the lights and out with your knives, boys,' Oberleutnant Sedelmeier tells his men.

Narvik may count as the Germans' Achilles Heel, but everywhere else *Weserübung* has been carried out in true *Blitzkrieg* style. 'The audacity of these German moves, in defiance of Britain's superiority in seapower, staggered the Allied leaders,' states Liddell Hart.

At none of the bridgeheads along the west coast of Norway had the Germans landed more than 2,000 men. The army needed only three divisions. The British countermeasures were indeed confused, and on several occasions bad luck dogged their attempts to recover the initiative that they had lost. Admiral Hotblack, chosen to command the Expeditionary Force, left the Admiralty at midnight to pay a visit to his club. He suffered a heart attack and was found unconscious on the stairs. A successor was immediately named. He died in a fatal air accident on the approach into Scapa Flow.

The British chance of destroying the Germans' hold north of the Arctic Circle by a swift strike had been wasted. In the first place, the British possessed no suitable land forces, then the Admiralty fought shy of committing an adequate number of ships, and finally there was a lack of co-operation at the highest level of command.

Then a landing party was put ashore on the wrong island. By the time the British had re-oriented themselves, the German mountain troops had been saved by a metre-and-a-half deep fall of snow. Nevertheless, General Dietl's situation continued to look desperate though reinforcements had been sent by air, mountain troops who had been given a seven-day crash course in parachuting.

Nothing was getting through by sea. To run a supply line by land over hundreds of kilometres of glaciers and peaks was impossible. During the interval, the defenders of Narvik had acquired two batteries of artillery, but they had no shells.

And it was at this point that the Franco-British operation actually came into being. On April 14th, 24,000 Allied soldiers landed in Harstead and swiftly headed towards Narvik.

The conquerors of the town were forced to withdraw, giving up the town and the harbour to the enemy. Their end seemed to have come.

The German mountain troops have taken refuge in their natural element. A band of lost souls, more often on the run than on the attack, still threatened by Norwegian snipers.

The men of Sedelmeier's company stare skywards. The good weather will certainly bring enemy air attacks, but it may also bring drops of fresh rations and equipment by the Luftwaffe.

'Here they come!' yells Foigele.

The others have also seen them: the skies are full of Ju 52s, and the soldiers are full of hope. They watch as the parachutes open and the metal cannisters dangling beneath them glint in the spring sunshine. Men slaver with hungry anticipation only to look helplessly on as the wind carries their supplies far away from them.

'What a bastard!' oaths Bachmaier. 'What a total, bloody bastard!'

'Three volunteers,' calls Oberleutnant Sedelmeier.

All of them line up, even the wounded. Their commander picks a handful of men. Then he takes them off with him, striding a few paces ahead of his volunteer unit. They walk one behind the other in Indian file. If possible they keep to cover, if not they move quickly over the flat stretches of scree and offer themselves as moving targets.

The quiet is uncanny, unnerving. From time to time a man's boot dislodges a stone and causes a small avalanche.

'There,' the Oberleutnant says, lowering his field glasses.

He stabs a finger in the direction of a gleaming aluminium container. 'We'll make it,' he says by way of encouragement.

'No sweat,' growls Huber impassively.

'I'd go to the end of the world for a decent bloody meal,' says Bachmaier.

They pass under a cliff. A thin shot rings out, piercing the deceptive quiet.

'Up there,' Huber says. Then he sees Foigele topple, begin to slither down the loose slope, twist once more and collapse to roll down to the bottom and a lonely death.

'I'll get the swine for that,' the Oberleutnant grates, and races on.

The others follow him, bounding as if on hot coals, keeping the Devil's own lookout.

Then they halt: the container is straight ahead of them, on the far side of a sort of crevasse, sure as hell to be right in the sniper's sights. Between them and the supplies is a narrow bridge, more like a rickety plank.

'We're going over that?' Huber mocks.

'That or turn back,' the officer snaps back, and he steps onto the creaking bridge. He turns. 'Follow one at a time!' he barks. 'The thing won't support two men!'

The others stand around, staring at the bridge and at Oberleutnant Sedelmeier, then gawping down at the yawning crevasse cut into the rock of the mountain.

The officer is almost at the far end of the bridge, is moving like a high-wire artiste, arms stretched out for balance.

Then a shot rings out.

Bullets hammer into the splintered wooden structure, hacking chunks from the bridge. For a moment Sedelmeier looks as though he is riding a swing. He crashes against one of the thin steel hawsers securing the bridge on the far side. For a few seconds more he hangs swaying on the cables. He manages to hold on long enough to see his men open fire on the snipers' nest.

Then his legs collapse beneath him. He plunges into the abyss, one victim among the 1,317 who died in the battle for Norway's iron ore.

The mountainmen give up on the container, but not on the position among the heights. Several times it seems that they will have to surrender. But each time they are resupplied from the air. They are cut off from God and man, but they hold their position, as if they were sure of a miracle.

The miracle happens. On June 8th, twenty-eight days after the siege began. The mountainmen can hardly believe their eyes. The enemy is embarking to leave, is evacuating the port and town of Narvik, is giving up the whole of Norway. Hitler had unleashed his *Blitzkrieg* in the West, and now the English need every man they can get.

Narvik remained in German hands until the end of the war. The navy, on whose urging the plans for 'Weserübung' had first been drawn up, now possessed the strategic positions that it had desired in Scandinavia, but had been weakened by the blood-letting there to such an extent that it could no longer exploit them.

Admiral Canaris's estimate of the cost turned out to have erred on the side of optimism: the casualty list included one heavy and two light cruisers, ten destroyers, six U-boats, one gunnery training ship, two minesweepers, two reconnaissance boats, four auxiliary ships and a dozen transport vessels. The two battleships *Gneisenau* and *Scharnhorst*, as well as the *Lützow*, the light cruiser *Emden*, the gunnery training ship *Brummer*, and the armoured vessel *Admiral Scheer* were put out of action for some time to come because of mechanical defects or enemy action.

The orgy of blood-letting and bravado had led to a matchless victory – but a victory that brought not a single advantage for the Reich.

Bloody Friday

Just before midnight is when the boys really get going. The discreet little whorehouse is, for what it's worth, the only place of its kind within thirty kilometres of Quenz-Gut, headquarters of the Brandenburgers. It's here that the lads of the special unit snatch what pleasures they can – with interest.

Unteroffizier Jonas, pulled out from Rumania at twenty-four hours' notice, is on the slim side so far as build goes, so when it comes to girls he tends to prefer a contrast: right now he has a big blonde on his lap, and he's massaging her through the undone buttons of her blouse like a piano maestro coaxing Mozart out of a baby grand. His mate Wengler is set on having his way with a quiet brunette, and Unteroffizier Regus looks as though he's going to have to be satisfied with what's left over, because as usual he's been a little too slow off the mark.

The three Brandenburgers have got pockets full of money, leave until the next morning, and so they are drinking like there's no tomorrow. There is, of course. As is proved by the appearance of their Hauptfeldwebel in the bar. Looking for them.

'Hey, big girl, eh?' he says slyly to Jonas.

'You can look, but you can't touch, Sar'nt-Major,' says Jonas with a dash of pride. He shifts position so that the NCO gets a good eyeful of the lady's ample wares. 'Too late, mate.'

'The Fatherland has need of you, Casanova,' grins the Feldwebel, feasting his eyes.

'Why me?' Suddenly the Unteroffizier knows he's in

trouble, and it's a question of saving what he can from the wreckage.

'That's what I ask myself too,' the Feldwebel leers. 'C'mon, love her and leave her! Hurry, man!'

The Prophet shambles out of the bar behind the other two. The damp, misty May night in this Year of Our Lord 1940 suddenly reeks of beer as they clamber up into the Feldwebel's truck.

'Nearly bloody well there,' Jonas blusters. 'Feeling my way down to the equator... and then you screw up my chances...'

'Tell it to the Führer,' the Feldwebel chuckles.

'The Führer doesn't go with women,' says big Wengler with a grin.

'The poor bitches can't keep up with him,' the Prophet mutters sagely. Then the Opel truck pulls away from the whorehouse.

'You're being transferred,' the one-man press-gang from Brandenburger headquarters explains at last.

'That's news I could have kept until tomorrow,' complains Regus.

'Think what you like,' the Feldwebel growls. 'Fact is, you're off on your travels tonight, gentlemen. From now on, no mail, no phone, no leave. And no sneaking off for a night.'

'Can we take the odd piss?' the Prophet moans, aping the Feldwebel's delivery.

The NCO lets that one go, and the rest of them subside into silence. Because they know, when headquarters go to the trouble of hauling them away from their pleasures, something's up. And if something's up, then it means trouble.

These men's job is deception. No crawling about on the parade-ground for Jonas and the others, no bull. Talk back to a Hauptfeldwebel the way they just have in any other unit of the Wehrmacht, and you'd have your arse in a sling. Not in the Brandenburgers. The banter hides mutual respect.

These men have learned to get their stuff together damned quickly, and to take even swifter leave of their comrades. 'Look after yourself, mate.' Forced smile. Embarrassed handshake. And the code is really saying, 'Till the next time . . . or maybe in Hell . . .'

In the darkness and the fog, the column of trucks rolls southwards. There is no shortage of rumours. But in this outfit, no one asks questions and no one gives answers. The place that the Brandenburgers end up in doesn't look too exciting: a camp in Asperden, near Goch in Westphalia. But the surroundings are irrelevant to them, because their barracks are sealed off from the world as if they had the plague.

Nothing happens on the first day. They meet old acquaintances, see a few new faces. But Jonas, as usual, has got things sussed. 'Bleedin' Dutchmen,' he says.

There they sit, well out of the action, and their only battle is with old-fashioned boredom.

Meanwhile, though, everyone is beginning to realise that this so-called 'special school', for all its intricacies, has a thread running through it: except for the new arrivals, everyone here seems to speak a bit of Dutch, a few perfectly, but all of them enough to hold their own.

'Now listen!' bawls the commander of this quarantine station, an Oberleutnant. 'You'll do as you are told and from now on you'll speak nothing but Dutch. You'll eat, sleep, drink, shit Dutch. Work hard, friends. The better you speak the language, the more chance you'll have of seeing your old mothers again.'

'And why's that?' hazards Regus.

'I ask the questions around here,' the officer snaps back. 'From now on, I don't want to hear a word of German. From now on there'll be no cursing 'cept *Got verdomme*. Got that, you villains?'

'Yes, Herr Oberleutnant,' they chorus.

And then they get to know a new man, Private Franzen. He is a pleasant boy with watchful eyes that are a little too close together. Only one thing unusual about him: Franzen, by reason of having been born over the border, has served in two armies. First in the Dutch, then in their own. His job now is to drill them in the regulations, rank distinctions and peculiarities of their neutral neighbour's army.

The West is filled with the calm before the storm. 'Case Yellow' has been postponed a total of twenty-nine times, but this time it is for real. And the soldiers being trained in the hermetically-sealed camp at Asperden are to play a vital role as a fifth column.

They know that their time in these bleak barrack-huts will be limited, but they accept the job they will have to do. It is May, but spring passes them by. They are seeped in everything Dutch from dawn until late at night – and even their dreams are filled with the dangers to come.

On May 8th, shortly after 23.00 hours, the officer of the watch's telephone rings. The NCO on duty lifts the receiver, answers with his name and rank.

'The tulips are wilting in Holland,' says an unknown voice.

'Is that so?' the Unteroffizier growls. 'Fascinating.'

'Repeat the message!' barks the caller. 'And tell your chief. The tulips are wilting in Holland!'

'There's a nutcase on the line,' mutters the Unteroffizier as he wakes the Old Man, repeats the bizarre message, and watches in astonishment as the Oberleutnant is drastically transformed.

'Wake all the men!' he bellows. 'Emergency!'

Within ten minutes the entire outfit is up and ready at four different assembly-points. The first group – including the Prophet, big Wengler, Franzen, a new man, and Unteroffizier Regus – gather in the canteen. But there's no schnapps on offer today, only the prelude to a mission they know will be near-suicidal.

'Amazed, eh, you weary lads!' says Leutnant Gerber to his flock. It is his way of encouraging them. 'This is the kind of experience only Brandenburgers get to enjoy.' The officer is not a day over twenty-three; he has long, storklike legs topped by a trunk that is more than a little too short by comparison, and a complexion smooth as a girl's. The ruthlessly ambitious young officer is known to his charges as 'the virgin'.

Big crates are hauled over from the weapons store, containers that someone has taken the trouble to nail up, secure with iron bands, then lock and lock again. As the men from the barracks staff unload the crates, cursing and sweating, their Silesian Feldwebel stands by grinning, proud as a mother hen and several times as ugly.

Leutnant Gerber breaks the first seal with due solemnity, as if he were opening a birthday hamper. 'Fancy dress,' he drawls, pointing to the open crates, which are packed with a variety of stuff: uniforms, priests' outfits, civilian suits, overalls, all carefully sorted and labelled with each individual's name.

The young Brandenburgers fall upon the loot as if this were a lucky dip; and the more thoughtful among them realise why their measurements were taken so precisely the previous week.

Along with his mate Wengler and the Leutnant, Jonas puts on the uniform of a Dutch gendarme. Müller is transformed into a farmer, Maier becomes a parson. The living end, however, the final straw, is Unteroffizier Regus, kitted out in the habit of a sturdy Dutch nun.

'Oooh, sister,' the Prophet guffaws. 'You're the most clapped-out nun I've ever seen.'

They damned-near die laughing, but suddenly the whole thing switches back to deadly earnest.

'Now listen good, boys,' says the Leutnant, standing among them in his gendarme's uniform. We're going for a little trip across the border to put on a show for the Dutch. Four gendarmes will be carting off fifteen suspicious individuals found close to the border. Franzen and I will go in front, the Prophet and Wengler will take the rearguard. The idea is that we are going to hand these unfortunates over to the military somewhere behind the lines. And if the Dutch don't smell a rat, they'll get a kick in the backside.' The bad joke almost misfires, and Gerber continues quickly, 'So. We shift ourselves along the Mook-Graave road until we get to the bridge over the Maas Canal. We must have that bridge by 05.35 hours at the latest, and our job then will be to hold until the Panzer Division that'll be following arrives to haul us out of the shit.'

'Sounds easy,' mocks Regus, the nun with the dark-brown voice. 'I hope there aren't too many trees along the road.' Everyone knows what he means. If they get themselves caught, the Dutch could well string them up from the nearest suitable greenery.

'Come on,' the virgin says contemptuously. 'We've faced worse odds.' He pauses. 'In any case, this is a volunteer mission. Anyone who wants to can pull out.'

He stares along the line of men. No one moves. Sure, this or that man may have cold feet, but no one is about to admit the fact.

'Good,' the Leutnant barks, satisfied. 'Then jump to it, comrades. In the name of madness!'

They grab weapons, papers, rations. They are soon sitting crammed into a truck, nineteen of them, heading west. They know that their chances of surviving this mission are slim. And the war they will be unleashing in Holland will carry their trademark.

The night is warm, the air is scented with hay, spring has arrived at last. But soon the smell of death will overlay the scent of blossom. For most of the men of the covert unit travelling through the lines of Army Group B on this night of May 8th/9th 1940, there will never be another spring. The juggernaut of death is hungry for new theatres of operations: Holland, Belgium, Northern France.

'Shine that bloody lamp of yours over here, will you, Jonas,' says Leutnant Gerber. The black Büssing truck bounces over the pot-holed road while the young officer's finger traces an unsteady line on his map. 'So, this is roughly where we'll be,' he murmurs. 'I'd guess we should arrive there in about ten minutes. And then it's off over the border while your Dutchman's not looking.'

His men are dressed up like carnival characters, but this time it's a life-or-death masquerade.

'So how far is it to this bleeding bridge?' asks big Wengler, a Dutch gendarme right down to the exotic frogging on his tunic and the gleaming white gloves.

'About four hours. Going at it like lunatics.'

'And how many men are guarding the bridge?' the private probes stubbornly.

'Ask your friend Franzen,' says the virgin, jabbing a finger at the man whose name is supposed to be Vandhoek, and who was a Royal Dutch Infantryman before he answered Hitler's call.

'As many as you can get into five bunkers,' Franzen says.

‘Bunkers?’ Jonas echoes anxiously.

‘Only little ones,’ says his mate in an attempt to reassure him.

Then there is silence for a while. Until someone lets out a dry fart, a perfect expression of everyone’s opinion.

‘Who was that?’ asks Gerber, and Unteroffizier Regus grins quietly.

‘Any more questions?’ The squad’s commander asks, eager to close the debate.

‘Yes,’ Jonas says. ‘How will the Dutch actually know there’s a war on?’

‘We’ll tell ’em. With our machine-pistols,’ the virgin rasps harshly. ‘In any case, the British fleet is already heading for Holland, and the Dutch have given the Tommies permission to march through their territory.’

‘You actually believe that, Leutnant?’ Wengler asks.

‘That’s not my department,’ says Gerbler. ‘All I have is an order, and the order says to tell you that.’

Suddenly the heavy truck grinds to a halt. Shouted orders. Curses. Questions. A Feldwebel of the Military Police lifts the curtain at the back of the truck, shines his torch inside. Its beam traps Unteroffizier Regus, and the M.P.’s face lights up, as if he has just nabbed Mata Hari and a bunch of her best friends.

‘Papers?’ he demands brusquely.

‘Don’t piss around,’ snaps the squad’s commander. ‘Fetch me Major Penzlau here. And be quick about it.’

The Feldwebel is not one of the Wehrmacht’s brightest souls, but it occurs to him that he may have bitten off more than he can chew. He puts a heavy guard on the weird mob in the truck and hurries off.

Jonas stares out over the tailgate, sees the infantrymen downing schnapps. By the bottle. ‘Christ, look at those bastards,’ he snarls enviously. ‘Getting their courage from a bottle.’

Then the M.P. returns. With a craggy-looking major. ‘Greetings, desperadoes,’ he says, shaking Gerber’s hand. ‘Keep the hoi-polloi away, will you, Feldwebel?’ he tells the M.P., and then he distributes the goodies he has brought with him: red arm-bands so that they will be recognised by the German spearheads, tablets to stop them coughing, German machine-pistols and machine-guns, because the Dutch weapons aren't good enough. Finally he beckons to a waiting civilian. Admiral Canaris's Abwehr hauled this man out of jail: a smuggler with a string of convictions, he is going to be their guide across the border.

Gerber nods. 'All right, mate. Take us to the promised land.'

They head into the woods. One behind the other. The roads are blocked with vehicles. Long columns of infantrymen wait patiently for miles back. The Brandenburgers are in the middle of one of the biggest concentrations of troops in history. One hundred and thirty-six divisions, including ten Panzer Divisions with 2,580 Panzers and auxiliary vehicles, are laying low and awaiting the order to attack. Seventeen divisions are defending the West Wall, forty-seven are to act as a mobile reserve, and seventy-two will actually carry out the offensive. In the north, along the Dutch border, is the Army Group Bock (B); south from there, between the Saar and Aachen, is Rundstedt's Army Group (A), which will be the hammer of the operation; while Leeb's Army Group (C), opposite the Maginot Line, will at first concentrate on diversionary attacks to keep the French busy. Two Air Fleets with 3,534 aircraft are ready for action, 1,462 bombers and 1,016 fighters, fighter-bombers and others.

The Allies in France can call upon 3,000 tanks and 2,500 aircraft. One hundred and thirty-seven French and nine British divisions are ready to defend what they hold. In the event of a breach of neutrality, they will be reinforced by twenty-two Belgian and twelve Dutch divisions.

'A comparison between the opposing forces gives the following picture,' writes Herbert Michaelis in his classic work, *The Second World War*. 'The 3,500 or so aircraft of the German Luftwaffe had an advantage of 1,000 planes over their opponents, but their superiority was even more marked when one considers their tactical possibilities . . . So far as numbers of divisions are concerned, and ignoring all differences in quality, and makeup, the strength of the Germans and their Allied opponents was roughly equal. But the introduction of the twenty-two Belgian and twelve Dutch divisions altered the balance to Germany's disadvantage. Moving on to tanks and other combat vehicles, the Germans lagged behind French numbers by some 420. Such estimates do not give us an impressive picture of German strength, particularly when we take into account the fact that France possessed the modern, extensively-improved defence system of the Maginot Line, that Belgium could fall back on the Albert Canal and the Maas-Dyle Line, with its many strongpoints, or that the Netherlands, with its policy of "Fortress Holland" and its capability of flooding certain districts, seemed a tough nut to crack.'

The Allies had been reckoning with a German offensive this spring, and since the Mecheln Incident the Belgians and the Dutch were also forewarned – particularly since the Abwehr major Hans Oster had already warned a Dutch officer, Major Gijsbertus Jacobus Saas, of the impending invasion. But, as in Norway the previous month, the Allies pay no attention to this gift presented to them by a convinced opponent of Hitler. They continue to assume that the German attack – as in the First War – will consist of a straightforward push to all points west. The Mecheln fiasco had, however, caused the plans which never gained Hitler's whole-hearted approval to be changed. In the process, the dictator returned to a proposal first put forward by Erich von Manstein, later to become Field Marshal, though the plan had not been well received initially, and its originator had been banished to an insignificant command in the East.

Manstein's study document, which suggested using strong concentrations of armour to break through the Ardennes and cross the Meuse, from there smashing their way to the sea in 'Operation Sickle', completing a huge pincer movement by cutting off the Allied forces that have moved north to go to the aid of the Dutch and the Belgians, was the basis of Hitler's gamble in May 1940.

It was a bold concept, but so fraught with risks that the traditional-minded elements within the General Staff could not warm to it. Even Panzer experts considered the Ardennes impassable. Guderian was called in to advise; he came down on the side of Manstein, and so the die was cast.

A number of elements were essential to the plan's success. Firstly it must not rain, or the Panzers would stick fast in the mud and the Stukas would not be able to bomb a path through for the armour. The crossing of the Meuse, Waal and Lek rivers would have to follow quickly, which meant capturing the bridges intact. In Belgium the fortifications along the Albert Canal, a forty-metre wide waterway with smooth, sheer banks, would have to be overrun. The terrain by the canal would be unusable for Panzers if the infantry did not succeed in seizing the crossing-points at Canne, Vroenhoven, and Veldwezelt, which Intelligence reports indicated were wired with explosives, and putting the key fort of Eben Emael out of action.

Hitler possessed a simple recipe for ensuring success: Eben Emael and the bridges on the Albert Canal were to be taken by airborne commandos, while the Meuse bridges were to be secured by the boys from the Brandenburg Division in fake uniforms. While most of the would-be invaders were still asleep, these suicide squads, 'Hitler's young men' (Winston Churchill) were already well on their way.

The night is still uncannily quiet as Gerber's raiders approach the border. The men feel the tension coursing through them like electricity as they duck, one by one, through the wire onto Dutch territory. They sneak silently across a meadow. Five minutes later they assemble on the edge of a wood.

'That's it, then,' whispers their guide. 'Here you are, and the rest is up to you.' He gestures at the nearby road.

Leutnant Gerber nods, without taking his eyes from his infra-red field glasses. 'They can't all be stupid, the ruddy idiots,' he murmurs incredulously. He does not trust the stillness. He can feel the bile rising in his throat. This time there's not even a radio link, and if the German assault on the West is postponed for the thirtieth time, the Leutnant and his eighteen men will end up dangling from the very bridge they are supposed to be seizing this morning.

They reach a railway embankment. They have now

penetrated four kilometres into Holland. Undiscovered.

'No shooting except on my orders,' the Leutnant orders. 'No smoking. No talking, and if it's really necessary, not a word of German!'

'Except for you,' grins Jonas.

The virgin pretends not to hear, looks at his watch. It is 01.45 hours. He can see the slow train from Groesbeek steaming towards them. On time, fully-lit, half-full. Taking farmers back from market, housewives back from visiting relatives, workers off the late shift. A couple of lovers are standing at the window of the second carriage; the girl, a well-stacked blonde, is pressed so hard against the body of her thin young man that her curves are pushed flat.

'Jesus, will you look at those tits,' says Franzen, then repeats his observation in Dutch.

'Shut your trap!' hisses Gerber.

His is commanding just one of the four independent commando squads that have crossed the border on this Bloody Friday. The four suicide parties have no communication with each other, and no link with the German positions on the other side. They are totally on their own, without protection under international law, a new phenomenon in war, as hard on themselves as they are on the enemy.

The first squad is heading for the bridge at Gennep, the second for the crossing near Nijmegen, the third is to seize the crossroads near Plaasmole.

The script for this gangster story was written on a green-topped desk in Berlin; Leutnant Gerber and his men are both actors and statistics, and they will be paid with the rope or a bullet unless their luck holds.

They continue on along the road, marching hard for a couple of hours or so. Two phoney gendarmes ahead, two behind. Five ranks of three men each between. Guns concealed under their coats. Only the phoney gendarmes are able to carry them openly. It is more difficult for the others, particularly Unteroffizier Regus, who has to conceal a machine-gun under his flowing nun's habit.

Not a Dutchman in sight. Or is there? The beam of a car's headlights cuts through the early-morning twilight. The

Leutnant hesitates, then orders, 'Take cover.' His men move like lightning to hug the ground. The car passes. No sign of recognition. The night is still peaceful. Another thirty minutes. The birds are already in full-throated song as the commando squad reaches its objective.

First they take cover again, to grab a breather. Jonas sits silently cursing their feathered friends among the branches above them. Big Wengler jabs a finger at his forehead: it's not the birds, but Jonas's nerves.

Gerber takes a look at the bunkers. Not exactly the last word in defences, but they are big concrete boxes with evil-looking machine-gun barrels poking out of the slits in the walls. No guards in sight. The *mynheers* seem to be fast asleep. You can almost hear them snoring. And between the bunkers the bridge over the Meuse-Waas Canal, sound enough to take German Panzers, so long as the Dutch don't blow her first.

The Leutnant looks at his watch. 'We still have twenty minutes,' he tells them. 'Now pay attention, my merry band of warriors. Three men will tackle each bunker, heading straight for 'em with no messing. You'll storm those cement shit-houses and call on the Dutchmen to give themselves up.'

'And if they don't?' asks Maier, the fake parson.

'Then you'll chuck a hand-grenade in, what d'you think?' the virgin snaps. 'But only if strictly necessary. I'd prefer a silent movie.'

'I'd prefer it even better if I were two hours older,' growls Jonas.

'Me too, mate,' the officer answers irritably. He orders Franzen, the most fluent Dutch-speaker, to take the lead. 'It's up to you,' Gerber explains. 'When you take out a cigarette and say, "Who'll give me a light?", everyone chucks away their coats and heads for those bunkers. O.K.?'

Six minutes to go. The last cigarette before the storm. Gerber nods. The suicide squad moves out. Street theatre. Director: Admiral Canaris. Eighty metres. Seventy . . .

There really is not a single guard on the bridge. Sixty metres to go. Then they are in direct line of fire from the bunkers. Another forty metres. Franzen in the lead, followed by the Leutnant, and then the others.

Thirty metres to go. A sleepy Dutchman comes out of one of the bunkers to take a leak. He sees the bizarre procession, stands watching in amazement. Then he recognises Franzen, his old comrade from the 11.R.I. based in Horn. 'Blimey, Vandehoek!' he bellows.

Franzen walks up to him, apparently ignoring everyone else, and fumbles for his cigarettes.

'Christ, old mate,' Pierboom chuckles. 'You ended up with the crocks, Vandehoek?'

'You can see we're all busy here,' the Brandenburger answers in fluent Dutch. 'Caught a bunch of suspicious characters.' He takes his cigarettes out of his tunic pocket and gestures with the packet. 'Who'll give me a light?' He has given the codeword – fourteen minutes before time.

And then all hell breaks loose. Pierboom is stone-cold sober, but suddenly he realises he can see nothing but grey mice – field-grey mice. The next moment, the 'gendarmes' are clad in the uniform of the German Wehrmacht. The parson has army trousers on under his cassock, and even the nun is performing a sort of striptease.

The sergeant has no idea what is happening, but he gets over his horror quickly enough to attempt a jump back towards his bunker to raise the alarm. But Wengler is already lurking behind him. Both men hit the ground, while the others head for the five concrete pillboxes.

The battle is short and one-sided. Not a shot is fired. The men in the bunkers are still sleeping their cosy, neutrals' sleep. They are wrenched from the land of dreams so abruptly that none of them has a chance to go for his weapon. Astonished, they raise their hands and shamble out of their bunkers. They still have no idea whether they have been attacked by men from Mars or are still living through some crazy nightmare.

Only Sergeant Pierboom, overpowered and disarmed, has put two and two together and figured 'Vandehoek' for the traitor. He spits in the man's face at the first opportunity.

'Wrong again, as the hen said to the sex-starved duck,' grins his former friend. 'I'm German. Always was. I only joined your lot on orders from the Wehrmacht, to –'

'Cut that crap,' oaths Leutnant Gerber. 'Just tell our prisoners that they'll be all right so long as they behave themselves.'

The last Dutch defenders clamber out of their positions, put their hands in the air. Pallid faces. Sleep-heavy eyes. No resistance. For this bunch of Hollanders the war is over before it can begin.

'Giving their all in the land of nod,' quips Maier.

'I've a feeling that this has been the easy bit,' Wengler says grimly.

And the Prophet adds sagely, 'Let's just see, shall we?'

Leutnant Gerber is lounging against the handrail of the bridge, watching as two specialists from the squad dismantle the explosive charges planted by the Dutch.

'Ready, Leutnant,' Unteroffizier Regus reports.

'You may smoke and talk,' the officer answers. He exudes confidence, but inside he is more than a little anxious. His enemies now are not the Dutch defenders but time. If the German invasion is postponed again, or the offensive starts late, he will be sitting on his lovely, captured bridge, and he might as well be in the arsehole of the world.

He looks over the bridge, places sentries at both ends. He has to keep back four men to guard the captured Dutchmen, so that his total combat force is no more than fifteen.

05.25. Time seems to be passing so slowly. These men have nerves of steel, but there is nothing worse than a war that is not yet a war.

05.28. Where the hell are the Panzers? The Stukas? The artillery barrages? All around them there is nothing but a hideous, cruel silence that tears at the nerves. And those damned birds singing.

'There was a soldier/On the banks of the Volga ...' Jonas mutters, mockingly quoting a well-known filthy song.

And then something happens that was not in the script.

The field telephone buzzes. 'Franzen,' shouts the Leutnant to the fluent Dutch-speaker.

The Private appears at the double, picks up the receiver.

'Sergeant Pierboom is not here at the moment,' he says. A question from the other end. 'I think he is taking his early-morning shit, Sir,' Franzen answers carefully.

The men at his elbow grin, but then they see the drawn face of the man on the phone and the grins evaporate.

'Understood,' Franzen confirms. 'The Sergeant will ring you back.' He hangs up and looks at Gerber. 'Full-scale alarm because of German spies in civilian clothing,' he says. 'A group was captured near Gennep. All shot out of hand.'

'Poor devils,' says Jonas. A brief requiem.

'How far is it to Gennep?' Regus asks.

'How far is it to the nearest telegraph pole?' growls Wengler.

Nothing happens for three more minutes. Nothing at all. Except that the young soldiers pack their lungs full of cigarette smoke, but then shells and bullets are far more damaging to your health.

'The Dutch are coming!' yells someone at the far end of the bridge.

They scramble to action stations, watch a swarm of Dutch infantrymen pounding towards them, steel-helmeted, bayonets fixed. As if they were on the exercise yard, but as exposed as cockroaches on a kitchen floor.

'Let 'em come on a bit,' says Gerber. 'No shooting before I give the order.'

Maybe 1,200 metres between them and the Dutch. Maybe 1,100.

'Fucking idiots,' Jonas moans. 'We can't just mow the bastards down. They're probably straight out of training. It would be a slaughter of the innocents, I tell you.'

'Fire the first round over their heads,' Gerber orders. 'Then they'll hit cover, if they've got any sense.'

'And if they haven't?'

'Then they'll turn us into mincemeat in no time,' says the Leutnant sourly, and looks at his watch.

Jonas peers behind him in the direction of Graave.

'Those idle sods have overslept,' growls Regus.

'Drunk too much schnapps,' Wengler agrees.

'Wait for it!' says Jonas, the Prophet. 'Here goes!' A prophet indeed. He lifts one hand. 'Abracadabra!'

At that moment – exactly 05.35 – the skies are transformed into an abyss of flame. The artillery have unleashed drumfire. Panzer engines have roared into life. Aircraft are swooping low ahead of the spearheads. Infantrymen are clambering out of their foxholes. The war in the West has begun.

'Christ, Prophet,' yells Regus above the din. 'With that trick, you could earn a fortune in the circus!'

'Fire at will!' Gerber orders.

His men open up with all they've got.

The Dutch throw themselves into cover, but they are no rookies, and neither do they lack the stomach for a fight. They return the Germans' fire and move slowly forward. Two hundred of them. Maybe 300 – against a nineteen-man squad, four of whom will have to guard their prisoners.

Regus is the first to catch it. A bullet in his forehead. Right in the centre. The Unteroffizier is dead before he hits the ground, looking as though he has suddenly grown a third eye.

'Jesus, that's it!' shouts Wengler from his machine-gun post.

'What's up, big man?' the virgin yells.

'Out of ammo,' Wengler confesses. 'Have to use me nail-file.'

The others, too, have reached the end of their tethers. And the Dutch are only 700 metres away. Attacking by the book, with one giving covering fire while his neighbour moves forward. The German commander estimates the distance, reckons up the number of seconds he has left.

Suddenly the advance stops. Apparently without reason, but just at the right moment.

'See if you can do something with the Dutch machine-guns in the bunkers,' Gerber yells, and takes another look through his glasses. What's going on? Why aren't the Dutch still moving forward, just when their goal is in sight?

'No problem, Leutnant,' bellows Jonas.

Maier is behind him, dragging out two full boxes of ammunition.

The roar of engines. For a moment Gerber is terrified that the Dutch are about to bring up tanks. Then he sees the two big trucks moving up on the far side, slowly moving into position, probably with machine-guns mounted on them.

'Look out!' the Leutnant warns. 'Fire at those trucks!'

At that precise moment the Dutch open up, and the bunch of lost souls on the bridge are in big trouble. The men manning the commandeered Dutch guns respond sparingly.

The three wounded men are cared for by Wengler, the squad's makeshift medic, as best he can, while the others carry on fighting, waiting for the German Panzers to come. In an hour. Or never. Or maybe a minute too late.

The battle is only ten minutes old, but for the rangy young Leutnant it is no longer a fight for some anonymous bridge but for survival.

Left and right of the road, the infantrymen of the Royal Netherlands Army have taken cover, flat as flounders on a dish. The pair of big trucks are moving forward along the highway, festooned with heavy machine-guns and loaded with soldiers, who at 500 metres are giving all they have. The pot-holes in the road are making proper aiming impossible, and so the *mynheers* are spraying the terrain with bullets pretty well indiscriminately, figuring that some will hit the target.

Trucks are not tanks, even when they try to behave like them.

'Take your time, Prophet,' says Leutnant Gerber. He puts his field-glasses to his eyes. His mouth is like a thin gash surrounded by downy beard. And his complexion is no longer milk-white but grey as an elephant's hide. 'Either those fellows don't want to live, or they're falling-down drunk,' he pants.

'I'll sober the bastards up,' Jonas growls, raising the stock of the machine-gun to his shoulder and taking aim. Specks of light dance in his sights. The spring sunshine is neutral: it screws up both sides' aim.

Jonas presses the trigger almost lazily. A burst smashes into the engine-casing of the foremost truck, strokes the driver's cabin. A jet of flame shoots out of the radiator; the petrol tank explodes. The flames lick hungrily on. Dutch infantrymen leap from their burning 'tank'.

The second lorry won't make it past its companion. The road is too narrow. Under fire from the Prophet, the driver risks a painfully-slow U-turn. The wind carries the sounds of screams, whistles, bellowed orders across the bridge.

'Christ, Jonas, that was fantastic!' bellows Maier, the dirtiest priest the world has ever seen. His joy makes him careless: he jumps up from cover like a football fan saluting a goal – except that the shooting going on here is no game.

A Dutch sniper catches Maier in the neck. The bullet slices through the carotid artery. A jet of blood thick as a man's finger gushes out, fast, slow, in the rhythm of the man's pumping heart. Maier's expression changes to one of terror as he stares down and sees the stream of blood pouring down onto his battledress tunic.

'Wengler!' Gerber bawls at the medic. 'Where the fuck are you? Do something!'

'Easy to say,' the big man growls back sourly.

'Bandage up the man's throat before he bleeds to death.'

'You must be crazy, Leutnant!' Wengler shouts. 'Might as well stick his head in a noose.'

'For Christ's sake, man,' the virgin moans. There's a crack in his voice no one has heard before. 'Do what you like, but do something!'

'I didn't invent this bloody war,' the big man says. Then to the men around him, 'Come on, get weaving!'

They carry Maier down into Bunker II. The man's face is wearing a silly, almost apologetic grin, but life is pouring out of him like beer from a leaking barrel. Wangler stuffs a wad of bandages over the wound. It is soaked through within seconds. The whole operation is useless. The poor swine has maybe six or seven litres of blood left in him. Maybe with a blood-transfusion kit, the big man thinks, or a tracheotomy and an oxygen-tent . . . And meanwhile his comrade's life is ebbing as he lies there in Wengler's arms. The best they can hope for is that he will lose consciousness before the end.

Occasional Messerschmitt fighters flit to and fro from over the battle zone, flying low. Sirens sound to their left and right. Combat alert. Only behind them, on the road that should be packed with approaching Panzers, is there absolute peace.

'I wish it was night, or the Prussians were coming,' moans the Prophet, who has a quote for every occasion.

'Shut up!' bellows Gerber, without taking his field-glasses from his eyes. 'Our friends from the rival team have had enough. They're making themselves scarce.'

'Got some other dirty trick in mind,' says Private Franzen, alias Vandehoek.

'The *mynheers*'ve got troubles of their own,' the Leutnant observes sagely.

'Wouldn't mind having their problems,' growls the Prophet.

And then the truth dawns. A roll of thunder. The enemy's tactics become as clear as day. The Dutch have brought up artillery and are now getting ready to blow the bridge to bits at their leisure.

The first shells land away from the target, but the gunners have got plenty of time to find their range. When they do, it will be thank you and good night.

'Come here, Franzen,' Leutnant Gerber says, with a wolfish smile that fails to reach his eyes. 'Let's get rid of some excess baggage.' They squirm their way over towards the hollow where the Dutch prisoners are being kept under guard. 'You get hold of your friend Pierboom,' the Leutnant pants. 'We'll send him over to the other side. He can tell his mates that they'll be massacring their own people if they carry on shelling us to shit like this.'

The shells are landing closer. Slivers of shrapnel whistle over their heads as the Leutnant and his interpreter reach the hollow. The Dutch prisoners, the men who literally slept through the outbreak of war, are huddled together far too closely.

'Spread out, for God's sake,' the virgin yells to the two guards. 'One direct hit and you'll all be buried in a mass grave.'

He stares at frightened, oddly apathetic faces. A little hate in those eyes, perhaps. Franzen starts speaking Dutch to Sergeant Pierboom. At first the man refuses to answer.

'Don't be so dumb,' his ex-comrade cajoles him. 'It makes sense. You'll be snatched from the jaws of death, eh?'

The sergeant thinks about it, nods, slowly gets to his feet.

'Let him through!' Gerber shouts to his men. 'And now run, as fast as you can, mate!' He watches as Pierboom sets off, first at a leisurely pace, then faster and faster as he moves through no man's land towards his own lines.

Ten minutes later, the Dutch artillery actually ceases firing. The earth trembles for a while afterwards, the air reeks of blood and cordite, their ears are deafened.

'There, how 'bout that?' says Gerber, cock-a-hoop again.

'Leutnant, your arse is where your brains should be,' says the Prophet insolently. 'That prick will tell them that there's only half-a-dozen of us left. And once the Dutch know that, they'll be back to chop us to bits with their penknives.'

'But until they come, we survive,' the Leutnant retorts. 'Got that?'

'Panzers behind us!' yells Wengler. 'German ones!'

'See?' the Leutnant says proudly. He turns, looks through his field-glasses. 'Panzers is a slight exaggeration,' he murmurs, adjusting the focus. 'One Panzer, in fact.' He spots the black cross on its turret. 'But at least it's one of ours.' Maybe it's the first of the spearhead. Or it's hanging back for reasons of its own. But a Panzer is a Panzer. And it has a radio aboard.

'Give 'em a nice wave with your red arm-band!' he bellows to the big man.

Wengler does the best he can, ties the recognition-flag to his machine-pistol and waves it frantically. But the men in the Panzer are either blind, or deaf, or thick, or drunk. Or all of those things.

Instead of moving to secure the bridge, they open fire on the position with their turret-mounted machine-gun. Then the Panzer starts up its engines and saunters jauntily off in the opposite direction.

'This can't go on,' grates Gerber. 'We shall have to encourage our comrades to hurry up a little. I want a volunteer.' He looks at the remnants of his unit. Who is dispensable? No one. 'How d'you feel, Franzen?' he says finally. At this stage of the game, a Dutch interpreter is the last thing he needs. 'You get your skates on and find the nearest German unit and ask them whether we're being expected to fight the war all on our own. Got that?'

'Sure, Leutnant,' the Private answers uncertainly. 'In a German uniform? Or a Dutch one?'

'That depends who you run into first,' says the virgin with

a grin. 'Far as I'm concerned, you can wear your wedding suit. Best of luck, boy . . .' And he despatches the man into the wilderness of war.

'Take a look at that,' oaths Jonas. 'All from your brilliant ruddy idea.'

Even with the naked eye they can see that the Dutch infantry are preparing to advance once more. This time there will be no stopping them, because they know that there are only a handful of men holding the bridge, and that the Germans' ammunition is running low.

So the Dutch move forward, from the left and right, strengthened by sapper units. They are gathering for their final attack, taking their time but doing the job thoroughly, a job that will be lethally effective – unless Private Franzen works a miracle.

While the Brandenburgers were still holding the bridges that would cost most of them their lives, there were others getting to grips with the enemy, fighting against disorganised, though vastly superior forces. Shortly before 'X-hour', 05.35 hours, assault groups of parachute troops went into action.

The sapper platoon II, FJR 1, under the command of Oberleutnant Rudolf Witzig, was woken by alarm bells at its quarters in the Hilden flak barracks near Düsseldorf. The men were hauled off in trucks to the airfield at Cologne-Ostheim, where Germany's latest secret weapons, heavy transport gliders, were waiting for them.

They were loaded aboard the gliders.

At 21.00 hours the Oberleutnant reported them ready for takeoff and then sent them off to get some sleep.

During these hours before the balloon goes up, there is no chance even to think of a stroll through Cologne's fleshpots, though the men are sick of being confined to barracks. The big job that is being demanded of them began in isolation and boredom. There has been no leave for months past. They put up with it, knowing that they were nearer to heroes' deaths than chasing skirts.

'Sweet dreams, and make 'em quick,' says Oberleutnant

Witzig, tipping his cap to them. 'First thing tomorrow, we'll be up and busy.'

'Another ruddy false alarm. Or am I wrong?' growls Private Wanner.

'Who do you think I am? Lord God Almighty?' the Hauptfeldwebel answers. 'What's the bleeding etiquette when you're a smoker?'

They all offer packets of cigarettes at once. They have pocketsful of the things. And their brains full of heroic fantasies. They are the cream of the most modern branch of the Wehrmacht, like the Brandenburgers, a special unit with their own morality and expectations – expectations that this war will throw whole countries at their feet, medals on their chests, and girls in their beds.

02.45 hours.

Alarm bells.

By 03.30 hours the entire outfit, assault section 'Koch', are lined up in full order: eleven officers and 427 NCOs and other ranks, dispersed among forty-two transport gliders. They will be steered by the best glider pilots in Germany, artists of wind-driven flight. The men have been split up into four assault groups within the section. They have been training for it in the Czech bunker complex under the Altvater for months, and now the combined parachute and glider attack is about to become deadly-serious reality – except that the Belgian defences are a lot tougher than those they have been practising on, and will not hesitate to fire back...

The assault group 'Steel' under Oberleutnant Altmann – two officers and 114 men – is under orders to launch an airborne attack from low altitude and take the steel bridge at Veldwezelt. The assault group 'Concrete', led by Leutnant Schacht, is to secure the canal bridge at Vroenhoven, and the assault group 'Iron' under Leutnant Schächter is to mount a glider attack on the bridge at Canne. Assault group 'Granite' – two officers, twenty-eight Unteroffiziers and fifty-six men – has been given the toughest job: they are to make a landing on the plateau inside Europe's strongest fortress, Eben Emael, in the middle of 1,100 well-trained garrison troops, and disable its gun-turrets.

At the Luftwaffe bases near the border, there is an air of feverish activity. During the night, planes carrying specially-trained men on board have been making sneak-flights to the Dutch and Belgian coasts to lay hundreds of aerial mines, to deter a landing by the British Fleet come the opening of hosilities in the morning.

They are also working round the clock at the Reich Propaganda Ministry in Berlin. Dr Goebbels' 'mouth-pieces' are busily cobbling together the legend that the German Wehrmacht moved into Holland, Belgium and Luxembourg only at the last moment, to prevent a threatened invasion by the French and the British – as if Hitler had not decided to ignore the neutral status of these countries months beforehand.

Stukas are being loaded with bombs, and the nippy Me 109s – so far the most successful aircraft of the war – are being fuelled. But even more distant airfields and garrisons hear of the alarm, hours before 'X-time'. In Southern Germany, the order drags the crews of squadron KG 55 away from a mess-evening. The 3rd Group, stationed in Gablingen, are enjoying a film in Augusburg, but the movie is one without a happy ending. In the middle of the performance, the lights flicker on and the usherette informs all the Luftwaffe personnel that they must leave the cinema immediately to take part in an emergency exercise.

They grumble and curse; dummy-runs of this kind have cut into their free time on dozens of occasions in the recent past. During the next few hours they will not be in action, but will end up crouching over sandpits, practising bombing French airfields until they are sick of it. But soon they realise: this is the real thing.

All 4,000 paratroopers are ready for action, with the assault group 'Koch' first in line. The paratroopers are about to embark – the short Norwegian interlude apart – on their first big operation. Units of this élite force are to drop into 'Fortress Holland' according to a painstakingly worked-out plan and to attempt to seize the installations before the Dutch have a chance to flood the polders, before their government can flee from the Hague, and before the oil storage tanks at Rotterdam can be set ablaze. At the same time, planes will launch a series of devasting bombing raids in an attempt to knock out the 100-aircraft strong Dutch Air Force before it can take to the skies.

The assault group 'Koch', however, is heading for Belgium.

It was Hitler himself who first suggested to the commander of his parachute troops that Europe's most modern fortress could be taken by airborne assault. General Kurt Student, not exactly the most pernickety of men, and a commander who had often complained that his paras had not yet been used properly, nevertheless had only one answer: it was impossible.

'Go home, sleep on it, and come back tomorrow,' the Führer said as they parted.

Student consulted his commanders: they were all for trying it. Since then men had been in training for the current mission, and since then they had stormed fortress after fortress - places they weren't even allowed to know the names of, for security reasons.

Now they stood waiting, kitted out in their usual sloppy fashion, lined up in three rows. They were burning with a desire to prove themselves, even if it cost them their lives. They were always in the vanguard, whether it came to living or dying, a close-knit, desperate outfit. Even normal training is a test of courage for these men they call 'the green devils' after their green camouflage-suits. Even in peacetime, the para's badge served as proof that a man was ready to make a dozen crazy jumps at practice-attacks, or was prepared to break his neck coming out of an aircraft. Hit the deck, roll forward, roll back, snap off the 'chute, then reach for your weapon... It was drummed into them like their two-times table.

Their only fear was to lose face.

They are more scared of humiliation than of a thousand landings on top of Eben Emael, the fortress they are to attack today - and no one will refuse to jump.

At 04.30 hours the first engines start up. The Jus warm up slowly, finally move off up the runways. The towlines pull taut. A jerk, and the DFS 230 transport gliders are off the ground, then climbing like huge kites.

Every ten seconds a towplane and a glider take off from the airfields at Ostheim, on the right bank of the Rhine, and Butzweilerhof on the left bank. The noble Ju 52, known as 'Auntie Junker', is already a familiar sight, but the transport gliders that she is towing are still secret; they weigh 900 kilos, can fly at night; have a gliding-speed of 124 kilometres per hour, can land to within an accuracy of twenty metres, silently, with their wide-span wings. There are between eight and twelve men crouched in each glider, perched on the long bar that runs down the middle of the thing, one behind the other like hens in a coop. They have the rising sun at their backs and the man in front of them's neck to stare at. Their water-bottles contain what they call a 'jumping cocktail': half coffee, half schnapps.

At 04.35 hours the last Ju takes to the air, joins its companions and heads towards the enemy, to seize a fortress that in the opinion of Allied experts could become a new Verdun if the Germans were to try to attack it.

Eben Emael, a defensive complex covering some forty-five hectares, embedded in a high plateau, could hold off any enemy. The labyrinthine structure's jutting artillery casemates, 'Sedan's little brother' (Raymond Cartier), are linked to each other by 4.5 kilometres of underground tunnels and corridors. Built over a period of some thirty years along with the Albert Canal and dominating the line from Aachen to Maastricht to Brussels, it is inaccessible by road. Here, so its builders had calculated, whole German divisions must bleed to death.

Hitler had added a twist of his own to the Manstein-plan, a bold stroke that would give his Panzers free passage: the covert units from the Brandenburg Division would secure the Meuse crossings, while from the air his paratroopers would seize the impregnable fort in an astonishing military coup.

The engineers who had constructed Eben Emael as the northern cornerstone of the fortress-complex of Liège had thought of every possible means of approach by an enemy – except the use of parachute troops. In 1930 the Red Army showed off such units to the world, calling them 'locust soldiers', but they were not taken seriously. The first parachute troops in Germany appeared at the parade to celebrate Hitler's birthday in April 1939, and they were conspicuous only by their peculiarly-shaped steel helmets.

Only a surprise-attack from the air would put the fort out of action swiftly, and such an assault would succeed only by achieving total and absolute surprise. Right from the outset, Koch's men had to accept that if any of them broke his vow of silence, deliberately or inadvertently, he would be subjected to the death penalty. And, in fact, two paratroopers were considered to have transgressed in this way, were sentenced to death, but were pardoned after the fall of Eben Emael.

A half-hour before the offensive begins, and all the Jus are airborne. The transport gliders have to be towed at a great height, and therefore they take precedence over the other transport Ju 52s, which will drop their human cargoes from a minimum height of ninety metres. The soldiers, once they have jumped, will hang helplessly on the end of their chutes for fifteen seconds. Their most vulnerable moment will come when they land and have to struggle to discard their chutes. If the enemy has not gunned them down by then, they will be able to assemble and attack him from behind, going straight for his jugular.

An armada of forty-two planes travels westwards, guided by a 73-kilometre long string of beacons as far as the Reich border. Estimated flying time: 31 minutes. Weather conditions: excellent. For his correct forecast on this day, the Luftwaffe's chief meteorologist, Diessing, will be awarded an engraved gold watch by the Führer himself.

The NCOs responsible for pushing the boys through are already waiting at the hatchways, checking their watches. As soon as the signal comes from the pilot's cabin, they will jump – a jump that will take them, in these last seconds of peace, into the midst of war. First to go will be the 'Granite' group. The first disaster: the pilot of the Ju spots exhaust fumes from another plane very close to him. To avoid a collision, he stands his crate on its head and dives. The transport gliders on tow have to follow the manoeuvre, no easy task.

The towing-line snaps, the glider pilot pulls up his plane

and ends up on an opposite course heading back towards German territory. Squad II are out of the paratroops' première performance at Eben Emael, including Oberleutnant Witzig, who had been due to lead the attack.

Back on their own side of the border, the glider lands in a meadow. First at the run, then picked up by a car, the young officer makes for the nearest telephone, to order a substitute aircraft for him and his men, as if he had missed a suburban train and was determined to catch the next one. No Ju available for miles around. Finally a response from Gütersloh. Witzig dashes back to his men and has them fix the meadow up as an improvised airstrip.

Another two transport gliders are forced to make emergency landings when their towing lines snap. Leaderless, with their equipment decimated and their force weakened even before a shot has been fired, the gliders of 'Granite' group approach Eben Emael. They do not know that the Belgian commander had been warned several hours previously of an impending air attack.

Disgruntled flak crews stare anxiously at the night sky. So far as they are concerned, one thing is certain: as long as they hear no engines, there will be no bombs. Their superiors are nervous, constantly urging them to extreme vigilance.

Cajus Becker recounts in his book *Attack–Altitude 4,000*, 'Suddenly, to the east, huge, ghostly birds are swooping towards them. They are already at very low altitude, obviously preparing to land. Three, six, nine silent aircraft . . .

Within a minute, all nine gliders have landed in their preplanned positions, despite the machine-gun fire being poured at them from all sides. All over the plateau, squads are leaping from the gliders and setting to their lethal work.'

Immediately after the landing, a radio message is sent to Hauptmann Walter Koch, who has set up his command-post in the midst of his four assault groups: 'Objective attained'. Seventeen minutes after their first landing and sixteen and a half minutes after the beginning of the offensive in the West, the leaderless 'Granite' group has destroyed all the observation and gunnery turrets on Eben

Emael with hollow charges. The last to be blown is Turret 31.

There is hand-to-hand fighting in some nearby living-quarters, in which Unteroffizier Unger and Private Wanner lose their lives. The attackers force the Belgians down into the underground complex and pursue them through the tunnels.

Then the next wave arrives: Ju transport aircraft, coming in very low. Parachutes billow and float earthwards. Those Belgians who catch sight of them are forced to change the direction of their fire, to cope with a new enemy in their rear. They cannot know that the 'paratroops' are only dummies festooned with bandoliers to look like heavily-armed soldiers.

In the meantime, the assault group 'Concrete' has arrived at the Vroenhoven canal crossing. The men do not bother to regroup after landing; as soon as they are free of their parachutes, they head straight for the bridge, rifles at the ready. Private Stenzel is the first to reach it, sees that Belgian sappers are in the process of blowing the bridge.

He leaps straight down into the midst of the enemy, tears the detonator-box out of the officer's hands. The three most important canal bridges remain undamaged.

The assault group 'Iron' enjoys less success. As they land, a huge explosion rends the air. Their objective has been blown. The 115 'green devils' are involved in fierce fighting, in which they lose twenty-two men. The 'Steel' group has a happier time in securing the bridge at Veldwezelt.

Wherever paratroopers rain from the sky, the defenders first have to overcome their complete astonishment, and this costs them valuable time. The next waves of paras take the positions on the Grebbe and the Peel. 'Green devils' are already fighting in Rotterdam, and above all they are holding the crucial bridges until the German Panzers arrive.

'The forces defending the borders were dead, or prisoners, or so overcome with consternation that they were in no condition to undertake the destruction of the vital bridges. The German paratroopers swiftly broke all resistance, and held their positions until the arrival of

German spearheads that were pushing towards Maastricht,' writes Raymond Cartier.

At 08.30 hours that morning, there is a new surprise at Eben Emael. In the middle of the battle, a transport glider sails over and crash-lands under heavy fire. The first man to jump from the DFS-230 is Oberleutnant Witzig, who promptly resumes his command as if nothing had happened.

The Belgian Major Jottrand radios to order the guns to open fire on his own positions. While the heavy Belgian artillery is bombarding its own fortress, the Germans withdraw to the protection of the demolished armoured domes. It is a grotesque situation: 1,100 Belgians are imprisoned in the underground complex, and above them the 'Grante' assault group probes like a hungry cat at a nest of mice.

The German Panzers sweep forward.

All the parachute units are relieved, one after the other, last of all the conquerors of Eben Emael, who have suffered only six dead and twenty wounded.

The issue may have been decided swiftly at the key points in Belgium, but it still hangs in the balance at the bridge over the Dutch Meuse-Waal Canal, where the handful of Brandenburgers are holding out under Leutnant Gerber.

'You don't need your glasses, Leutnant,' says Jonas. 'You can take a peep with your own fair eyes and see what they're going to do with us in a minute.'

'Shut your miserable trap, Prophet!'

'And what would you prefer, old man?' Jonas continues relentlessly. 'Hanging or shooting? Personally . . .'

The young officer ignores him, puts down his field-glasses. He has a reputation as a professional optimist, but with the situation as it stands he can feel himself slipping. If he includes himself, then his total strength at the moment consists of five exhausted soldiers, but Private Aschke and Brenninger don't count, because they have to stay guarding the Dutch prisoners. So all he has left in this machine-gun emplacement is big Wengler and this Prophet, who is getting gloomier by the moment. Seven men are dead, among them fine fellows like Unteroffizier Regus, Maier, and Müller. Maybe two of the six wounded could still manage to haul ammunition, but the commandeered Dutch bullets will soon run out, too.

'I've got an idea,' says the virgin, and crawls cautiously out of the emplacement.

'Another?' grunts big Wengler.

The gawky Leutnant with the over-long legs works his way over to where the prisoners are being kept under guard. He looks down at their ashen, unshaven faces, sees the hopelessness in their eyes. He nods down to them. 'You're in luck, lads. You're off back home to mother, pronto!' He waves Aschke and Brenninger towards the emplacement on the bridge. But the Dutchmen still do not understand. He is, of course, speaking German. They stare fearfully at his machine-pistol, suspecting the worst. '*Got verdomme*,' he bawls, remembering the Dutch he was forced to speak before the capture of the bridge. 'I won't hurt you! Just clear off! Double-quick!' he shouts in their own language.

Gradually the enemy infantrymen realise that they are being set free. They set their numb limbs in motion and move off, still glancing behind them as they move forward.

The virgin squirms back to the bridge. The freed soldiers are now halfway over, waving nervously and calling out to the foremost Dutch units.

'That should hold them up for about a minute,' says Jonas.

'Christ, you're a mathematical bloody genius, Prophet,' hisses the leutnant. 'You ignore the fact that we are now five able-bodied warriors here.'

Brenninger has moved quickly to take over the second machine-gun.

'If we pool everything,' the sergeant says. 'We've got 261 rounds left.'

'But a whole load of grenades,' the Leutnant says comfortingly.

'True,' Aschke answers with a thoughtful grimace. 'But if I were you, I'd stick 'em up your own sweet arse and give yourself a trip to heaven, Leutnant.'

The enemy attack resumes. One firing, one moving forward, parade-ground stuff.

'Gentlemen, this time we'll have to let them come very close, to save ammunition,' orders Gerber.

The Dutch are using tracer-ammunition. The thin trails of flame make death a visible thing. The ammunition is soon running so low that the Germans manning the machine-guns are forced to put the weapons on single-shot, and Gerber is already holding the grenades ready.

But then they come. You can hear them before you see them. Fighter-planes, Messerschmitts. They sweep in low, engines howling. Their shadows flit over the ground. And their wing-mounted machine-guns hammer away at friend and foe alike.

They peel off, then come back.

Wengler loses his nerve. 'Someone must have addled their brains!' he screams, leaps out of his trench, waves his red arm-band and stands, feet planted squarely apart, right in the path of the Messerschmitts. 'You arseholes! You morons! You frigging bumpkins!'

He gets no further. A burst slices through him, zipping across and down from his left shoulder to his right thigh. He crashes to the ground. He feels nothing, has no idea what is wrong, stares in terror at the bloody mass of intestines seeping out of his torn body, tries to push them back in with his big hands.

It is too much for Aschke. He turns, throws up in the mud beside him.

The Me 109s turn again.

'Move!' the Leutnant bellows. 'Everyone into the bunker!'

He is dragging his right leg behind him. He has a bullet through the thigh. Aschke has been wounded in the arm. Jonas is examining himself incredulously from top to bottom. All the others lie dead or dying by the bridge that they had been ordered to hold.

'C'mon, into the front parlour!' Gerber screams. 'Make yourselves comfortable!'

'Comfortable' is hardly the word, if only because Maier is

lying bloodless and very dead under a blanket in the corner.

The Leutnant stands at a firing-slit, stares out in the direction of home. After all, he sent Franzen over there to fetch reinforcements. 'Don't understand where the fellow's got to,' he growls.

'He's in a warm, soft bed and dreaming of the final victory,' the Prophet mutters sourly, but he doesn't believe what he is saying; he knows his comrade too well. Franzen will risk his hide to help them.

In fact, Franzen is still underway, two kilometres to the east. He has already seen a German despatch-rider thunder past without noticing him. He has come close to running up against a bunch of demoralised Dutch troops. The trouble is that whichever side he encounters may well shoot first and ask later.

And so Franzen hits upon the idea of continuing this part of the war in his underclothes. He tears off the remnants of his uniform. Pants and vest are neutral, he thinks with a grin, and emerges from cover just as a German armoured scout-car comes rumbling along the forest track.

'What sort of a queer bird is that?' says the ensign in charge. 'Stop,' he tells the driver.

Franzen stumbles up to the vehicle. 'I am a Brandenburger,' he pants. 'Branden-Brandenburger.'

'Is that something you eat?' growls the driver. 'Or a cocktail?'

But the ensign has understood. 'Come on, get in!' he says to the man in underpants.

The commander of the scout-car has heard talk somewhere of undercover operations. The whole thing had been so secret that no one knew any details. Immediately before the offensive had begun, he had heard a report that the Dutch had rounded up all four Brandenburger units.

'But the bridge is still intact!' Franzen bellows. 'Christ, my mates are up to their necks in shit and . . .'

'Step on it!' the ensign orders his driver.

As the heavy vehicle lumbers forward, he sends a radio message to the effect that the bridge over the Meuse-Waal Canal is still intact. He gets no farther with his report. They are travelling so fast that the driver has no chance to check the road. He runs over a mine. It explodes right under him. The vehicle is tossed into the air and goes up in a sheet of flame.

'Poor devils,' says a company commander who sees it happen.

The bridge is still standing, as if by a miracle. The Dutch have other worries now, for the German spearheads have reached them. Artillery is being hauled into position all around the bunkers. Sappers are working their way towards them, preparing to knock them out one by one.

Leutnant Gerber, Jonas and Aschke are catching merry hell from both sides, but the greater threat comes from the German advance parties for whose arrival they had longed with such fervour. The men in field-grey are doing everything strictly by the book, aiming their guns for the firing-slits. Covered by the artillery, the sappers work their way over and hurl explosive charges through to the interior of the bunkers.

They have completed work on the empty neighbouring bunker; now it's the Brandenburgers' turn. Aschke holds out the red arm-band, waves it frantically, but a burst of machine-gun fire hacks off his arm.

'They're out to kill us,' moans Jonas. 'So there'll be no witnesses to the undercover operation.'

'You're crazy!' the virgin screams.

Another second and they will have had it. Jonas had only one thought: to avoid suffocating or being blown to bits in this concrete hell. He grabs his handkerchief, goes to the exit, tears open the door, stumbles out straight into the firing-line. They'll see white, surely, he thinks wildly; the handkerchief, white, white, white... Surrender, the end, and... shit...

'How did he get there?' someone asks. 'Cease fire!'
For a moment there is a pause in the bombardment.

'The bridge,' Jonas wails, and then says the password, 'The tulips are wilting in Holland –'

He just has time to glimpse the first Panzers roaring over the bridge, then everything goes black and he crumples to the ground.

The sapper Hauptmann stares down at the wounded

lunatic, and slowly he begins to realise that something has gone terribly wrong. He says, as if to himself, 'The tulips are wilting in Holland.' He watches as Jonas is laid on a stretcher and carried away from the battlefield. He gazes after the last survivor from the Meuse-Waal Bridge, and he shakes his head.

On this bloody Friday before Whitsun, the people of Europe sit glued to their radios and follow the news bulletins, though these are compounded mostly of lies; for tactical reasons, real successes are often left unannounced, while phoney victories are trumpeted over the airwaves. The French Minister of War, Maxime Weygand, who had been about to resign, decides to remain in office in view of the situation. He wires the commander-in-chief of the French forces, General Maurice-Gustav Gamelin, his intimate enemy, 'From now on there is only one goal: Victory!' The widely-hated general wires back a bombastic response, 'I can only give one answer: France!'

'The fiasco began on a note of pathos,' as Raymond Cartier has remarked.

As expected, the British and the French move over the border to aid their neighbours. By now they are too late to help the Dutch, but long columns of British and French troops cross into Belgium, scarcely harassed at all by the otherwise omnipresent Luftwaffe. The Allies do not realise that the German planes have been ordered to spare them, to encourage their advance into a well-laid trap.

Guderian's Panzer units are already racing at extraordinary speed through the few roads that cross the Ardennes, heading for Sedan. They are waging a kind of war never before seen in history, in accordance with a principle that General Rudolf Schmidt repeated to Rommel. His then commander told the man who would become the 'Desert Fox', 'There are always two alternatives, and the more audacious is always the right one!'

The Wehrmacht suppresses all reports of its breakneck progress in order to avoid alerting the Allies to its real aims. And, in the event, the French continue to be unaware of danger for some time. While the generals in command of the advancing German forces drive with their men in their command-vehicles, or flit about the battlefields, dodging enemy flak in their little Fieseler Storchs in order to gain a close-up view of the developing situation, the French generals are still dining handsomely at their headquarters well to the rear, waited on by white-gloved orderlies. They are fighting the same war their fathers fought, according to the same rules, without realising that the old rulebook was torn up when the Germans crushed Poland. Everywhere is Poland now: Panzers and bombers working in partnership, Stukas bombing the roads open, sending trained gunners panicking for cover, men fleeing impregnable positions for their lives.

The first distinguished victim of the German attack in the West is the British Prime Minister, Neville Chamberlain. He is forced to resign in favour of Winston Churchill, who forms an all-party cabinet and brings a new quality of determination to the struggle against Hitler. In a speech that still counts as literature, he promises his people blood, sweat, toil and tears.

'We have before us an ordeal of the most grievous kind. We have before us many, many long months of struggle and suffering. You ask: What is our policy? I will say: it is to wage war, by sea, land, and air, with all our might and with all the strength that God can give us: to wage war against a monstrous tyranny, never surpassed in the dark, lamentable catalogue of human crime... You ask: What is our aim? I can answer in one word: Victory – victory at all costs, victory in spite of all terror, victory, however long and hard the road may be; for without victory there is no survival...'

That same Bloody Friday also witnesses a horror around which Goebbels throws a smokescreen of lies, and which is therefore overlooked by most writers.

In the afternoon, the combat squadrons *Greif* (KG 55) and *Edelweiss* (KG 51) are about to take off for their third mission of the day. Their crews are none too pleased. They are seeing none of the fine weather that Northern France is enjoying. During their first operation that day, they spent the time flying aimlessly around in the fog. Only on their second had they actually dropped any bombs. Now they have been ordered to attack targets in Southern France.

The instruments have been checked, the engines warmed up. Final operational briefing. One more cigarette, a gulp of coffee. They clamber up into their aircraft, five men to each He 111, a no-frills bomber capable of a speed of 275 knots. It takes twenty minutes for it to reach an altitude of 5,000 metres, its operating limit is 2,800 kilometres, and it can carry a bomb-load of 2,000 kilos.

The engines snarl into life.

'Best of luck, Herr Leutnant!' the groundcrew leader calls up to the Flight commander of the third group.

It is 14.30.

Twenty combat planes take off from their bases at Landsberg and Bad Wörishofen, assemble at 1,500 metres above the peak at Memming and fly in close formation towards the storm clouds that are hanging above the Black Forest. The ninth Flight, commanded by Oberleutnant Schifferdings, loses its way and is attacked by Swiss fighters over the neutral town of Solothurn. It is nearly a total disaster. Going something like a bat out of hell, suffering from seven direct-hits from cannon-fire and his fuselage peppered with machine-gun holes, the Oberleutnant escapes and makes an emergency landing just across the German border.

Leutnant Seidel and his Flight are completely on their own. Their target is the airfield at Dijon-Longvic. Flying blind. Only occasionally does a gap appear in the clouds beneath them, and then they spot a village or settlement. The Leutnant compares them with his documents aboard. The photos he had been supplied with are indistinct, and from high altitude all these flea-bitten dumps look alike somehow.

To judge by the time, Seidel reckons that they must have reached their objective. A moment later, the clouds open. And there is a city beneath them. It must be Dijon. The flak is making no attempt to fire at the Germans, but then the French often get caught on the hop, and even their fighters are not up to much; the Frogs don't have their own air force, and the army commanders in charge of their pilots have little understanding of how to use them in action.

'We've arrived!' shouts the Leutnant into his headset. 'Make ready to attack!'

It is true that the flying-time has been about right, but Seidel does not know that instead of flying in a straight line he has flown in a circle, and that he is not over France but over Germany. The city beneath him is not Dijon but Freiburg. The target, now once more half-obscured by wispy cloud, is not an airfield but a children's playground in the suburb of Stühlingen.

The city in the south-western corner of Germany has already put on its best face for Whitsun. The cinemas are showing *Operetta*, with Willi Forst, and *The Postmaster*, with Heinrich George and Hilde Krahl. The shop windows are still filled with goods, even the food stores, though the population - compared with pre-war times - has been put on half-rations.

The average consumer receives 700 grams of meat a week, 280 grams of sugar, 110 grams of jam, 150 grams of pot barley, semolina, sago or other cereals, and a fifth of a litre of milk per day. Every four weeks, they are allowed 125 grams of soap and 100 grams of washing-powder.

Passers-by stop and stare at the displays in the windows of the clothes shops. It is not the price that is crucial in the decision to purchase or not, but the possession of a Reich Clothing Card. Each citizen has 100 points to spend in a year, for which twenty are needed for a shirt, sixty for a suit, sixteen for a pair of ladies' woollen knickers, eight for a roll-on girdle, three for a tie, twenty-five for a night-dress, and one for a handkerchief.

A mass of schoolchildren are gambolling around the playground at Stühlingen. Adults watch their antics, scolding, laughing, putting their hands over their ears at the din. Suddenly they all glance skywards. Loud engines. There is nothing in sight; the aircraft must have disappeared into the clouds, and they must be their own, because no warning-sirens have sounded.

Freiburg's air-raid observers on top of the Lorettoberg

identified the unseen aircraft as a Flight of German He 111s as long as an hour ago. True, it is unusual for combat aircraft to carry out training raids on inhabited towns, but perhaps all other available airspace is occupied because of the offensive in the West.

16.11. The He 111s are no longer flying in wingtip formation; the left- and right-hand two-engined aircraft have slotted themselves in behind their leader in a typical attack position.

A sudden roar drowns all the street noise, swiftly grows louder, more threatening. The sound is like an express-train hurtling into a tunnel at top speed.

The first bombs make contact with the playground. The children scatter in blind panic, rushing towards the Colmarer Strasse, straight into the eye of the storm of bombs that is raining down on the hapless city. It is a massacre. The children are blown apart by direct hits, smashed against the walls of buildings by waves from the impact, and bomb-splinters tear into their tiny bodies, slicing through limbs and arteries. Passers-by who rush to their aid are crushed by falling masonry.

Now, at last, Freiburg's sirens wail, and the population flee into their air-raid shelters.

The attacking planes turn away eastwards. The smoke clears to reveal a mass of dead and injured civilians. Finally the police cars, the ambulances and the rescue crews arrive. The injured children fill the air with their heart-rending screams - and the silent ones will never scream again.

Sixty-nine bombs have slaughtered twenty-two children, thirteen women and twenty-two men, caused serious injuries to twenty children, thirty-four women and forty-seven men. Twenty-two bombs - by grim good fortune - failed to explode. The disposal experts who defuse them can see immediately that they are of German manufacture. The markings indicate that they were from the Luftwaffe base at Landsberg.

There, an hour earlier than planned, Leutnant Seidel comes into land - having led, all unawares, an attack on a German city of some 108,000 souls.

'Where the hell did you get to, sluggards?' bawls the

group commander at his subordinate.

The truth very quickly becomes apparent.

'We must arrive at the horrifying conclusion,' stated the group commander in his secret report on the affair, 'that after lengthy wanderings, Leutnant Seidel wrongly identified the city of Freiburg as his objective, the city of Dijon . . .'

The commander-in-chief of the Luftwaffe, Hermann Göring, orders a full legal investigation that same evening, but Propaganda Minister Dr Josef Goebbels has another idea, and succeeds in having it adopted: the fiasco will be laid at the door of the British. His well-oiled propaganda machine immediately begins issuing hate-filled tirades against the British 'child-murderers' and 'incendiarists' in an effort to stoke up anti-British feeling.

'The German Luftwaffe will avenge this action, which is in breach of all international law, in full measure,' shrieked the leader-articles that appeared the next day throughout the tame German press, by order of the Minister. 'From now on, any further enemy bomber raids on the German population will be answered with the employment of five times their number of German aircraft against an English or French city.'

The Weekly Newsreel went to the limit of bearable horror in showing the victims: children, always the children. The big Freiburg lie was maintained until the end of the war, and occasionally freshened up for another airing. Those who knew the truth, sworn to absolute secrecy, remained silent. And Leutnant Seidel, the main actor in the tragedy, died in action over the British city of Portsmouth on August 12th 1940.

Victorious Fiasco

Death stalks the countryside this spring. The green meadows are being crushed under Panzer tracks. Cordite poisons the scent of chestnuts in bloom, and the soldiers of the British Expeditionary Force tear the elderflowers from the branches to decorate their helmets. The stables and water-meadows resound to the painful mooing of unmilked cows, deserted by peasant owners who have fled before the advancing armies.

In Northern France the church bells are ringing - not always because German Panzers are nearing the villages, but also because in Catholic France May is the time when schoolchildren celebrate their first communion. France at Whitsun 1940: girls in white frocks and lads in dark suits and their first long trousers run screaming through the line of battle, dropping prayer-books, rosaries and candles - only to be crushed by the juggernaut of war.

The twisted Whitsun message in the year of our Lord 1940 is: March and die, kill and be killed, play Cain and Abel - even though one of the British commanders, waiting impatiently for reinforcements, ammunition, fuel and air support, hastily tears open a despatch envelope, to read that all England is praying for him and his soldiers.

The battle is raging on a 280-kilometre front between the North Sea and the Maginot Line, which has already been penetrated at a number of places. The majority of German combat vehicles still consists of light Panzers; the entire ten Panzer Divisions can still call on only 349 Panzer IIIs and 278 Panzer IVs. Stukas are clearing the way through. Armour is thrusting forward. As soon as the advance comes to a halt, air support is summoned. The Luftwaffe controls the skies, but they have paid a high price for that dominance. Three hundred and four aircraft are lost on the first day of the offensive in the West, another fifty-one are damaged, and 267 pilots, all trained in peacetime to a standard that will never again be equalled, have given their lives.

For the first time, the Panzer regiments encounter the French 'Somua', a heavily-armoured, slow-moving monster that frequently runs out of fuel but acts as a sort of mobile fortress in the battle.

Hauptmann Ernst Freiherr von Jungenfeld from the 35th Panzers is one of the first to do battle with the enemy, near Merdorp. The commander of the Sixth Company, nicknamed 'pampas' by his men, recounts, 'As I try to get my bearings, I see a French Somua coming up right behind me, completely concealed by a hedge. I and my Panzers disappear very fast. We swiftly revolve the turret and take a bearing on our dangerous opponent. I am now in a position to observe that my opposite number is doing exactly the same thing. I almost beat him to it by a few seconds, but as I fire the first burst my magazine jams. I have problems reloading. Then the first shots hit our Panzer, somewhere to the rear of the engine. We, meanwhile, are all working frantically to unjam the gun. Then we are hit a second time. Lang, my radio operator, suffers a serious wound in the back. He is moaning and writhing and can no longer help. Dürr and I struggle to get the damned gun into shape, for we have no intention of giving up without a fight. We are hit for a third time. The fuel tank. A huge jet of flame shoots through the Panzer. Now there is nothing more to be done. We must get out, because at any moment the thing could go to blazes.'

At the positions along the Dyle, near Gembloux, the first classic tank battle of the Second World War is in progress. The German advance has been halted by a determined French artillery bombardment. The Panzers have withdrawn to new attack-positions on either side of Baudecet. But the French guns keep hammering them.

'The Frogs are acting a bit sharp today,' says Kudritzky, the lively lad from Essen, to his mates.

'They'll soon calm down again when the Stukas arrive,' Gütler answers. 'In any case, what do I care whether we get to Paris this week or the week after?'

'The madamoiselles will be waiting for you,' chips in Seelmann with a leer.

'Maybe for you,' Gütler says irritably.

'For us all,' Kudritzky intervenes to restore the peace.

'D'you think we'll have a chance?' asks Seelmann.

'When there's women around, there's always a chance,' Kudritzky observes, drawing on his meagre stock of experience.

Gütler grunts cynically. 'If you've got the cash, sure.'

'What the hell,' says the lad from the Ruhr coalfields. 'Joy in your heart and your pockets full of money.' He nods to the others. 'I'm off to take a shit. Don't piss off to Paris while I'm away, will you?'

Kudritzky strolls into a half-ruined farmhouse in a nameless village, because a latrine among the ruins is more comfortable than what Mother Nature provides. Firstly, a small dog bites his leg out of sheer terror. Then he opens the wrong door; a stark-naked Frenchwoman, gesticulating wildly, bawls her head off at him, anything but a picture of Gallic charm.

Kudritzky returns, his task unfulfilled, reckoning the order to attack could come at any moment. Gütler has picked up a frightened hen; he is holding it in his arms like a baby.

'What the hell is that?' asks Kudritzky.

'Her name's Susie,' Gütler says. 'I'm taking her with me.'

'In your Panzer?'

'Where else?'

Kudritzky frowns. 'The creature'll just crap all over the lot of you.'

'So what?' says his mate slyly. 'You can clean away the shit, but how else are you going to get a fresh egg for your breakfast in the middle of a battle?'

The advance rolls on.

'During the past three days, the Regiment has destroyed or captured 53 French tanks,' writes Hans Schaüfler in *So They Lived, So They Died*, the chronicle of the 35th Panzers.

'The French were defeated because they committed their armour singly or in small groups, and because their tanks were not manoeuvrable enough. But their armour plating is much better than ours... The enemy's artillery is far superior. It can put up a defensive barrage as heavy as any from the First War. The Panzers rumble on.'

The men are back in their Panzers and moving ahead at top speed – or as their own private language has it, 'giving them carbide'. They don't have to drive far to the battlefield, tanks against tanks, and death grabbing his fill of both sides. If they are to break through, the Stukas will first have to smash the French artillery. Heavy shells crash into the tormented earth. Human beings glow like torches in the flames of burning vehicles.

Advance. Retreat. Attack from the flank. A swift war of movement. Breakthrough. Again and again, the boys of the Panzer units put their lives on the line. They tell themselves that the war will soon be over, and then there will be no more 'heroes' tinsel' being doled out. They plough on crazily through the storm of war, as if heroes' deaths were in short supply.

A frozen moment of horror: Kudritzky watches as the Panzer III in front of his, manned by his mates Seelmann and Gütler, turns into a pillar of flame. He is forced to stand by while the crew tries to escape, though in the end only one living thing gets out of the inferno. Before the battle roars on, he sees one small, fragile creature scuttling terrified between the lines: Susie, the hen.

'Although the Allies were still holding on to the Dyle Line on May 15th, the Belgians' hasty retreat served to convince them even more strongly that the main German thrust would come at this point,' writes Charles Messenger. 'They continued to concentrate their attention on the Dyle, though for a long time now their main concern should have been with the Ardennes, further to the south.'

General Maurice-Gustave Gamelin – described by the French minister Georges Mandel as a 'military bureaucrat' and by his subordinate, the British Air Marshal Arthur

Barret, as a 'popeyed, fat-bellied little grocer' – is insistent. He firmly believes that the Germans, as they did in the First War, will concentrate everything on a breakthrough on the northern flank. He still does not realise that the fatal blow will come from a quite different direction.

Gamelin, in common with most pre-war German military leaders, considers that the Ardennes, heavily forested and mountainous and with poor road connections, are impassable for Panzers and present a natural barrier that more than compensates for the gap in the Maginot Line. But Panzer generals such as Heinz Guderian and Erwin Rommel have had the courage to whistle at the kind of wisdom they teach in military academies.

Friends and enemies alike were amazed at the speed with which the German Panzer Divisions crushed all resistance and careened on through the Ardennes Forest, without giving a thought to securing their flanks. 'I did not comprehend,' Churchill later admitted, 'the violence of the revolution effected since the last war by the incursion of a mass of fast-moving heavy armour. I knew about it, but it had not altered my convictions as it should have done.'

By the evening of May 12th, Guderian and his Panzers had reached Bouillon, the last, small town on Belgian soil. The general set up his headquarters at the Panorama Hotel, whose walls were festooned with outsize hunting trophies. From here he enjoyed a glorious view over the valley of the Semois, but he was unable to pay much heed to the landscape, for Gamelin had realised that disaster was threatening his southern flank and had begun to organise a counter-offensive centring on Sedan.

First the French hurled their air force against the invaders. Bombs exploded all round the hotel. Windows caved in. The Panzer general was injured by flying glass; he only just avoided being struck by the massive head of a wild boar, which fell from a wall during a bombing raid. The general laughed, then went straight back to his main concern: the crossing of the Meuse at Sedan.

'An avalanche had been set in motion,' writes William L. Shirer. 'An armoured force so concentrated, with such mobility and striking-power, had never been seen in war before, and it smashed the French armies to pieces . . . The defenders had no chance against this terrifying phalanx of steel and fire and its accompaniment of Stukas . . .'

They defended desperately, with 'unsung courage' (Alistair Horne), but the *Blitzkrieg* was unstoppable. Rommel's 7th Panzer Division moved even faster than Guderian's units. By 16.00 hours on May 12th it had already reached the Meuse at Dinant. The future 'Desert Fox's' tactics were decided according to Rommel's maxim, 'I have found again and again that in encounter actions, the day goes to the side that is the first to plaster its opponenet with fire. The man who lies low and awaits developments usually comes off second best . . . This applies even when the exact position of the enemy is unknown, in which case the fire must simply be sprayed over enemy-held territory.'

Rommel is constantly at the head of his forces in his specially-converted Panzer III, which serves him as a mobile command post, or swooping above the front in his Fieseler Storch. His division reaches the Meuse only two days after the beginning of the offensive. At one stage, Rommel and his command vehicle, cut off from the main force, drive into the middle of a French bicycle unit and are saved only by the quick action of an adjutant.

Gamelin, following the classic tactic of a commander in trouble, at first refuses to admit the existence of more than a few minor German bridgeheads, 'adjustments of the front', and small-scale breakthroughs. But he secretly issues orders for the town of Sedan and the left bank of the Meuse to be defended at any price. Once German Panzers get across the river, the road to Paris will be open; the French commander has still not grasped that in 'Operation Sickle', the coast is the real objective.

The murderous struggle of Panzers against concrete defensive emplacements begins at twilight on a mild summer evening. The first round of blood-letting ends only when the armour has used up all its ammunition. One weapon that has proved formidable on level ground is the 8.8 anti-aircraft gun. The fact that it was also capable of use against surface targets had been a chance discovery of the Wehrmacht in Poland. One day, finding themselves under attack from a cavalry unit, the crew of a flak battery had no choice but to use their 8.8 – it was that or be ridden down. The devastating results when their gun was used in this way had astonished them and their superiors.

Now, however, the flak barrels are being aimed with great care and deliberation at the French firing-slits. They have knocked out gun after gun. The defenders have been blown to smithereens, suffocated – or if they're lucky, captured before the fire destroys them. The 'impregnable' Maginot defensive complex, reckoned perfect by experts the world over and built at a cost of billions, crumbles like an eggshell at the first – at the latest by the second – assault.

The next morning, the battle intensifies again, turns into a massacre. The Luftwaffe's ugly birds of prey are circling 10,000 feet above the town, awaiting their chance. Suddenly the Ju 87s plunge earthwards, their sirens howling, straight for their pin-point targets, as if they were intending to ram them. No more than 100 metres above the ground, they drop their bombloads and climb again, just when it seems they must crash, but the psychological effect is more damaging than any bombs. Those of the enemy who survive the attack follow the motto *sauve qui peut*, dump their weapons and stumble away from their positions, moaning and cursing, not infrequently with their officer at their head. By nightfall, the Germans had established themselves on the far bank of the Meuse and by dawn the next morning had constructed means to transport the Panzers across the river.

'Towards midday the intensity of the attacks increased,' writes Alistair Horne in his book *The French Campaign 1940*. 'The Luftwaffe now sent in hundreds of aircraft in close formation. Feldwebel Prümers of the 1st Panzer Division, who was still being subjected to heavy artillery bombardment, observes with fascination the arrival of Richthofen's Stukas, "Three, six, eight, oh, there were even more behind – and more planes to the right, and more . . ." A quick glance through the field-glasses – Stukas. What we were due to see during the next twenty minutes was one of the most powerful sights of this war. Squadron after squadron climbing to a great height, going into attack formation, one behind the other, and there – there – the first dives straight down, followed by the second, the third – ten or a dozen altogether. All at once, like birds of prey, they fall on their victims and release their bombloads against their targets. We can see the bombs quite clearly. It is literally raining bombs in the defensive positions and in the town of Sedan itself.'

The French fighter squadron *Cigognes* (Storks), a legend in the First World War, attacks a formation of German dive-bombers as it returns from a mission over Sedan. The French have only out-of-date Curtiss fighters, but they succeed in shooting down twelve Stukas of the first wave and then start on the next, which is only just setting off to attack the French positions. Several Ju 87s are destroyed before they can go into action; the rest turn back without having dropped their bombloads.

But other Ju 87 squadrons are busy over Sedan, guarded by Messerschmitt fighters, and they are smashing strongpoint after strongpoint. The defenders are still fairly raw troops. The French general, Edouard Ruby, says of their conduct during air attacks, 'The gunners stopped firing. They just threw themselves to the ground. The infantry cowered in their trenches, deafened by the noise of the bombs and the screaming of the Stukas. They had not yet developed the instinctive reactions that would enable them to stay at their anti-aircraft guns and fire back. Their only concern was to keep their heads down. Five hours of this nightmare were enough to reduce their nerves to shreds . . .'

Sedan cannot hold, and at Dinant Rommel, 'a man who did not keep office hours' (Len Deighton), is not content to mark time. His men wade through the shallows where they can swim to the far bank, cross in dinghies and rafts under withering enemy fire. The river is damned by sluice gate no. 5 near the island of Houx. The gate has been left intact, because for the French to have blown it would have lowered the water level and made fording easier for the Germans. The gate is captured – the French had left one solitary machine-gunner to defend it – and under cover of darkness Rommel's advance guard moves across the walkway and up the steep bank towards the heavily-wooded heights beyond.

Once established, they are reinforced, and the advance to the West continues.

At Sedan, Guderian's Panzer soldiers have also reached the far bank, crossing on rafts, planks, floating bales of straw, and establishing bridgeheads on both sides of the captured town. Counter-attacks have been beaten off. The offensive is continuing inexorably.

Gamelin realises that he will have to commit all his reserves, particularly all available aircraft, in order to halt the German advance. He appeals for help to the British Air Marshal Barret, the commander of the 'Advanced Air Strike Force', asking him to find a means of demolishing the pontoon bridges that the Germans have thrown over the Meuse, over which combat troops and supplies are flooding into battle.

The English offer seventy-one Fairey Battles and Blenheim bombers. The French contribute 250 aircraft to this suicide mission.

The air armada flies the length of the Meuse valley, keeping low enough to have a good view of the pontoon bridges, high enough to at least avoid the fire from German 2-cm flak. Those few who survive the mission will call their objective ' the valley of death'. First comes Squadron 12, the 'dirty dozen', which has already fought in the bloody encounters around Maastricht. Then come the Blenheims, straight into the concentrated 3.7 cm flak fire coming from the German positions. They are caught by the gunners, shot to pieces in flight or crash in flames. Those left unharmed by the flak are dealt with by the predatory Messerschmitts.

The slaughter lasts for barely half an hour. None of the pontoon bridges are hit. According to German figures, the Allies lose 200 aircraft; Allied sources claim the toll is forty bombers and fifty fighters. The British Fairey Battle squadrons lose twenty-four of the thirty-one aircraft sent into action. As the official chronicle of the RAF says, 'The RAF has never suffered comparable operational losses, before or since.'

Runstedt, commander of Army Group A, is an eye-witness to the ground-air duel as he crosses the bridge over the Meuse at Donchery while on a tour of the front.

Standing beside Guderian, the Colonel-General asks, 'Are things always like this here?'

'To that,' says the Panzer commander, 'I can honestly answer: Yes.'

The French Prime Minister, Paul Reynaud, is shown the card of an officer who committed suicide out of shame at France's defeat. It reads, 'I am taking my own life, Monsieur Prime Minister, so that you will know that all my men fought bravely, but that one cannot send soldiers into battle against tanks armed only with rifles.'

The German Reich Radio, meanwhile, kept up a barrage of victories, heroes, place names. The amateur strategists at their school desks and on their barstools found it hard to stick their little flags into their maps fast enough. Within four days of the first attack, little Holland was finished. All her pleas for help to the Allies had brought no reward. As early as May 13th, German Panzers stood at the gates of the oil port of Rotterdam, preparing to rescue the surviving paratroopers holding out there.

Colonel Scharroo was negotiating the surrender of the town with Leutenant-General Schmidt. The Dutch officer insisted on playing for time and delaying the final capitulation, thereby taking a big risk, for 600,000 civilians lived in the city, whose oil port was already in flames. At 10.40 hours, two German officers were sent to Dutch headquarters. The Dutch led them through Rotterdam with their eyes bindfolded. But it was 12.40 hours before they met with Colonel Scharroo. He promised them that he would send a negotiator under flag of truce at 14.00 hours.

General Schmidt sent a radio message to the 2nd Air Fleet: 'Attack postponed because of negotiations.'

The radio operator fiddled with his transmitter. Interference on the air-waves; he failed to get through.

13.30. Combat Squadron 54 takes off from Delmenhorst, Quakenbrück and Hoya-Weser on an attacking mission. One hundred He IIIs take to the skies. Time of attack 15.00 hours. Target: a triangle north of the Willem Bridge over the Meuse in Rotterdam. A liaison officer had agreed the objective in discussions with the 39th Panzers on the spot the previous day.

14.15. Finally the message postponing the attack gets through. But the radioed order for the planes to spare Rotterdam and to attack a pre-arranged alternative target never gets through. The two formations of planes fly onward.

The chief-of-staff of the 2nd Air Fleet, Oberstleutnant Rieckhoff, hurls himself into an Me 109 and chases after the errant squadron. But he cannot make up the lost time. The city's horrific fate is sealed.

14.45. The mood in the German command post near Rotterdam is tense and irritable. Still no confirmation that the air raid has been called off. The skies are cloudless, but a billowing fog hangs over Rotterdam, and smoke continues to rise.

The roar of engines. Squadron Kommodore Oberst Lackner and his 53 He 111s reach Rotterdam in full attack formation. Generals Schmidt and Student leap out of their command-post below and personally fire red flare-signals with their flare-guns, but the attempts at warning are swallowed by the thick smoke.

Death whistles towards its target from the open bomb bays of the Heinkels. The high-explosive bombs set buildings on fire. Stored oil feeds the fires, which eat their way through the wooden-framed buildings of the old city and from there through the whole of Rotterdam.

The second wave arrives: forty-six Heinkels, led by Oberstleutnant Höhne. The officer gives the order to attack. The automatic release-mechanism clicks into action.

At this moment he sees the puff of a red flare beneath him. Though his aircraft and its two companions are already dropping their bombloads, Höhne tells the following aircraft to turn back. He reported later, 'I have never flown on another mission whose circumstances were so dramatic.'

Forty-three bombers attack an alternative target. But the ninety-seven tons of bombs dropped on Rotterdam have unleashed appalling effects in the densely-populated city. Women and children are slaughtered as they take refuge on the streets, in cellars, in makeshift shelters. The Fire Brigade, equipped with old-fashioned hand-pumping equipment, is forced to watch helplessly while their city burns to the ground - 11,000 buildings in all, which incorporated 25,000 dwellings, leaving 80,000 people homeless.

General Schmidt presents his personal apologies to the High Burgomaster of the city and to Colonel Scharroo for the attack, which he had not wanted, but which he could not prevent. A chivalrous gesture, though admittedly it will not bring the 900 or more dead civilians back to life again.

Because of a communications failure, the Allies announce the number of victims as 30,000. A chain of unfortunate circumstances has been transformed into a symbol of inhumanity that will contribute heavily to the escalation of the air war. On May 15th, Churchill raises the ban on attacks against civilian targets in Germany, and that same night ninety-nine bombers attack strategic points in the Ruhr industrial area. On May 15th, Holland surrenders; Queen Wilhelmina and her ministers flee to London and form an exile government. At this moment, the German bridgehead at Sedan is already fifty kilometres across and twenty-five kilometres deep.

The next day, the armoured spearheads of Army Group B also smash their way through the positions on the Dyle. On the other flank, Guderian's and Rommel's Panzers are now 100 kilometres west of Sedan and rolling across open, undefended terrain. Not a single French military unit stands between the spearheads and Paris. The French still have their *Armée de l'Air* which despite its losses remains a formidable force. The factories are working overtime. Trained pilots are plentifully available. So far in the conflict they have shown courage and spirit, but their military commanders do not know what to do with them.

'Organisation on the ground was a scandal, air-raid warning procedures were practically non-existent, and the anti-aircraft batteries were a joke,' writes the American author Martin Caidin in his book *The Me 109*. 'Dozens of brand-new fighters stood idle at airfields in the hinterland, worthless in any air battle because of missing windscreens, propellors, or other important parts. No attempt was made to rush these parts to where they were needed. Meanwhile, however, the frontline airfields were under constant, merciless attack by the Luftwaffe. The Allied pilots lacked ammunition, fuel, and spare parts, a situation that was well known to the German Secret Service... At the time of the battle for Dunkirk, the German army seemed to be moving forward so quickly on the ground that the panic-stricken French troops and supply-units swiftly set fire to all fuel and ammunition dumps, while any number of French pilots landed at airfields that were already deserted and in flames – a fact for which their own people were to blame'.

Among the French fliers, two men who later became famous writers – Sergeant Romain Gary, crewman aboard a 'Bloch 210' bomber and Captain Antoine de Saint-Exupéry – underwent experiences that they would never forget. At the airfield in Bordeaux, where Gary landed after his final mission, he found himself in the midst of an exotic collection of aircraft crowded among the runways. 'The field had been turned into a sort of exhibition-ground for every sort of aircraft type that had flown for the *Armée de l'Air* during the previous twenty years. It was as if, before it died, France's airforce was recalling its past. ... I saw a young naval pilot whose chest was covered with the most impressive array of medals that I have ever seen, clamber down from his pilot's cabin. In his arms he carried a sleeping small girl, whom he must have kept on his knee during the flight. I saw another pilot climb down out of his "Goeland" aircraft in the company of ladies who were quite clearly inmates of some third-class provincial bordello. I looked into a "Simoun" and saw a white-haired NCO sitting with a lady in trousers with two dogs, a cat, a canary, a parrot, two rolled-up carpets, and a painting by Hubert Robert that was propped up against the side of the pilot's seat... I saw – and I shall never forget them – the faces of my comrades, the men who piloted the Dewoitine 520 and Morane 406 fighters, who returned badly shot-up from their last missions to watch their young commander tear the *Croix de guerre* from his uniform and stamp on it. I saw some thirty generals standing waiting quite pointlessly by the control tower... And everywhere the strange collection of aerial fauna that was about to take to the air one last time...'

Captain de Saint-Exupéry was a reconnaissance pilot, one

of that breed who believed that clear orders and precise co-operation between the various branches of the armed forces might have saved the battle for France, 'It is the end of May 1940, in the midst of retreat and defeat. Crews are being sacrificed at such a rate that is is like pouring glasses of water on a forest fire. And what is the value of an individual life when everything is breaking down? There are fifty reconnaissance crews left to cover the whole of France, each consisting of three men. Twenty-three of those crews are in our group, II/33. In three weeks we have lost seventeen of those crews. We have melted away like wax in the sunshine. Yesterday I said to Lieutenant Gavoille, "We shall only begin to understand it after the war." And he said to me, "Surely you cannot consider surviving this war, Captain?"'

Paris hosted a state visit during May. Churchill, with an escort of fighters, flew into the French capital. As he assured his hosts that Britain would fight 'to the last bullet', he watched documents already being burned in the courtyard of the Quai d'Orsay. The entire world expected that the Germans would be in Paris within two or three days. Surprisingly, they turned and headed for the Flemish coast.

On May 19th, this 'military tourist excursion' (Raymond Cartier) reaches Abbéville and the mouth of the Somme. Operation Sickle is almost complete.

The sixty-eight year old commander-in-chief, Gamelin is sacked and replaced by the seventy-three year old Maxime Weygand, 'a tired, shrivelled-looking little man, of whom an acquaintance said that he looked like a retired jockey' (Len Deighton). Marshal Henri Pétain, an eighty-four year old hero of the First World War, becomes Deputy Premier. Weygand, hitherto with the Army of the East, takes two days to arrive in Paris, where he appears in breeches and highly-polished riding boots and makes no attempt to hide his contempt for all politicians.

The German Panzers roll on. On many occasions, the over-cautious Rundstedt attempts to halt them. He is not always alone. Even Hitler, a natural gambler, is worried when the mobile columns move ahead of supplies, transport, etc. The armoured columns are reluctant to move at a less breakneck pace, and continue to operate more or less on their own initiative – the Panzer generals have become modern *condottieri*.

By May 20th, the attack has carried to the Somme, leaving a million Allied soldiers and a million civilian refugees – who were a constant hindrance to Allied movements – trapped north of the 'sickle'. On May 22nd, Lord Gort's troops attack near Arras and are driven back after heavy fighting. Two days later, the Germans are on the La-Bassée Canal. The British Expeditionary Force under Gort, an old war-horse from the First War, who has put on a lot of weight in the meantime and had reckoned with a 'cosy, pleasant sort of war' (Raymond Cartier), has fallen into a trap. At Dunkirk the British are heading for a catastophe without equal. Only a miracle can save them. There the Allies, mainly British, have been forced back into a narrow bridgehead. The ammunition is getting scarcer with each day that passes; all members of the Expeditionary Force have been put on half rations, and fuel is running low. The only thing available in huge quantities is, for some reason, whisky.

London, without consulting her French allies, considers whether to withdraw her forces back across the Channel. Lord Gort opposes an evacuation, 'When I became a soldier, I could not have believed that I would one day lead the British Army to its gravest defeat,' he wired his government.

Nevertheless, the 'miracle' of Dunkirk began in the last week of May.

On May 23rd, Göring contacted Hitler. He felt that the skills of his Luftwaffe had been seriously under-exploited and demanded that he be given the pleasure of decimating the British trapped in Dunkirk.

It was not Göring's bombast alone that caused Hitler to commit a decisive error. He was afraid for his Panzers, with their overheated engines and exhausted crews, and he knew that Flanders is not perfect operating terrain for tracked vehicles.

On May 24th, the dictator finally halts his Panzers along a line running between St Omer and Gravelines. The crews obey reluctantly and with bad grace, only a few kilometres from their objective, and sit there and twiddle their thumbs. The enemy is in sight. But the Luftwaffe is about to steal their victory.

In London, the long faces match the grim weather. On May 26th, the cloud is so thick over the city that Big Ben disappears into the fog. Those politicians, bankers and businessmen trooping today into Westminster Abbey in their dark suits know enough about military situations to realise that the bad weather is, in fact, the only bright spot in the gloom.

The evacuation of Dunkirk is preceded by a Service of Intercession, in London. Everyone who is anyone is present at the nation's premier church, to join in prayer at the tomb of the Unknown Soldier. It is a short, quiet and dignified ceremony, though whether it is a symptom of piety or impotence is arguable. No tension showed in the face of the new Prime Minister - still only sixteen days in office - though it certainly did not suit Churchill's temperament to be sitting on a hard pew at this stage of the battle. In planning the evacuation, he had spent a long time - perhaps too long - trying to assuage his French ally.

Now the Prime Minister was ready to order the beginning of 'Operation Dynamo', the withdrawal of his élite forces across the Channel under the noses of the German bombers. His Admirals had calculated that only one soldier in ten would reach Britain alive - perhaps 45,000 in all. Winston Churchill did not hesitate to accept such a fearful human cost. In war, results count more than losses.

In the half-light of the Abbey, his broad, heavily jowled features are as if carved from wood. Those around him notice no urgency, certainly no sense of panic, not even resentment against the many old political enemies of his who are here today, and who through their weakness consigned the Republic of Czechoslovakia, Poland, Denmark, Norway, Holland, Belgium, Luxembourg, and France to suffer under the German jackboot. Perhaps they now realise that their weaknesses enabled an Austrian corporal to think of himself as a man who would conquer the world. Many of them, however, would still be prepared to come to an arrangement with Hitler even now - not because they like him, but because they cannot bear their fine golf courses being turned into dummy airfields to lead the German bombers astray.

'The Englishman hates showing his feelings,' wrote the wartime Prime Minister in his memoirs, which won him the Nobel Prize for Literature. 'Nevertheless, in my stall in the Choir I could feel the pent-up, passionate emotion, and also the fear of the congregation, not of death or wounds or material loss, but of the defeat and final ruin of Britain.'

At 18.57 on that same day, Vice-Admiral Bertram Ramsay in Dover issued the order for 'Operation Dynamo' to begin, the massive feat of organisation that was to bring hundreds of thousands of British and French troops from their threatened bridgehead to the safety of this offshore island.

The British dub the bizarre fleet that sets sail that Sunday evening the 'armada of minnows'. The Admiralty had commandeered tugs from the Thames, lifeboats from luxury liners, lobster-boats, fishing boats, sloops and barges, private yachts and excursion steamers. Dutch coasters and British channel ferries alike are pressed into service in an apparently hopeless cause, for no one expects that the evacuation will succeed. Each night, the ships leave the ports in the southern and the south-eastern parts of Britain. Many who possess a private motor-boat suddenly disappear from their offices in London, join the 'minnows', and chug their way over the Channel to Dunkirk. Only sailing-boats cannot go, for there is not a single breath of wind. 'The sea showed itself yet again to be England's best friend, and remained completely calm,' writes Raymond Cartier. 'The slightest swell would have made the beach unusable and reduced the numbers of those evacuated by half.'

On May 27th the siege of Dunkirk begins with a devastating bombing raid. Then thick cloud descends. The weather cares not a fig for the Führer's orders. For the next two days, the commander-in-chief of the Luftwaffe has to put up with rain, gales, and fog. The pilots curse. The mechanics and the ground crews are delighted, for many machines had been in an appalling condition and some had lost as much as 50% of their nominal strength. The men hang around their aircraft, stare up at the sky until their necks ache. The bad weather holds, and so does their ill-humour.

'Well, Richtofen,' says Colonel-General von Kluge, commander-in-chief of the 4th Army, to the commander of the VIII Air Corps. 'Have you taken Dunkirk from the air yet?'

'I haven't even attacked it yet, Herr Colonel-General,' answers the furious air force commander.

The bridgehead held by the British is still 150 kilometres across. The bases from which the German aircraft operate are up to 500 kilometres distant. Closest to the enemy are the fighters and a few Stuka squadrons. The nippy Messerschmitts have often been known to land right on battlefields that are still being fought over. They can take off on grass tracks, and the pilots of the fighter units JG 27 and 51, which share the airfield at St Pol, fly eight, nine, or more missions in a day. The record at the moment stands at thirteen takeoffs in twenty-four hours, and there is often only a half-hour interval between takeoffs.

Fighters are voracious consumers of fuel; only a lack of it can restrict their activities. When it runs low, they have to wait for 'Auntie Ju' to fly in more – and this at a moment when the British have come up with a surprise: the 'Spitfires', a hitherto-protected aircraft that is the equal of, if not superior to, the Messerschmitt. Now they are swimming in fuel and cannot take off because of the fog.

A few days before the sun had been shining and the fighters had no fuel. Only one, half-filled aircraft waited on the edge of the airfield. It belonged to Hauptmann Galland, later General of Fighters, who at that moment was furious at having to deal with a mass of red tape in his command-post, a commandeered circus waggon.

'They're coming!' a hefty groundcrew Feldwebel shouts, and the sound echoes through the airfield like a clap of thunder.

The men stare skywards. A tiny point. The first transport

aircraft comes in view, grows larger. Then the next. The foremost 'Auntie Ju' approaches, makes ready to land. In a leisurely, self-satisfied swoop.

'They're taking their ruddy time,' someone oaths.

And then no one is speaking any more. Because they see the 'Spitfires', the British Air Forces's latest wonder-planes. They are on the attack, three or four brown birds of prey. A whole flock. They plunge down on the defenceless Ju heading the convoy.

One burst – a ball of fire.

The wreckage from the transport aircraft falls on the horrified men waiting below.

And the rest will fare no better.

Above them, the pilot of the second Ju is playing for his life. He pumps the heavy plane, forces it groundwards, then hauls it up again, with great difficulty, over and over again. And with barrels of petrol on board...

Hauptmann Galland dashes across the airfield, leaps onto the left wing of his Me, tears off the cockpit cover, swings himself into the pilot's seat. As he starts his engine, his mechanic jumps out of his split-trench, kicks away the chocks, connects up the electric-starter cable.

The pilot presses the starter. The Me bounces forward. The propeller turns, faster and faster. The machine zips across the grass surface, reaches takeoff speed, leaves the ground.

Galland's Me remains only just above ground level; it seems as if he must collide with some nearby trees. He is sticking close to the surface so as to remain unseen by the Spitfires until he is ready to take up his attack position.

The second Ju 52's left-hand engine is burning. Suddenly the entire stern of the aircraft is one sea of flame – but she still keeps flying.

At last the plane falls out of the sky, crashes into a wood near the airfield. A huge pillar of flame marks the site of the crash. The three-man crew brought the materials for their own cremation.

Above it all, Hauptmann Galland is on the attack. He has a Spitfire in his sights, is taking aim, blasting with his wing-cannon. Then, obviously by order, the entire flock of Spitfires turns off westward – and at this moment the third Ju 52 lands unscathed.

The well-secured barrels in her hold are carefully rolled from her belly. Fear gives way to 'business as usual'. The empty Messerschmitts are immediately filled up.

Galland's Me lands. The pilot clambers down from his cockpit. He is a wiry officer: dark eyes, neat moustache on his upper lip. Hauptmann Galland is already a legend for his victories in the air, and he is still producing the goods – even though he bears little resemblance to the 'nordic' type that his Führer is so obsessed with.

For sixty hours the Panzers sit motionless at the gates of Dunkirk. For thirty-six hours, not a single bomb falls on the bridgehead. The Channel is packed with shipping, but the numbers saved on the first day seem to justify the most pessimistic estimates: only 7,669 British soldiers reach the coast. On Tuesday, the air offensive has to be postponed again, because of rain – and 17,804 British and French reach the island. The landing-points on the British coast are almost like fairgrounds. The men who have escaped the hell of Dunkirk find themselves greeted by brass bands, subjected to wordy speeches of welcome by local mayors. Pretty girls present them with flowers and kisses. They are given hot tea, rum and cigarettes. If they didn't know it before, these men, so ragged and grimy that they look more like pirates than soldiers, now realise that it was worth fighting their way across the beach at Dunkirk.

Twenty-four hours later, after two and a half days, the Panzers start their engines again. Hitler has ordered one last, ruthless assault on Dunkirk, and now the decisive battle will begin – a battle from which both Germans and British will emerge as winners and losers.

The atmosphere of the thousand-year-old port is one of a lull before the storm. Then the Panzer engines roar, the artillery begins to bark, and soon the aircraft will also arrive. The wind has torn away the veil of cloud: Dunkirk faces a Bloody Wednesday.

From the Rhine-Main area, from around Düsseldorf, from hastily-constructed airstrips in Holland, the airborne hordes come. The sky is black with aircraft. It is like the end of the world.

Slowly the attackers approach their objective, move out across the Channel around Dunkirk, looking for the fattest prizes among the mass of ships beneath them. The Stukas are greediest. Eight hundred and forty-eight ships of all kinds, protected only by one destroyer, offer themselves as targets. The deadly birds switch on their automatic bomb-releasers and their sirens, test their diving-breaks, tip and dive like falcons at 600 kilometres an hour, straight down on their targets...

The Stukas attack again and again, diving at a ninety-degree angle onto the ships, banging on their diving-brakes at 2,000 feet. But their dive ends only at 500 feet. At that moment, these vultures of war are at their most vulnerable.

Attack: one, two, three Ju 87s. Each has chosen a fat steamer as its victim, but at the last moment the target wanders out of the dive-bombers' sights. The ships are moving hard astern into a semi-circle. Their bombs splash harmlessly. Their pilots haul the Stukas up, force them into a climb, try another 'tumble'. They will sow death – or suffer it.

Former luxury liners disintegrate amidships, two over-crowded destroyers go down in the filthy waters of the Channel, seven are seriously damaged. The ferries *Queen of the Channel*, *Fenella*, *Normannia*, *Lorina*, *King Orry* are bombed to pieces. Hundreds of shipwrecked men flounder between the still-floating carcasses of these great ships, where they will suffocate and drown, or perhaps be rescued only to be attacked again. Stukas that have been disabled by anti-aircraft fire smash into the decks of their burning victims. The losses on both sides are appalling – the war is consuming its own heroes.

Permanent action-stations for the Heinkels, Dorniers, Junkers and Messerschmitts. Dunkirk is a witches' caldron heated by a thousand fires. Cordite blackens the faces of the defenders, blood dyes the harbour-basin red. Dead men with bloated bodies and staring eyes float close to burnt-out ships.

Oil storage tanks explode. Huge walls of black smoke obscure the target as the next wave of aircraft comes in. The post office is in flames. The town hall is burning. The docks are shattered. The harbour has been so badly damaged that its gates cannot be closed at low tide. And the air raids continue. The bombs keep falling, crushing human beings' lives, and their dreams, their children, their homes.

The fighter branch of the RAF, Fighter Command, has given the Germans a nasty surprise by suddenly conjuring up the Spitfire. Both their pilots and their aircraft are now the Germans' equals, perhaps even superiors. He who has the better eyes, the swifter reactions, the stronger nerve – and the luck – is now going to be the victor in the man-to-man air battles, and no matter whether he is British or German.

The 200 of the first batch of Spitfires, which are given their baptism of fire over Dunkirk, have one great advantage: they are able to take off from nearby bases on the British coast, to make short hops across the Channel, and their short approach makes them omnipresent. And the same is true of even the slower 'Hurricanes'. Fighter Command sends sixteen squadrons in over Dunkirk. They shoot down 262 German aircraft, at a loss to themselves of 133.

Suddenly the British have command of the air, however localised. 'All German calculations had assumed that Professor Messerschmitt's plane would prove the better of the two,' writes David Irving in his book *The Rise and Fall of the Luftwaffe*. 'But now the Spitfire wrought havoc on the German fighter squadrons and the bombers approaching Dunkirk were easy prey.'

The German Panzers cannot make progress. The defenders are fighting for their lives with verve and courage. British soldiers stand on the once-elegant beach of Malo-les-Bains with their feet already in the water, patiently waiting for hour after hour, being bombed, harried and strafed by fighters. There is no cover, but at least the sand swallows the bombs, deadens the explosions.

The slaughter continues right through the night.

The destoyer *Wakeful*, an uncomfortable old tub, has already brought 600 members of the Expeditionary Force safe and sound to Britain. On Wednesday at 00.30 hours she moves in to pick up another load of lost souls. Captain Ralph Fisher watches anxiously from his bridge. He has been warned to expect German U-boats on the prowl.

Suddenly he sees two pale strips of water pushing towards his ship: torpedoes.

'Hard to stern!' he bellows.

'But it was too late,' writes Richard Collier. 'A torpedo struck the *Wakeful* exactly amidships. The old destroyer broke in two with a loud grinding noise: prow and stern both jutted out of the water.

The 640 soldiers on board were doomed; they sat below decks, trapped. But in some cases their death-agony would last for hours. Captain Fisher and other survivors were picked up by the Scottish fishing-steamer *Comfort*, others by the minesweeper *Gossamer*.'

The men commuting between death and freedom press on. New convoys are constantly leaving Margate, Dover, Portsmouth and Sheerness. More amateur skippers join the throng. 'Good luck,' say the harbour masters as they despatch a ship. 'Just sail in the direction of the gunfire.'

'Such an armada as this had never before been seen,' writes Richard Collier. 'Manned by the famous and the obscure, young and old, it was an international fleet. A Dominican monk steers the yacht *Gulzar*. A clerk from the Bank of England reports for duty on a lifeboat wearing his bowler hat and striped trousers and carrying an umbrella. The Chinese steward Ah Fong prepares tea on the *Bideford*, and the Earl of Carven serves on the salvage vessel *St Olave* as Third Engineer. The minesweeper *Fitzroy* is manned by a crew of gaelic-speaking Irishmen with their own interpreter.'

Only now do the French realise that the British intend to evacuate all their forces through Dunkirk. There is an argument between the French Admiral Jean Abrial and the English commander.

'Who does this Lord Gort think he is, anyway?' rages the

Frenchman. He threatens to block the harbour and have the leader of the Expeditionary Force – technically his subordinate – arrested.

Dunkirk is hell, and its fires are greedy. Two million tons of oil run out of the shattered storage tanks and form a sea of flame one and a half kilometres long. The town has had no water supply for days now. Aboard the burning paddle steamer *Crested Eagle*, deck plates bend from the heat until they are 'like a turtle's back' (Richard Collier). 'Thousands of men on land watched in horror as the sailors, afire from head to toe, ran around her decks like madmen, or leapt screaming into the water.'

The drifting cordite made men's eyes water. Aboard the drifting wrecks, desperate figures fight for survival, and suffocate and drown. Oil tanks are still exploding. The town hall of Dunkirk is a heap of ruins. The main post office is in flames. The harbour gates cannot be closed. Corpses float in towards the beaches; their faces are black, they have staring eyes and swollen bellies. And the ugly harbingers of death from those skies continue to make screaming dive after screaming dive. Hundreds of British soldiers stand in the filthy water and calmly let the battle rage over them. One behind the other, queueing as if they were at a bus-stop in London. And corpses swim between the waiting men, bobbing among the waves, turning and twisting; a terrible sight that holds no terror for these men any more.

Sailors in small coastal vessels search the water with long poles, probing for survivors. Only smaller boats are left in the harbour now. In the twilight, as the air raids finally ease off, more and more boats join in the armada.

Not all the soldiers of the Expeditionary Force maintain the legendary British discipline. Captain William Tennant, the naval commander sent from Dover by Admiral Ramsay, encounters a small group of drunken soldiers in the centre of the town, led by a sergeant who is wearing a looted feather boa. A rifle bullet whistles past Tennant's head. He goes up to the Sergeant, takes away his weapon. 'Here, old boy,' he says, and offers him a hip flask filled with brandy. 'A sip of this and you'll feel better.'

The man is too astonished to offer resistance, and the

mutineers put themselves back under the commander's orders.

Lord Gort is still sitting in Bastion 32. On hearing that the Belgians surrendered on May 28th after brave resistance, his initial response is, 'The swine!' His northern flank is now totally at the mercy of the German Panzers. Rumours chase rumours, and panic is unleashed by false reports that German parachutists dressed as nuns have dropped near Dixmuiden.

The world knows full well that the battle being fought in the Straits of Dover is the battle for Britain's survival.

Two hundred thousand soldiers were still defending Dunkirk, while the others made ready, 50,000 at a time, for the evacuation. The British sailors ran out of steel helmets. To provide some protection against shrapnel, they stuck zinc buckets and enamel bowls over their heads. Battle-weary soldiers from the Expeditionary Force rode cows down onto the beaches and discovered novel methods of getting aboard ships. One man paddled over on a door, another used a wardrobe as a lifeboat. Many made makeshift lifesavers, and one came on an inflated car tyre, using his rifle to propel himself to safety.

The men standing in the water – for much of the time amused by one British soldier who performs card tricks non-stop – watch as men who had got on board the rescue boats are shot up by German aircraft. The dead are tossed overboard and the queue starts to move again, a line three wide stretching back for miles . . .

For those soldiers who survived, patience paid off. Even on Bloody Wednesday, 47,310 men reached the British side of the Channel. The bad flying weather on Thursday meant that 53,823 British and French troops escaped the inferno. And the rescue operation continued: the ships kept coming, turning . . .

On June 1st, the weather improves, and the decimated German bomber formations take off from their distant bases for the bloody final act, that will last for another four days. Among the attackers is the training squadron L I, which has set off from near Düsseldorf. It is supplied with the brand-new Ju 88, already acclaimed by the propagandists as the 'miracle bomber'. It can carry 2,500 kilos cargo (later 3,500), can reach 470 kilometres per hour (later almost 600), and has an operational range of 3,120 kilometres. The Ju 88 is mainly a medium-range bomber, but can be used as a dive-bomber, as a nightfighter and reconnaissance aircraft. The versatile aircraft has such heavy fire-power that it can face enemy fighters without escorts.

Nine days of horror are drawing to an end. The Germans are still eight kilometres from the ruins of France's fourth-largest port. On June 2nd, the last British soldier is picked up. On the night of June 3rd, eleven torpedo boats, thirteen mail steamers, two freighters, five paddle steamers and a huge number of small tugs and private boats, reinforced by 100 French fishing boats, go back once more. This time they go only by night and pick up 26,000 trapped men, the vast majority of them French. The Admiralty issues orders that 'Operation Dynamo' will end at 03.30 on June 4th 1940. Thereafter, the harbour will be made unusable by the sinking of block-ships in its entrance. The last survivors are crammed together in the armada of small boats. Thirty-four thousand combatworthy, if exhausted, soldiers are forced to stand on the shore and watch as the last rescue ships steam away. They face years of imprisonment.

Three hundred and thirty-eight thousand, two hundred and twenty-six soldiers, including 123,000 Frenchmen, have escaped to southern England, though mostly weaponless. The British have lost 272 ships, including nine destroyers, mostly as a result of air attacks. On the sandy beaches around Dunkirk they have left behind 50,000 vehicles, damaged and undamaged. Deserted cows bellow in the fields, surrounded by shoes, weapons, bicycles, lorries and incredible quantities of empty champagne and whisky bottles.

Only nine out of 600 tanks and twelve out of 1,000 big guns are shipped back to Britain. Supplies can be replaced, but not human beings. Hundreds of thousands of young soldiers, snatched from defeat in France, are now available for the 'Battle for Britain' that will follow. Thus for the

Germans, Dunkirk is a victory thrown away, and for the British a victorious fiasco.

After the battle in Flanders, France's back has been broken. Weygand and his troops fight on, have even overcome their 'Stuka-shock' to some extent, but once the invaders reach the coast, the campaign turns into a picnic. A sour French commander predicts that Britain 'will have its neck wrung like a chicken within three weeks.'

Ninety-two thousand Frenchmen have fallen in defence of their fatherland, 200,000 have been wounded. The British Expeditionary Force has lost 68,000 men and 1,526 aircrew, mostly fighter pilots.

'The determination of the British to fight on does not seem to have troubled Hitler's thoughts,' states William L. Shirer. 'He was sure they would see the light after he had finished off France, which he now proceeded to do. On June 10th the French government hastily departed Paris and on June 14th the great city, the glory of France, which was undefended, was occupied by General von Küchler's 18th Army . . . On June 16th, Premier Reynaud . . . resigned and was replaced by Pétain, who the next day asked the Germans, through the Spanish ambassador, for an armistice.'

At the end, Benito Mussolini joined in, a sorry hero, to carry out his own ludicrous campaign against the beaten French without making noticeable progress. As early as June 17th, Guderian's Panzers had reached the Swiss border. Any French attempt to continue the struggle would have been useless. From 21.35 hours on June 25th, the guns fell silent all over France. The Germans had taken 1.9 million prisoners of war and suffered casualties during the six-week campaign of 27,074 dead, 111,034 wounded, and 18,834 missing.

The forty-day campaign of the Battle for France, was over. Hitler's terms were communicated to the French negotiators on June 20th, in the same railway carriage in the forest of Compiègne in which the defeated Germans had signed another armistice in November 1918. The German advance continued beyond the Loire while the talks continued, but on June 22nd the German conditions were finally accepted. The armistice came into force on June 25th at 01.35 hours. It allowed for the German occupation of the country north of the line Geneva-Tours and along the Atlantic coast as far as the Spanish border, though it left the Fleet to be disbanded and the colonial empire in French hands. Vichy was also permitted to have a small air force and a 100,000-man volunteer army.

On the day of the surrender, Charles de Gaulle, a French tank officer and Secretary of State, fled to Britain, determined to raise an army of liberation and continue the struggle.

Hitler, meanwhile, was ruler of Europe. The Russian Foreign Minister, Molotov, summoned the German ambassador to the Kremlin and conveyed to him the Soviet government's heartiest congratulations on the victory in the West. In America, Britain's last hope, an election campaign was in full swing, and both candidates, Franklin D. Roosevelt and Wendell Willike, vied to convince the voters of their commitment to peace at any price.

The corpses of drowned men were being picked up from the beaches around Dunkirk even weeks after the surrender. Between the German 'empire' and the British Isles lay a water barrier that at its narrowest point was only thirty-six kilometres wide. Germany's military commanders were already discussing how they would launch a 'glorified river crossing' and succeed in landing in Great Britain.

Chronology

1939

1.9.39 German attack on Poland.

3.9.39 Great Britain and France declare war on Germany.
U-30 sinks the passenger ship *Athenia* without prior warning.

12.9.39 Hitler informs his generals of his intention of launching an offensive in the West when the fighting in Poland is over.

13.9.39 Two Soviet Army Groups march into Poland.

25.9.39 Bombardment of Warsaw.

28.9.39 German–Soviet Border and Friendship Pact signed in Moscow.

6.10.39 The last Polish troops surrender.

14.10.39 U-47 sinks the battleship *Royal Oak* in the naval harbour at Scapa Flow.

7.11.39 'X-Day' for the western offensive postponed for the first time (this will happen 29 more times).

9.11.39 Agents of the SD kidnap two officers of the

British Secret Service on Dutch soil near Venlo, in the process fatally wounding a Dutch officer, Lieutenant Klop.

8/9.11.39 Admiral Canaris, boss of the German Abwehr, meets with Rumanian government representatives in Bucharest and reaches agreement on secret measures to protect oil shipments to Germany.

17.12.39 A sea battle in the estuary of the River Plate puts an end to the successful raiding career of the armoured cruiser *Graf Spee,* which is scuttled against Hitler's express orders.

1940

5/8.1.40 Finnish forces wipe out the 44th Russian artillery division east of Suomusalmi.

17.1.40 Due to an emergency landing by two Luftwaffe officers near Mecheln (Belgium), the German plans for an offensive in the West fall into Allied hands.

16.2.40 The British destroyer *Cossack* attacks the German supply ship *Altmark* in Norwegian waters and frees 303 prisoners of war. The Norwegian government protests but refrains from intervention.

5.3.40 Hitler discusses Operation 'Weserübung' – the occupation of Norway and Denmark – with the commanders-in-chief of the three branches of the Wehrmacht.

28.3.40 The Allied War Council in London orders the mining of Norwegian coastal waters as a preparation for the occupation of Norway.

5.4.40 British attempt to block the passage through the 'Iron Gate' and halt oil shipments from Rumania to Germany is foiled by the action of the Brandenburg Division's special unit.

9.4.40 Operation 'Weserübung' begins.

24.4.40 The British land forces at Harstadt, north of Narvik.

2.5.40 British forces withdrawn from Namsos and Andalsnes.

10.5.40 The German offensive in the West begins. Prime Minister Chamberlain falls, and his old enemy, Churchill, is appointed to head a coalition government.
Freiburg is accidentally bombed by German aircraft.

11.5.40 German parachute troops seize the Belgian fort of Eben Emael.

13.5.40 General of Panzers, Erwin Rommel, crosses the Meuse near Dinant.

15.5.40 Holland surrenders.

19.5.40 Panzer Group Kleist reaches Abbéville.

24.5.40 Hitler calls a halt to the Panzers' advance towards Dunkirk and decides – at Göring's suggestion – to entrust the Luftwaffe with the destruction of the Allied bridgehead.

27.5.40 Beginning of Operation 'Dynamo': the British forces are evacuated to their native island with the aid of 848 ships.

28.5.40 The Belgian King Leopold III signs his country's surrender.

4.6.40 End of Operation 'Dynamo': 338,226 Allied soldiers escape from the trap at Dunkirk.

5.6.40 Beginning of the Battle of France.

8.6.40 German troops re-enter Narvik.

12.6.40 Following a sabre-rattling ultimatum, Soviet troops occupy the Lithuanian cities of Kovno and Vilna.

14.6.40 German forces march into Paris.

22.6.40 Franco-German armistice signed in the Forest of Compiègne.

25.6.40 Armistice in France comes into force. 1.9 million Frenchmen pass into German captivity.

Sources and Further Reading

Hanson W. Baldwin: Große Schlachten des Zweiten Weltkriegs. Lübbe-Verlag, Bergisch Gladbach
Cajus Becker: Angriffshöhe 4000. Stalling Verlag, Oldenburg
Cajus Becker: Augen durch Nacht und Nebel. Heyne Verlag, München
Cajus Becker: Das Bildbuch der deutschen Kriegsmarine 1939-45. Heyne Verlag, München
Cajus Becker: Verdammte See. Ullstein Verlag, Berlin
Will Berthold: Der Sieg, der vor die Hunde ging. Hestia-Verlag, Bayreuth
Will Berthold: Division Brandenburg. Heyne Verlag, München
Alex Buchner: Narvik. Heyne Verlag, München
Martin Caidin: Die Me 109. Moewig Verlag, Rastatt
Raymond Cartier: Der Zweite Weltkrieg. Piper Verlag, München
Richard Collier: Eagle Day: Battle of Britain, August 6 – September 15, 1940. J.M. Dent Ltd., London
Richard Collier: Sands of Dunkirk. Fontana, London
Richard W. Condon: Winterkrieg Rußland-Finnland. Moewig Verlag, Rastatt
Len Deighton: Blitzkrieg: From the Rise of Hitler to the Fall of Dunkirk. Cape, London
Len Deighton: Unternehmen Adler. Hestia-Verlag, Bayreuth
Wolfgang Dierich: Kampfgeschwader 'Edelweiss'. Ian Allan, London
Adolf Galland: Die Ersten und die Letzten. Heyne Verlag, München

Karl Gundelach: Kampfgeschwader 4. Motorbuch-Verlag, Stuttgart
Liddell Hart: Geschichte des Zweiten Weltkriegs. Fourier Verlag, Wiesbaden
Werner Haupt: Fallschirmjäger 1939-1945. Podzun-Pallas-Verlag, Friedberg
Hans Herlin: Verdammter Atlantik. Heyne Verlag, München
Andreas Hillgruber und Gerhard Hümmelchen: Chronik des Zweiten Weltkriegs. Athenäum-Verlag, Kronberg, und Droste Verlag, Düsseldorf
Alistair Horne: To Lose a Battle: France 1940. Macmillan, London
David Irving: Trail of the Fox: The Life of Field Marshal Erwin Rommel. Futura, London
David Irving: The Rise and Fall of the Luftwaffe. Futura, London
Robert Jackson: Dunkirk. The British Evacuation. Mayflower, London
Franz Kurowski: Der Panzerkrieg. Moewig Verlag, Rastatt
Kenneth J. Macksey: Guderian. Macdonald, London
Kenneth J. Macksey: Panzer Division. Ballantine Books
David Mason: U-Boat: The Secret Menace. Ballantine Books
Herbert Molloy Mason: The Rise of the Luftwaffe. Cassell
F. W. von Mellenthin: German Generals of World War II. University of Oklahoma Press
Charles Messenger: Art of Blitzkrieg. Ian Allan, London
Herbert Michaelis: Der Zweite Weltkrieg. Vertriebsgesellschaft Modernes Antiquariat, Wiesbaden
Martin Middlebrook and Patrick Mahoney: Battleship: The Sinking of the 'Prince of Wales' and the 'Repulse'. Allan Lane
Léonce Peillard: Die Schlacht im Atlantik. Heyne Verlag, München
Janusz Piekalkiewicz: Luftkrieg. Südwest-Verlag, München
Alfred Price: Blitz on Britain. Ian Allan, London
J. Rohwer and G. Hümmelchen: Chronology of The War at Sea 1939-45. Ian Allan, London

Hans Schäufler: So lebten und so starben sie. Das Buch vom Panzer-Regiment 35. Privatdruck
Walter Schellenberg: Aufzeichnungen. Limes-Verlag, München
Edward H. Simms: Jagdflieger. Motorbuch-Verlag, Stuttgart
Gerald S. Snyder: The *Royal Oak* Disaster. Mayflower, London
Edward L. Spears: Prelude to Dunkirk. William Heinemann Ltd., London
Time-Life-Buch: Der Angriff auf Rußland. Time-Life-International, München
Otto Zierer: Rot scheint die Sonne. Bastei-Verlag, Bergisch Gladbach

BLOOD DEEP

Colin Stubbington

A wrecked U-boat drifts into the stormy shallows off Britain's North Sea coast. U-31's reeking hull gives up a grisly cargo – and a clue to the Kaiser's most secret plan – to draw Greece into the raging conflict consuming northern Europe . . . *against the Allies!*

In the savage wake of Jutland the British are cautious about their battleships. They can only risk sending the mighty Aegean Squadron into Piraeus harbour if the seas are free of steel sharks. Ralph Caradoc's mission is to find the hidden U-boat base and blast it to kingdom come. But his old friend Kapitan-Leutnant Kirbschaus' mission is to send the Aegean Squadron to the bottom of the clear blue sea . . .

WAR FICTION 0 7221 82295 £1.75

FINAL HARBOUR

A NOVEL BY

HARRY HOMEWOOD

U.S.S. **Mako** is one submarine among many. In telling her tale FINAL HARBOUR speaks not only for its heroes. It speaks also for the unsung thousands of submariners who waged a bitter, hidden war beneath the ocean's depths.

Mako's crew is a cross-section of civilian reservists and trained seamen thrown together by the harsh dictates of war. Captain Hinman has welded them into a fighting team as deadly and efficient as the steel predator in which they sail. At sea they are united against the enemy they would die to defeat. But on shore they are different men cherishing different dreams and loving many women. And before **Mako** can win her war each of her crew must fight many battles of their own.

FINAL HARBOUR tells the story of a ship, the men who fought in her, and the women they left behind.

WAR 0 7221 4795 3 £1.95